Buried Bones

Also by C.K. Crigger

The Woman Who Series

The Woman Who Built a Bridge

The Woman Who Killed Marvin Hammel

The Woman Who Wore a Badge

The Woman Who Beat the Odds

The Woman Who Inherited Trouble

The Woman Who Went for Broke

Novels

Ault's Heir

Black Crossing

Hereafter

Letter Of The Law

Liar's Trial

Lost Girl Lake

Madame's Daughter

The Yeggman's Apprentice

Yester's Ride

The Winning Hand

And many more...

Buried Bones

PAINTER'S BAY
BOOK ONE

C.K. CRIGGER

Buried Bones

Paperback Edition

Wolfpack Publishing
1707 E. Diana Street
Tampa, FL 33609

wolfpackpublishing.com

This book is a work of fiction. Any references to historical events, real people or real places are used fictitiously. Other names, characters, places and events are products of the author's imagination, and any resemblance to actual events, places or persons, living or dead, is entirely coincidental.

Paperback ISBN 978-1-63977-645-0
eBook ISBN 978-1-63977-644-3
LCCN 2024942698

Buried Bones

One

A gunshot echoing from the hills overlooking the bay startled Rio Salo out of a sound sleep. Only the one report, though she listened long moments for more. She had a notion there might've been another but wasn't quite sure. Not that it mattered anyway. But usually an enthusiastic drunk from the saloon across the bay would empty his gun thinking to shoot a star and she'd have a hard time going back to sleep. Lord only knew she went short on sleep most the time anyhow.

From habit, Rio noted that it was still dark and it was raining. Raining hard, big drops beating on the hotel roof, and the wind blowing rivulets down her window in a blurry mess. Thunder, first like a split in the sky, then a long, low rumble, muttered in the distance. It hadn't been a gunshot that awakened her at all, she decided, but a crack of thunder.

Her little white dog, Boo, by name, had roused from sleep and sat at the end of the bed with his ears pricked.

He quivered at the next rumble of thunder and came to huddle close to Rio's side.

Eased—Rio preferred thunder to gunfire—she rolled over, drew the blanket up around her ears, and went back to sleep.

Minutes, or maybe hours later, hard to tell which, the second of the two bells hanging above her bed jangled. Once, twice, bringing her upright and casting aside the pillow in a startled rush. "What?"

For a few seconds the noise stopped, then began again. Only sustained this time, as if someone had their finger on the button by the front door and was pounding it in a timed sequence.

A sinking thought struck her. If she didn't hurry and still the commotion, an even worse situation was certain to develop.

Thrusting aside the blankets, her feet found the moccasins she used for slippers. "You stay put," she whispered to the dog. "And quiet."

Sticking her arms through the sleeves of the long coat she wore as a dressing gown, Rio lit a lantern with trembling hands. Running out of her room and down the hall, she buttoned the coat as she went on past the dark dining room and through the small lobby, and so to the door.

Once there, she hesitated. Not for the first time, she wished for a peephole where she could look out and see just who was there. She wanted the choice whether or not to open the door to them. This part terrified her.

But then, this was a hotel. Or it used to be. Drawing a breath, she drew a key from a hook hidden behind a hat rack and inserted it in the lock.

One of these days, whoever was on the other side of

the door was going to have evil intentions. He'd grab her. Strangle her, maybe. Or shoot her. Or...or...

She flung open the door. "Yes, yes, I'm here," she said. "What..."

Gusting wind blew rain into her face. Although a roof overhung the porch and wide front entrance, the structure didn't help when the wind blew hard out of the south. Rio blinked against the deluge, her lashes fluttering. Squinting, she made out two men standing at the door. One of them held the other on his feet, though he sagged as if to collapse. No doubt due to the great dark blotch staining the front of his shirt.

Rio might not be the best judge of men, but she could tell whoever these two were, they meant trouble.

Before she could slam the door shut, refuse them entrance, or even open her mouth, the man supporting the collapsing one pushed her out of the way and carrying the other with him, brushed past her.

"Shut the door and lock it," he ordered roughly. "And get us to a room out of sight. This kid needs care. He's been shot."

So maybe that had been gunfire she'd heard. Either that or a thunderous premonition strong enough to invade her sleep. Mouth open, she stood as if bolted to the floor. "Wait. What's happened. Who—"

He wasn't listening to her. "Quick, girl. He needs attention. Now."

"He needs a doctor." She'd seen the wounded fellow's face. Very young, pale enough to shine through the dark, drained, his eyes weren't even fully open. His legs bent like soggy straws.

"No doctor. You look capable. You and me. We'll tend him. Which room?" He turned toward the hall where the four downstairs rooms were located, almost as if he'd been here before. That or he could see in the dark as well as any cat. "Hurry. Which room?"

She pointed. "Straight through the lobby to the end of the hall." Did she even have a choice? And what did he mean? That she and he would tend the man's hurts? She knew nothing about treating gunshot wounds and had no desire to learn. Did he?

"Get more lights. We're going to need them. And hot water. We'll need that too. Bandages, towels, carbolic if you have any. And warm this place up. It's colder than a well-digger's ass."

Rio blinked at his language.

Taking a better hold on his partner, he was carrying the wounded man by now. "Move it, girl," he said, his voice harsh.

Rio could do nothing else. Locking the door behind her, she hurried, pausing a moment to glance up the stairs to where the family living quarters were shut off from the public rooms. She heard nothing stirring. Boo was blessedly silent. A relief.

Continuing through a side door, she entered the kitchen and lit a couple lamps. The boiler was in the cellar. She went down steep steps into the eerie dark and poked wood into the boiler's burn chamber. The apparatus not only heated the water but provided steam heat for the rooms. She'd have to boil some water on top of the stove, however, to obey the man's demand for hot water fast. At least an hour was required before hot water came out of the taps. The big restaurant stove, always banked for the night, provided heat much faster.

She went about collecting things she thought the harsh-voiced man would need if he planned on doctoring his companion himself. There was a good supply of medicinal items in one of the cupboards nowadays, always kept on hand. She got out a rimmed metal tray, put a clean cloth on it, and set out tweezers, scissors, bandages, iodine, alcohol, and a packet of the herbs used to help her father sleep. Or they had once, before he got so bad. There was a small knife, as well, with a short, very thin and sharp blade that reminded her of a miniature filet knife. Not, however, the best tool if she needed to defend herself.

Although, when she thought about it, the man hadn't threatened her. He'd just given orders, and she'd obeyed. She hadn't even asked questions.

If the wounded man required more than the herbs, she'd have to chance going upstairs, and she really didn't want to do that. Not yet. Although she would like to put on her clothes. A strange man in the hotel under these circumstances, with her in nightclothes? The vulnerability made her skin crawl.

Footsteps sounded behind her. Even so, she jumped when the man said, "That water about hot?"

Rio touched the side of the kettle. "Getting there."

He'd stripped of his coat, revealing a revolver tucked in the back of his britches as he turned and picked up the tray. "I'll take this. You bring the water as soon as it's ready."

"All right." She looked around then, seeing him for the first time in the light. His voice had led her to believe him older. He was a medium-sized man, with dark hair, dark eyes, dark complexion. He didn't have a beard, but he wasn't clean-shaven, either. Or not right now. Possibly he'd been living rough for a few days. His clothes, though wet with rain and stained with what she assumed was the other man's blood, were normal working man's clothes.

She opened her mouth to ask his name but he'd already turned and strode away, carrying the tray with the medical items.

The kettle had a little while yet before it boiled. She took the opportunity to run up to her room where she quickly dressed, Boo staring at her all the while. The plain blouse, her habitual ankle-length skirt, the wide belt that helped firm her back for the heavy lifting she had to do, and plain low shoes. Her pale blonde hair flowed loose. It took only moments to brush it back, give it a twist, and wrap a tie around the resultant tail.

Before going downstairs, she tiptoed to the room two doors down from her own and listened. Nothing. A good sign, she hoped. Maybe the storm had helped him sleep. That and the opium. Lord knows the old man's disposition fit right in with cold and rain.

Steam poured from the kettle's spout when she got back to the kitchen, Boo following hard on her heels. She let him out, then, carrying the kettle inside a basin, she made her way to the room she'd designated for the wounded man and went in.

The man didn't turn around. "About time. Get over here. I need your help."

No please, no thank you when she complied. Just the demand to follow orders. If she were brave, Rio thought, she'd tell him to get out, to take the wounded man and go. She had no obligation to do as he said. In pure fact, she suspected she'd be better off not to. If she had truly heard the shot that hit him, it could only mean one or two things. Either the law was after the pair, or they had a rival outlaw bent on killing off the competition.

A third thought struck. Unless the man was the law and had been on the losing end of a confrontation. But a lawman...wouldn't one be more polite?

Best, Rio decided, to keep her mouth shut and ask no questions. Just do as she was told. Hear nothing, see nothing, say nothing. Be a good little monkey.

She set the basin with the hot water on the side table and moved across the bed from him. Revealed now in the lamplight, she saw the wounded fellow was barely more than a boy, midteens maybe, with a sprouting of whiskers, but probably not yet shaving on a regular basis. Aware of those kinds of details lately, Rio could see a marked resemblance between her two unwanted guests. She also saw the younger one, the boy, was trying hard not to cry. Tears were squeezing out behind his closed eyelids, although the only sound he made reminded her of a dog panting.

"Unbutton his shirt. Hurry."

The cloth, sodden from the wash of blood most of the way down, proved reluctant to yield to her trembling fingers.

"For God's sake," the older one muttered, clearly impatient with her ineptitude. But at last, the boy's chest lay revealed.

The wound didn't appear as bad as what she'd been expecting considering all the blood. An irregular hole about a quarter inch in diameter, was all.

Taking a shaky breath, maybe the first one since she'd begun undoing the buttons, Rio stood back as the man ever so gently lifted the boy and removed the shirt.

He flicked her a glance. "Help me turn him onto his side."

She did, then gasped. "Oh."

"Don't you get sick. Not now. We've got work to do." He bent closer to the boy's ear. "This is going to hurt, Win. You've got to hang on. Hear me?"

The boy answered. "Mmmmm."

It could've meant anything in Rio's opinion, but the older one said, "Good man," as if it had been agreement.

The bullet had entered from the front, just below the clavicle. It had gone through to the other side. But not quite all the way through. The bullet, visible as a protrusion inside his body, had cut just through his skin, though plenty far enough to bleed. Bleed a lot. She couldn't imagine why it had stopped there.

"He needs a do—" she started, but he cut her off.

"I told you. No doctor. Nobody else. Just you and me, you hear?" Face set like stone, his narrowed eyes glared at her.

Accustomed to her father's glares, she wasn't as affected as she might have been otherwise, but nevertheless, she backed off.

She didn't see a choice. Not a good one anyway. Nodding, she couldn't help wondering what he would do when he didn't need her anymore. Kill her? Then why wasn't she more afraid?

"All right. First off, I want you to wash his wounds, front and back. I've got to see what I'm doing."

So that's what she did. And then, after he thoroughly soaped and rinsed his hands with more of the hot water, she held the boy propped against her while the man cut through his skin to the bullet, probing and cutting as he went. The boy, who remained conscious the whole time, all without uttering a sound, squeezed her hard enough she knew she'd have bruises. But at last, the bullet popped out. The wound cleaned and bandaged, she made a pill of the herbs and had him swallow it down with warm water.

Only then did he pass out.

He should've had morphine, she knew. He was bound to suffer when he came to. She started to say something as she cleaned up the detritus from the makeshift surgery and prepared to carry it away, but the man practically shoved her out the door.

"I'll take it from here. You can go. I think you know to keep your mouth shut about us being here. To anybody. Got it? Do that and you'll be all right."

"Yes. I understand." She wondered if he ever spoke in anything but staccato sentences. If he ever said please or thank you. If what he'd just said was a threat.

But, seeing as her hands were full, he did open the door.

In the kitchen, she saw the rain still beat against the windows. A cascade poured from the eaves with no sign of letting up, although the thunder and lightning had passed eastward. A hint of daylight showed in the sky rising above the line of trees sheltering the bay.

She was so tired and here it was, time for her day of work to begin. Demands would be made. And questions. Would there be questions asked?

She'd been warned not to speak of this, so she wouldn't. Besides, who would she tell? Her other patient?

With a shuddering breath, she lifted the lid from the stove's firebox and began to feed the bloody cloths and the shirt with the bullet hole in it into the fire. He'd told her to get rid of it and she would. She also washed the basin and other items and put them away, then took a mop out to the lobby and wiped up any remaining water spots from where the men had tromped through. When she was satisfied no traces remained, she made coffee and fixed a breakfast tray.

Not for herself. She'd lost all desire for food.

Her father, on the other hand, was bound to be awake by now, and he expected her attention to be prompt.

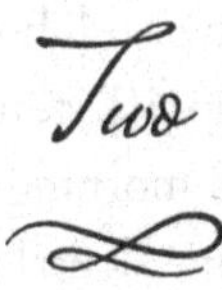

Fist raised, Rio stood outside the door to her father's room, knowing what to expect the moment she went inside. Her heart felt leaden in her chest and her stomach churned. Every day this got worse. The smells. The cursing. The unending grind. Why didn't he just give in and let the cancer take him? Put them both at peace. Gritting her teeth, she forced her lips into a smile, tapped lightly, and entered.

His room smelled of death. Not of blood, as if from a slaughtered animal or the room she'd just come from, but the kind of death you can't see, where an invisible sickness rots the body from the inside out. The kind that cuts a man down and makes him suffer. Him and everyone around him.

Elias Salo lay in a bed that dwarfed him as his flesh slowly melted away. His body and head canted to one side, like a slung-aside rag doll. He must, Rio thought, be dreadfully uncomfortable. Well, he was never slow about letting her know.

A large, strong man once, these last few months had

diminished him. Skin hung loose on his frame. His pale blue eyes had sunken into their sockets; his cheeks gone gaunt. Rio smelled the strong odor of urine. She'd have to change the sheets again first thing.

"Good morning," she said, holding the weak smile in place with an effort. The sick stench nearly overwhelmed her. "How are you this morning? The storm got a little noisy. I hope you got some sleep last night." He must have slept. At his insistence, she'd given him a second full dose of his morphine around midnight, then at his insistence, added an opium gum pill as a supplement.

He twitched feebly, though when he spoke his voice was still strong and loud. "How the hell do you think I am? I'm sick. I'm dying." A string of curses followed, which included most every foul word ever created. In two languages, no less. Anyone listening would've surmised this illness was her fault. He certainly seemed to blame her.

Would the man downstairs? Was he hearing all of this? He probably agreed with everything her father was saying. Dr. Clement, who treated Elias, had soon learned of the abuse and asked her once why she stayed.

What could she say? A sense of duty? Pure mule-headedness, a word she remembered her mother saying once. If she even remembered correctly. It had been fourteen years and she'd only been eight. Besides, she had no other place to go.

From long practice, Rio refused to let either his curses or his blame touch her. She'd quit caring about her father years ago, when she'd been a child. After a while, in a lesson she'd learned well, the heart and mind grew callouses.

"Lazy little bitch! Where have you been?" he went on, his mouth twisting with pain, with anger. "I called for you, girl. You're late. I knew you were down there just taking your sweet time. I'm thirsty. I need my morphine. I need it now. And straighten me up. I'm slumped over here like a sack of shit. Then change my bed. I had to piss, and you were too slow with the bedpan."

She wasn't late. To the contrary, not that she'd waste her time arguing. Grasping his thin shoulders, she braced herself against the mattress and drew him up, tucking a pillow in behind him. The time he could tolerate between doses of his drugs had grown shorter during these last few days. It wouldn't be much longer, she thought, until the cancer killed him. Or the morphine. He only held on because he kept expecting her half-brother Eino to arrive at the lake any day—this day by preference—ready and willing to take control of the business. Not that much remained of it except for the logging crew what with the hotel closed. Even before he'd become bedridden, Elias's irascibility had driven most of their hotel patrons away. Word had gotten around. Only the logging enterprise made him any money nowadays.

Every day that Eino remained away meant her father's temper grew more uncertain, and he took it out on her. As if her half-brother would care even if he knew. His attitude toward her had always copied his father's, which meant he'd ignored her the rare times he wasn't finding fault. She couldn't help thinking that if he'd died sometime, somewhere, in the last few months, it wouldn't break her heart. His silence deemed it possible. Even likely given Eino's propensity for causing fights.

"I've got your medicine right here." Her tray held a glass of cold water, a tiny porcelain salt cellar holding two brownish-colored hand-rolled pills, a mug of coffee, and a plate on which buttered toast, and a few rashers of bacon rested.

She went to set the tray on the bedside table but, his hand shaking, he grabbed the porcelain cup, tipped the pills into his mouth, and washed them down with a mouthful of water before she could act. Water spilled onto the sheet, soaking him. Oddly, he didn't seem to feel it.

"Get me another pill," he said. "You've been cheating on my dose. I need more morphine." He called his medication morphine, but he needed far more of the drug than the doctor's prescription allowed. Now he took contraband opium, as well.

Pushing the rest of her offering away, he came within an inch of drenching Rio with the steaming coffee, while managing to dump the toast on the floor. "I'm not hungry. Take that crap and throw it to the hogs."

A joke? He didn't own any hogs. Never had, never would.

"You're already taking twice as much of the medicine than the doctor prescribed," Rio said, just as she did every time he begged for more. "If you take too much, it could kill you."

"What difference does it make? I'm dying anyway."

Truthfully, she'd count his death a relief. The only problem with that being whether she'd get the blame.

She had one more argument, the only one, aside

from Eino's absence that might concern him. "You know I have to buy your opium pills on the sly. It's grown more dear now. I'm charged more every time, and Li Bai demands cash in hand."

Today, for the first time, Elias changed his tune regarding the cost, though he'd railed against it before. "It eases the pain and that's all I care about." He growled the excuse. Settling back against the pillow, he glared at her. "And fix my bed. What're you waiting for?"

He'd never once asked how she'd managed to acquire the extra doses of opium. Or even how she paid for them. She had to bargain with the Chinese cook on Washington Ames's logging crew. He got the drug from smugglers who brought it from the coast. Who they were and how he organized his part in the trade she didn't know and didn't care to ask, but it was, all in all, a humiliating experience. Dealing for it made her feel dirty and ashamed.

Yesterday, Li Bai had eyed her, his gaze lascivious as it moved over her body, then withheld the little tin box holding the opium until he had her money in hand. She'd wished to shrivel down to nothing so he couldn't see her. And he'd known.

"Opium hard to get," he said, grinning. "Comes from Canada. I pay more money, you pay more money." He cast a cautious look around as they met down by the wash house behind the cook shack. "They blame me if they find out and he die. Cost you more next time. You no pay, that is all. No more."

Sometimes Rio wondered if what he sold her was even the real stuff, considering the way her father complained. But eventually Elias's eyes would dilate and grow hazy, so she guessed it must be. And though he still moaned, at least his body grew slack and he slept, Not, apparently, without dreams.

Elias Salo had come to the eastern Washington territory with the army in 1879, where there'd been a small outpost set up on the shore of Painter's Lake. When his term was up, he'd managed, by hook or by crook, Rio didn't know which, to acquire a large chunk of the lake's north shore, most of which consisted of rather steep, though heavily timbered land. Counting on the picture-perfect setting to make his fortune, he got married, built the hotel, and prepared to start a dynasty. He even made a lot of money, but disappointment followed. His first wife died after bearing a son; his second wife ran away eight years after bearing a daughter, that daughter being Rio.

Rio, as she grew up, could only conclude he'd always been a mean, irascible man and it was no wonder her mother ran away. The only question was why she left Rio behind. It wasn't as if Elias had ever concerned himself with an unwanted girl child. As she remembered, even her mother had been more like an employee, valued because she singlehandedly kept the hotel afloat.

Though confined to his bed and growing weaker every day, he still ruled his little empire there at the edge of the lake. Or thought he did. He remained unaware that Rio gave the day-to-day orders, which mostly consisted of telling Wash Ames to use his own judgment when it came to hiring men for the timber crew, and even deciding where to work next.

"One of these years," Elias said over and over, to Rio and to anyone else who'd listen, "this land is going to be worth a fortune. A second fortune." He'd laugh then, and say, "I've made one fortune already. Me. A poor Finn from the old country. This land is my legacy. Mine and my son's."

He used to take great pleasure in bragging to his friends—when he still had some—about the money he'd made from the timber he'd cut and floated across the lake to the big sawmills on the outskirts of town. That, plus the success of the hotel until it began failing after Rio's mother left. He went from being the poor Finn who no longer had to count every dollar he spent to choosing not to spend any. Not much on himself, and certainly none on Rio. "I'm saving it all," he said, "for Eino. For my son when he comes home."

For a son who didn't care enough to even let his father know his whereabouts.

Rio didn't know why all these bitter thoughts filled her head as, without speaking, she bathed him, changed the bedding and straightened his thin, wizened body. Maybe because of the repetition since she heard him repeat the same story every...single...day. Months ago, she'd resolved to shut her ears, to never dwell on his complaints. She'd had to if she didn't want to let him break her—which she didn't.

When the drug finally put Elias to sleep and she finished cleaning his room, she went to care for her own small domain. No larger than the dressing room in the hotel's seldom-used premier suite, it suited her. It had a window where the prevailing breeze cooled her in summer, and it backed onto the chimney where a basement steam boiler provided the hotel's heat in winter. This past winter, it had seldom been fired. No need when her father's room had a small wood stove and she'd been responsible for keeping the fire burning. When it got cold, she just piled on another blanket and invited the dog to sleep with her.

Lord knows there'd been no guests to speak of lately. A few hunters in the autumn, but none since then. Rio had been grateful. She had enough to do caring for Elias, keeping the place up, and discussing the logging business with the timber boss. Which reminded her. She and Washington Ames had a meeting scheduled for first thing this morning, and if her inner clock hadn't gone wrong, Ames was already a few minutes late. Or she was.

Pausing to collect some notes she'd made for the meeting, Rio headed downstairs.

At the same time, someone, in an eerie repetition of her earlier, nighttime visitors, pressed the button and started the bell ringing.

It couldn't be Wash, she thought. He always came to the kitchen from the back. Besides, he knew, or guessed, about her problems with her father.

As she stepped to the landing, she heard the door at the end of the hall open. The man's head poked out.

"Keep your mouth shut if anyone asks about us." He spoke just above a whisper. "And don't play dumb with me. You'll know if it's us he's talking about." His head withdrew into the room but she didn't hear the door actually close.

By then, the person outside had his finger hard on the bell button. She dashed across the lobby and flung open the door.

"Would you kindly leave go of the bell! My father is ill and you'll disturb him." The words were out of her mouth before she got a good look at the man who stood on the hotel doorstep. They were words she might not have uttered if she had.

"Sheriff Donaldson," she said. Then, and against her better judgment, she added, "Can I help you?"

The sheriff, big, middle-aged, well-padded, and self-important, scowled at her. Rain dripping from the brim of a ridiculous-looking high crowned bowler hat was soaking into his well-cut gray suit, turning the wool almost black. "You've kept me waiting. I'm wet. Why is this door locked?" He shoved past her and entered.

Rio didn't move. She spoke to his back, doing her best to keep her voice from shaking. This man scared her. Always had, always would. "The door is locked to keep intruders out." She was proud of herself. She sounded quite cool. Emboldened, she added, "This is no longer a public facility, but a private home. Just as the sign outside says. I'm sure you wouldn't welcome someone barging into your house without an invitation."

He had to turn around to speak to her. "They walk in my house I'd shoot the..." He at least had the manners to quiet his rough language.

"No doubt." She didn't know if any of the men he was reported to have shot dead had walked into his house without invitation, but figured Donaldson's story would always be that they'd invaded and that he had a constitutional right to protect his property.

She couldn't help wondering if she used this same defense, she'd get off scot-free. Might be best if she didn't test the theory.

"Where is Elias?" he demanded, looking around the cold, dark lobby as if her father would appear at his demand. "I need to talk to him."

"He's become bedridden, I'm afraid. Upstairs. He's asleep. And I'd appreciate it if you'd leave him be. The pain keeps him awake much of the time as it is. Perhaps I can help if you'll tell me why you need to talk to him."

Donaldson's rather bulbous nose looked down at her, as if she were beneath his consideration. Except for his eyes. A dull, hard gray like river stone. Those undressed her and left her naked. "I've known Elias Salo for a good many years." His upper lip curled. "The day he'd give a pea-wit girl authority to speak for him is the day I resign from sheriffing."

Really? Then prepare to resign. She barely stopped herself from saying say so out loud. Besides, saying Elias had given her the authority did stretch the truth. Somehow, she'd just taken to doing things and he'd pretended not to notice. As much as he reviled the necessity, he realized he needed her help.

As if she were invisible and everything she'd said passed unheard between one ear and the other, the sheriff strode across the lobby and began mounting the stairs.

"Mr. Donaldson! Sir. Please do not disturb my father."

Her plea ignored, Donaldson, evidently familiar with the hotel's layout, turned to the left toward the family rooms. From there, he opened every closed door, including the one to her tiny hideaway, where he stood a moment, his nose pointing up and sniffing.

Rio shuddered. As far as she could tell, there wasn't much difference between Donaldson and Li Bai. Except the sheriff might be even more dangerous.

But he went on until he came to the end door. Opening it, he recoiled. "What the hell?" His roar of surprise was barely muted, and loud enough to penetrate Elias's slumber—or maybe stupor. He opened his eyes.

"Donaldson? What are you doing here?" Elias floundered, trying to sit up. "Here, girl," he said, "give me a hand."

Sliding past the sheriff, who stood blocking the doorway, for once Rio was happy to do as her father demanded. Better to deal with the devil she knew, meaning her rudely awakened father, than with a snake like Sheriff Thor Donaldson.

Once upright, Elias appeared more like himself. "What do you want that my daughter can't tell you? She's my eyes and ears since I got sick. I'm dying, you know. Doc says so and I feel it coming. I want to be left alone and in peace while I'm waiting for Eino to get home. Just don't mistake this. I'm still in charge."

It was a long speech for him. One Donaldson frowned over. "So if there'd been any strangers around here, looking for a place to stay, you'd have seen 'em, right? See'n as how you seem to be stuck here."

"The hotel is closed. No guests. Didn't Rio tell you?"

"That's not a yes or a no."

"I ain't seen anybody but the girl and my timber boss for a week. Until you. And I don't want to see you. We're done, Donaldson. You can leave." With that, Elias closed his eyes and from all appearances, went back to sleep. Rio knew different.

Rio had known her father disliked the sheriff but hadn't realized his feelings went this far. She'd heard Elias say he believed the sheriff responsible for half the crime in the county and he'd always been careful in his dealings with Donaldson.

He must believe he has nothing to lose, she thought. *But what about me?*

"Elias," Donaldson said, sharp and loud, but Elias didn't move.

Rio tucked the blanket higher around her father, as he always complained of the cold. Straightening, she said, "I'll show you out."

Donaldson stumbled going down the stairs, hissing his displeasure of the dark. "I'll take a look around first."

"No, sir, you will not. You've already disturbed my father for nothing. You didn't even ask a real question. See any strangers? What does that even mean? Are you looking for someone in particular or are you just curious about the hotel business? Or lack of business, since we're closed."

He stared at her. "Got a sassy mouth, don't you, girl? You forgetting who you're talking to?"

"I'm talking to you the same way I'd talk to anyone who entered my home uninvited and bothered my sick father."

He bent toward her, his murky pale eyes snapping. "I ain't just anybody. I'm the law round here. You do as I say or you can be in deep trouble."

She didn't answer. She couldn't. Instead, she walked across the lobby and to the door, holding it open with white-knuckled fingers. "Goodbye," she said, and was surprised when he walked out onto the porch.

But standing there, half in, half out, he still had one more thing to say. "I'll be talking to this timber boss. You'd better hope he backs up your story."

"What story are you talking about?" Rio knew her

voice rose. "I don't have a story. And you haven't said a single thing that has a point to it."

She'd had enough. She slammed the door behind him and twisted the key in the lock. More impressive perhaps, if she hadn't then leaned her back against the cool mahogany wood and fought off dizzying waves of blackness.

Three

A man spoke from across the lobby, his quiet drawl startling her. "What did Donaldson want?"

Rio jerked erect. "Mr. Ames?"

He stood in the doorway from the kitchen, Boo at his side. "Yes, ma'am, it's me. We've got a meeting this morning, don't we?"

"Yes. If you'll just give me a minute." Glory be, she didn't want him to see her like this, shaking, her face red—unless she'd gone white. Red for anger, white for fear.

A couple deep breaths later, she crossed the lobby and entered the kitchen. Washington Ames—Wash, for short—already had a pencil in hand with a scrap of used envelope sitting in front of him at the kitchen table in case he needed to make notes.

Rio didn't think herself capable of cohesive thought at the moment. She went to the stove, took two mugs from the shelf at the side, and picked up the coffee pot, waving it in Wash's direction. "Coffee?"

His eyes, an unusual dark blue in color, were fixed on her. Probing, wary. "Sure."

This was rote. She always offered coffee, he always said yes. Yes, also to the cream she set out, saying the cream was a treat, but no to the sugar.

Her hands still trembled as she set the cup before him and put a few licks of cream on a dish for Boo.

"Did he touch you?" His body stiff and tense, Wash watched her carefully.

No mistaking the *he* Wash meant. Looking down, she swallowed. "Just his eyes."

A wealth of meaning resounded in those terse words. Meaning she hadn't intended to reveal. "It's all right. I'll survive." Forcing a twitch of the lips to serve as a smile, she waved a hand. "Down to business, Mr. Ames. Were you able to discover why Mr. Hightower is late in reporting the evaluation? Or has he turned up after all?" This last sounded on a hopeful note. Their timber cruiser should have reported in yesterday afternoon, and last night would've been a bad night to spend camped in the woods.

"No. He hasn't reported in. Considering the storm last night, I gotta say I'm a bit worried about him." A frown creasing his face, Wash twirled his spoon in his coffee. "It isn't like him to just up and go to the next job and not let me know. Me or somebody. The Celestial crew likes him, calls him friend. Last timber cruiser we hired always managed to cheat the Chinese out of a few dollars. Hightower is honest with everybody, whether they work directly for your dad or whether we contract with the independents. He's been a steady worker for almost two years."

"He didn't just go on a toot?"

"Not him. He's not a drinkin' man. Agrees some with the ladies of the temperance league. If he isn't back by tonight, I'll go looking for him. He could've had an accident and be too hurt to make it back on his own."

Rio clasped her hands. "Oh, no. I hope he's safe."

Rio had taken Wash's advice and spoken to her father about logging the tract on the north side of his property this season as soon as the weather turned warmer, and the woods dried. The land was steep, and both she and Wash were unwilling to risk the horses in slippery, muddy footing. With last night's heavy rain, with the timber cruiser's report in hand, needed supplies could be brought in as they waited for the mud to dry.

Elias, sure about Wash's recommendation, hadn't even listened. He just nodded once. Good enough.

Trouble was, if their cruiser didn't show up with results of the evaluation, there'd be a delay. It all depended on if he'd been hurt. Or worse. "Can you find someone to take Mr. Hightower's place? If he's hurt, I mean."

Wash shook his head. "Could be tough. Give me a couple days as it might take a while. All the experienced fellers I know right off are busy and the rest can't add two plus two to make four. I might have to do it myself, though I'd rather not."

"All right," Rio said, sighing. "Let me know, and if necessary, I'll clear a new hire with my father."

Actually, she wouldn't. Within the last couple weeks, he'd lost any interest in the everyday needs of his company, seeming to believe he'd either already given his orders, or that his timber boss—meaning Wash—didn't need direction. Which he didn't, really.

But she would keep the charade going for the sake of the business. Salo Wood Products had a reputation to uphold. She, with Wash's help, had been running the outfit for several months now, and nobody seemed to have cottoned to her deception. Certainly not her father, although she believed Wash knew. Part of it, anyhow. And just to think of Donaldson's reaction terrified her.

Wash made a few notes on his envelope as they talked on, then folded it and tucked the paper, along with his pencil stub, in the inside pocket of his jacket. He rose, took a step, then turned back to study her a moment longer. "You gonna be all right, Miss Salo?"

Rio's lashes swept down to hide her eyes. Good glory! Did her every thought show on her face? She needed to get better at hiding them.

"I'm fine. The sheriff didn't scare me. He just made me mad." She uttered the lie with no hope of being believed.

And she wasn't, an easy tell going by Wash's shake of the head. But he pretended just like she did.

"You let me know if you're worried, and I'll take care of it." His smile touched her like a caress. "Can't have our boss lady held up by a man like Thor Donaldson."

She couldn't force an answering smile, but her innards gave a funny little jiggle. "And I can't have my timber boss jailed on some trumped-up charge by a man like Thor Donaldson. Ignore him. I'm going to."

The moment, she might've known, was spoiled when her father's bellow swam down the stairs. "Rio, where the hell is my medicine? I need my morphine. I need it now."

Wash already on his way out, stopped in his tracks. "Want some help?"

She couldn't bear for Wash to see—to hear—the way her father treated her. "Nah. You go ahead. We'll be fine here."

WASH, having come in just before Rio and Sheriff Donaldson descended the stairs, mulled over every word he'd heard of their spat. If spat is what one could call it. While he admired Rio's pluck at refusing to knuckle under the sheriff's bullying ways, he didn't think she'd paid enough attention to his threats. At the same time, he couldn't quite figure why Donaldson had pressed her about seeing strangers, or why he wanted to look through the hotel. To tell the truth, Wash was surprised the sheriff hadn't insisted. Whatever was going on seemed to have him worried.

But he hadn't forgotten Donaldson intended on talking to him. If he followed through, Wash planned to discover answers to a few of those questions. Meanwhile, he wanted the sheriff to believe he was catching Wash by surprise, so instead of taking the main road between the hotel and the barracks, he took a shorter route to the cook shack. One hidden from the view of anyone taking the road like Donaldson, who was driving a buggy, would have to do.

Donaldson, if he showed up at all, could find him there. Just as if he'd never been anywhere else.

The rain had stopped, although water still dripped from the trees overhanging the shortcut path through the woods. When he'd come this way earlier for the meeting with Miss Salo, in anticipating seeing her, he hadn't noticed, but now his gaze landed on footprints etched in the mud at the path's verge. Two sets, if he wasn't mistaken, one set larger than the other.

Who could those footprints belong to? This being a private path, one even the sheriff probably didn't know existed, Wash's own should be the only ones on here. They pointed directly toward the hotel, but there were none going the other way.

A few yards before he came through into the logging crew's camp, he found where the tracks had appeared out of the surrounding woods. Maybe there was something to Donaldson's curiosity about strangers.

Over on the road, he was aware of Donaldson's horse and buggy getting closer. With no more time to ponder the tracks, he slipped into the cook shack where he found Li Bai stirring something in a huge pot. A kind of stew, he figured, with the cook's own touch of foreign flavorings mixed in.

"Sheriff is coming," he said, and took note of the way Li Bai's head jerked up, reminding him of a wary rabbit sensing a hawk's hunting eye. "Looks like he's headed here." Or would be as soon as he found the bunkhouse empty.

"Here? What for?" A wealth of caution showed in the way Li Bai asked the questions.

"He probably just wants to talk, but if I was you, I'd forget my English." Wash winked at the Chinaman. "Or find a chore somewhere else."

Li Bai nodded. "Yes, yes. I go. You stir the pot two times. Yes?" He might not even have been mentioning the sheriff, he acted so careless.

Wash found a cup, poured some of the cook's

deplorable coffee into it, and tipped his chair back so he could see out the window. "I will."

Quick as one of those scared rabbits, Li Bai ducked around the back of the building. Congratulating himself on the nifty way he got rid of the cook, seconds later Wash heard Donaldson holler "whoa." Buggy springs squeaked as he jumped from the vehicle, his boots squishing in the mud.

Almost absently, Wash got up and went to the stove where he stirred the pot. Engrossed with the slosh of the spoon when Donaldson walked into the cook shack, he didn't look up.

As for the sheriff, he didn't bother to scrape his boots. Clumps of mud fell on Li Bai's clean floor.

"I been looking for you," Donaldson said. "Where you been? And where's the Chink?"

Wash shrugged. "He didn't say. Outhouse'd be my guess. Whatever he's cooking here, it sure smells good." And a second later, and without answering to his own whereabouts, "Anything I can do for you, sheriff?"

"Are you in charge around here, Ames? Because I've just been over at the hotel and that stupid girl don't know nothing about nothing. She may be pretty as a picture but she ain't got much sense. Only thing smart about her is her mouth. I'd like to—" Donaldson cut himself off mid-sentence.

Clenching his jaw tight and hoping no particular expression showed, Wash said, "Miss Salo is a fine-looking woman, that's for sure." He hadn't much—or any—patience for stringing this out. "You say you've been looking for me? Why?"

"You're out in these woods often enough. I hear

you're thinking about logging off Salo's quarter section up north. That true?"

And how, Wash wondered, had the sheriff come by that information? The crew hadn't even been told about it yet, the plan remaining between him, Hightower, and Rio. And maybe Elias, if he was cognizant enough to remember. But now, with Hightower missing, here Donaldson was asking probing questions.

His senses went on high alert.

"Possible," he said. "Depends on the cruiser's recommendation."

"Huh. Might be best if you was to pick another section." Donaldson pressed for an answer, his eyes icy.

Wash went just as cold. "Oh? Why is that?"

"Just sayin'. I've been hearing things."

"What things?"

Donaldson glared. "That's good advice. I was you, I'd listen."

"I don't think Salo's business is any of yours. Now, is there anything else?"

The sheriff huffed. "Cagey, ain't you? Yeah, I want to know if you've seen any strangers around the hotel lately. This morning, for instance. Early. Real early. A couple fellows who got no business in these parts. The girl said they ain't staying there, but I don't trust a thing she says."

"The hotel is closed," Wash said. "Has been since last fall. Miss Salo's got enough to do taking care of Elias, let alone looking after a bunch of hotel guests. Elias is a difficult patient."

Everyone who knew Elias knew that, so Wash wasn't telling tales out of school. He, and they, also knew Elias had no particular generosity toward his daughter, let alone gratitude for her care. Wash more than anyone else.

"Does that mean you ain't seen anybody?"

He nodded. "That's what it means." He noticed Donaldson didn't mention that Rio had forced him from the hotel, mostly by strength of will. Or even that he'd been upstairs to talk with Elias and come back down dissatisfied. But then, Wash didn't say he'd witnessed it either.

He had a few questions of his own. "These strangers, sheriff. Who are they and why are you looking for them? What do they look like and what've they done? I take it they're wanted by the law."

A strange look, almost a smirk, spread across Donaldson's face. "They're wanted by the law, all right. I dunno what they look like. I was just told about them and that I'd best take them in, dead or alive. As for what they done..." He drew in a breath. "Murder."

Just like that, Wash knew he was lying. Oh, not about the law, or only that Donaldson himself most probably was the only law wanting to take them in. Best if dead, from the way he talked. But as to their crime? That was the question. Had there been a murder? Wash hadn't heard of anyone turning up dead.

"Who's been murdered?" he asked. The missing Hightower crossed his mind.

"Keeping it quiet for now," the sheriff said.

"Well, then..." Wash took out the silver pocket watch he carried in a vest pocket and looked at it. "I've things to do. I'll be keeping an eye out for strangers and let you know if I see any. But now I need to hitch up a team and get a load of grain for the horses hauled to the camp up north. So, I reckon we're done here?"

Donaldson took the hint and headed for the door. "Yeah, we're done. For now. And Ames, you watch yourself. Make sure you report to me. Only to me."

As with most everything the man said, there seemed to be a threat behind his demand and Wash heard it clearly.

Wash followed the sheriff outside and watched until Donaldson hefted himself in the buggy. Only then did Wash mount his horse and turn him toward the barn where he planned to pick up the team and wagon. He hadn't been fibbing about that. But first, he stayed long enough to watch Donaldson drive away and gain the main road toward town.

He'd forgotten to give the stew pot its second stir. Hadn't forgotten about those footprints he'd seen in the woods though. Murderers running from the law? Witnesses running from the killer? Or simple folk making their way through the woods?

Four

Upstairs in the hotel, Elias writhed as the pain settled deep in his bones. Both femurs ached with unremitting agony, until finally, he could stand it no longer. Reaching over to the side table, he picked up the cowbell and shook it. The bell was connected with a wire that caused smaller bells, one in Rio's bedroom and one in the kitchen, to peal.

"Rio," he called out, "Rio. Get in here, girl. Bring my pills. I need my pills."

"Coming. I'm fixing you a tray." Her voice floated up to him from downstairs, but as usual, it took a couple minutes before he heard her light footsteps on the stairs. She needed a little time to set up his tray, or so she said, but he didn't believe her. Why didn't she always have one ready? He didn't like waiting.

Tears of pain leaked from behind Elias's half-closed lids, but he sensed when Rio entered the room. He even heard her little gasp.

This time, the tray held not only his little brown pills—only two of them, damn her, when she knew he needed three. At least three—but also some steaming soup and applesauce, rich with the scent of cinnamon.

Pap, he thought in disgust. Food for a baby. But about all he could get past his dry throat nowadays. He couldn't swallow real food. It didn't matter. He wasn't hungry anyway. He just needed his pills.

Why didn't Eino come home? Where was the boy? He couldn't hold out much longer. Not in this shape. The cancer was eating him alive. Self-pity brought tears to his eyes.

"The morphine is gone but I've got your opium right here," Rio said. "Let me help you up." Her arms stretched around him, heaving him into a more upright position.

No matter how he tried, for some reason he always ended up as this twisted hulk.

"My morphine," he moaned.

"Yes, yes. Here." She thrust the little salt cellar into his hand and held a cup of water ready. No glass this time, he noticed. She'd given him a tin cup instead. Unbreakable even if he threw it across the room. If he could throw anything that far. Maybe he'd throw it at her. He wouldn't mind seeing her bleed. Not mind at all.

"More. I need more of my medicine." He was begging, ashamed, yet angry, too, when she didn't rush to obey him. "Dammit, girl, two isn't enough. You know it isn't."

"Eat first."

Rio's insistence got the soup bowl under his chin, but his hand shook so hard she ended up spooning a bit of the broth into his mouth. When he just couldn't eat any more, when it took too much effort to swallow anything besides his medicine, he brushed her away.

"One more pill," he said. "Just one more and I'll try to make it do until afternoon."

Clamping her lips together, she finally looked him full-on in the face. It was something she hadn't done for weeks as his sickness grew. "There isn't any more. This was the last Li Bai will give me. I'm sorry, but I don't have the money to pay for more. The price went up. Every time I go to him for more, it's gone up."

Elias started to get angry, to berate her. Damn the girl! She was lying. She had to be. But then, with a hopeless sort of realization, he knew she wasn't. She'd get the pills for him if she could. Oh, not for the sake of easing his pain but simply to shut him up.

He supposed she had run short of cash now the hotel was closed. He'd have to tell her his secret. He'd been saving the money for Eino—and there was plenty of it—but now he gave up. He couldn't stand to be without his drugs. Not even for Eino.

"There's money," he whispered.

"I know. Your bank account is healthy enough. I am not cleared to get money from the bank, if you remember."

She'd asked him to put her on the account, but he'd gotten angry. He'd said no, that he would dole out money to her as he'd always done. He'd said women didn't know what to do with money except spend it on fripperies, and that bank accounts were for men. He was still of that opinion, even though matters had changed when he got so ill. Perhaps he could set up a deal with the bank to release a certain amount to her each month. Enough for his medicine.

The thought eased his conscience. Come to think of it, he didn't remember giving her any money for quite some time. He'd write to Masterson at the bank and get the letter sent today with the authorization. But that wouldn't kick in for a couple of days. She said this was the last of his drug. He had to have more. Today. Now.

"No," he said. "There's money here. I always keep some on hand at home. In case a deal comes up that needs worked right away." His eyes drifted shut as the opium began numbing his pain. He forced them open again. "You go away now. I'll get it when you've gone."

She went silent as she stared down at him. Then, "When I've gone?"

For some reason, her query made him angry again. "Yes. When you've gone downstairs. It's a secret. Not for you, you spying little..." He stopped himself. "Go on. Get out."

Her breath came and went, came and went. And again. Slowly, she turned and left the room. She didn't close the door behind her, but then she never did. It remained open during the day so she'd hear if he called. Which he often did.

It didn't matter. He clearly heard her footsteps retreating down the stairs, upon which he struggled to get out of the bed. It wasn't easy and he cursed the weakness making such a simple act incredibly difficult. But he managed to stagger to the tall armoire standing across the room.

Elias was sweating when he got back in bed, several bills and a few coins clutched in his hand. He pulled the blankets around him, chilled from his foray out of the bed, and promptly slumped sideways. It didn't matter. He was used to it now.

Sleep, dreams, and numbness took him away without realizing when the money spilled from his opened hand.

RIO, desperate and a little afraid of what might happen if she didn't have money in hand soon, went downstairs all right, but taking every precaution, she removed her shoes and came right back up, her footsteps silent on the stairs. It was easy to peek through the five-inch opening between the jamb and the door's edge to where she had a perfect view of Elias's room reflected in the dresser mirror.

She watched him fight his way out of the bed and go to the armoire. Once there, his legs shaking under his nightshirt, he moved his spare pair of shoes and lifted a board on the bottom of the cupboard. He fished around in there for several moments, then replaced the board and staggered back to the bed, money visible in his hand.

The secretive old devil.

So. Now she knew. After being afraid to mention money to him for the past ten days, when she'd spent every cent of her lifetime savings to buy his drug, he'd had plenty of money right here. What a fool she'd been. What a fool he'd made of her, just like always. She could almost feel the callouses on her heart growing thicker. Whatever loyalty she'd ever felt toward him, toward Eino, flew away.

Her father fell into a heavy drugged sleep almost at once. Rio went to the bed then and without him even stirring, withdrew a couple bills from those he'd dropped in the bed. It hadn't looked as though he'd actually counted the money, and if he had, she could always argue he'd miscounted. He'd mentioned several times that his vision was often clouded nowadays. Shoving the bills into a pocket, she left the room as silently as she'd come.

Boo, who knew never to let Elias see him, sat at the bottom of the stairs. Her unexpected—and unwelcome—guest awaited her there as well. As an indication of her weariness, Rio came near to panicking when she saw him—the man, not the dog. Her eyes widened in dismay. It seemed impossible, but she'd almost forgotten he and his wounded companion were in the room at the end of the hall. There hadn't been a peep out of them since she'd taken the boy's shirt to burn. Not from the wounded boy and not from the man. The middle-of-the-night surgery felt more like a dream, a bad dream, than anything to do with real life, and for a moment she wondered if she'd imagined it.

Evidently not since when he spoke he didn't strike her as dreamy in the least.

"Did you tell him about us? Did you tell anyone?"

His gaze traveled toward the upper floor, so he must mean her father. It occurred to her that he'd probably overheard her conversations with both Donaldson and Wash Ames. "No."

"You're sure?"

Rio'd had about enough of men questioning her today. And only Mr. Ames had been anywhere near polite. "I'm sure." It came out as a snarl and a little louder than she'd meant.

He put up both hands as though to fend her off, which only made her angrier.

He jerked his head toward the stairs. "Is that your father up there? You positive you didn't tell him?"

"Yes, it's my father up there, and yes, I'm positive." Her lips tightened, which, though she was unaware, deepened a dimple at the side of her mouth. "He's sick. I don't tell him anything. If it concerns me, he doesn't care anyway. Never has, never will." Aware she'd just said some things she had no business telling a complete stranger, she picked up her shoes from where she'd left them on the bottom step and backed away from him.

The speech silenced him. His look softened, until she figured he'd probably heard her father yelling at her this morning.

She took a breath. "Is he—your brother—any better?" Easing away from the stairs, she headed toward the kitchen. Unfortunately, he moved along with her.

"What makes you think he's my brother?"

"Isn't he? The two of you look similar." She'd spoken more to fill the silence than anything, but evidently her assumption of their relationship made him frown.

He smiled a little then, as if giving in to her observation. But then he said, "He's not so good."

The less than cheerful answer made her a little nervous. "He needs a doctor. A real doctor."

He shook his head. "No."

"I don't want him dying here," she said, well aware of how harsh that sounded. "When will you be leaving?"

"I don't know. When he's better. You got any more of that concoction you gave him last night? He's in a lot of pain and it seemed to help a little. I wish..." Then he gave a snort, an inexplicable sound under the circumstances, and shook his head. "How far is the nearest town? I need to buy some supplies. Or if I give you some money, maybe you could go buy some for us. I don't want to leave him alone."

"And I don't leave my father for any long shopping trips. The town is just across the lake. You'll have to go yourself. You know how to row a boat, don't you?"

"I do, but your boat would be a dead giveaway that you have guests."

He had a point.

They'd reached the kitchen. He stopped in the doorway as she pulled out a chair, seated herself, and put on her shoes. Rio supposed he didn't want to leave the boy by himself, but that might stem less from the state of his health, than to keep their presence here secret. Her curiosity soared. How and why had the boy gotten shot? What were they doing out in the woods? Salo's woods, if she wasn't mistaken, in the middle of the night? And who had done the shooting? Who were they, anyway?

From the grim look the man gave her, she hesitated to ask.

"What do you need?" She hoped it was something she could give them. Anything to get them out of the hotel. They had to be the men Sheriff Donaldson was looking for, and she didn't want him coming back and saying he was going to search. A cruel man, he'd take pleasure in making her suffer for it if he found out about them occupying a room in the hotel. And probably make her father suffer, as well, no matter how sick. Elias had never made any bones about disliking Donaldson, and the sheriff was known as a vengeful man. His position gave him license to wallow in his cruelty.

The man looked surprised that she'd ask. "Are you offering to help?"

"No...yes...maybe."

He didn't question her half-answer. Holding up a hand, he curled his fingers one by one as he ticked off a list. "I need trail food, ammunition for a .44, bedrolls, a shirt and medicine for Win, a couple horses."

His list was longer than she liked. If they had been traveling or camping or whatever they'd been doing on the Salo property, what had happened to their things? In the middle of the night, no less? Had they been on foot? They must have started out better prepared than it sounded.

"I can give you food, a bedroll, a shirt, and some medicine. About the ammunition, I'm not sure, and the horses, probably not."

"Probably not?"

She lifted her chin. "I cannot."

He said something under his breath she didn't hear. But what she saw was the way he lifted his nose and scented the soup. Neither he nor the boy had had anything to eat today. That she knew of, anyway. Or maybe, for all she knew, they'd been hungry longer than that, considering the way they'd showed up here with nothing.

The boy, she reflected, should eat and drink to rebuild his blood and regain his strength, if he were able.

As if to reinforce her conclusion, a pitiful call came from down the corridor and the open door to the fourth room. "Beck, where are you? Beckett?"

Beckett. So now she had a name. Boo's funny little floppy ears pricked.

"He sounds weak," she said, taking pity on both men, even though it went against her instincts. "I made soup. You should have some. You and your brother."

"It smells good. I know he's hungry. If you can just spare some for my brother, I'll be grateful."

"There's plenty for you both. Eat as much as you like." She'd made the soup from the least desirable parts of an old hen, saving the best for her supper. It was the work of a minute to set out a couple bowls and spoons, a packet of crackers and put the pot and the ladle in the middle of the table. Making a motion of invitation with her hand, she gathered her jacket from a hook beside the back door and prepared to go out.

"Aren't you eating?" Beckett eyed her warily.

She sighed. "Not just now. I have to—I have a chore to do first, before my father wakes up again. Just help yourselves."

"A chore?" The question held a wealth of suspicion.

"Oh, don't worry. I won't tell anyone you're here. Why would I? You're just regular hotel guests as far as I know. And I never ask anything personal of the guests. They come, they pay for lodging, and they leave." Shrugging, she tugged open the door and left Beckett staring down at the soup.

Five

Going by foot, the main cook shack where Rio planned to meet Li Bai, as well as the way to the crew's bunkhouse, took about twenty minutes provided she walked fast. Calling to Boo, they hurried along. Part of the path followed the shoreline of the pretty bay cut into the banks of Painter's Lake. At the boat landing, instead of a separate mill pond, the logs were deposited directly into the lake and lifted into the sawmill from there. The finished lumber was floated on rafts to the other side of the lake to be loaded onto rail cars.

Li Bai would soon be gone if Rio didn't hurry. He usually did most of his cooking at the headquarters cook shack in the early morning, then packed it by mule to wherever the logging crew was working. Then all he and a helper needed to do was heat it up. She supposed that somewhere in the woods, he met his Canadian supplier for the drugs.

Wash Ames had once told her Li Bai insisted the one cook shack was more efficient than having two separate facilities, one at the sawmill and one at the logging site, but Rio had a notion Li Bai insisted because of his other job. Meaning the opium business, of course. She didn't know how it all worked, although she'd heard her father discussing the topic with other men a time or two when he wasn't aware she could hear them. That had been how she'd known to contact the Chinese cook when Elias began requiring more of the drug than the doctor would prescribe. He'd do anything to keep his pain at bay. What she did know was that this gave Li Bai more opportunity to openly serve his opium customers.

One might think Li Bai would be grateful and give his boss—or his boss's emissary, meaning her—a break on price. The thought made Rio huff. The man was a greedy soul, and ruthless besides. She hated him.

The sun had come out as she walked, and Rio reveled in the warmth on her shoulders. Better yet, the storm had cleared the air of smoke from the sawmill and burning slash. The noise of birds having a heyday in trees struck her as a cheerful sound, especially when mixed with Boo's eager little yips joining in. One thing marred her errand, the mud from last night's drenching rain underfoot.

At the cook shack, she found the Celestial securing the packs on his two mules, though they were so lightly laden, he really only needed one. The other, she suspected, was to carry a different cargo. She'd barely caught him in time.

He didn't seem particularly welcoming when he spotted her and Boo, especially Boo, on the path. Boo didn't like Li Bai and Li Bai didn't like Boo. The man threw up his hands and shook his head. "No, no, missy. No drug today. No credit. You get money first."

"I have money. Enough for three days worth of the drug. All right?"

He squinted at her. "Where you get money?"

On the verge of telling him the truth, Rio hesitated. Her temper flared at the thought of Li Bai, a Chinaman, having the nerve to question her. What if it occurred to the shifty little man that it might be easy to creep into the hotel and seek out Elias's cache? She wouldn't put such jiggery-pokery past him.

"A friend," she said. "I got a loan. Eino will pay him back when he returns." Let him make of that what he will. If he knew anything of her half brother, he'd know enough to doubt whether Eino would concern himself with paying his father's debts. But then, where she got the money had no reason to count with him. Being ready to hand some of it to him should be enough.

And it was.

———

THE HOTEL WAS EERILY silent when Rio and Boo slipped in through the back. Carefully, she wiped her muddy shoes on a mat, then walked on tiptoe into the kitchen, as silent as a thief. Noticing a chill, she lifted the lid into the stove's fire box as gently as if candling eggs as she restoked the fire, hoping to prevent the metal from clanging.

To her surprise, the big restaurant kitchen was as tidy as if she'd done the cleanup herself. The soup pot sat at the edge of the stove top, its contents still warm enough to eat. She went to fetch herself a bowl and found the ladle, spoons, and bowls she'd set out for Beckett and Win washed and stacked on the work counter. The table had been wiped free of crumbs, the cracker packet folded over and neat as a pin.

Sharing with Boo, she had just finished her soup and was contemplating a second bowl—after all, she'd had an early, and extremely upsetting start to her day, and needed fuel—when she heard a noise coming from the room where the brothers had taken up residence. A sound familiar to her after contending these last months with her father, that of someone thrashing helplessly in the bed. And was that...crying?

She stood up. Should she go see if she could help? She started, then stopped and listened again. The crying was coming from the boy, Win, and he sounded as if he were in terrible pain. But surely his brother would tend to him. And he, she felt certain, would not appreciate her concern—or her questions. He'd ignored every one she'd asked so far.

Though she listened, she heard no talking. Just the stifled crying. Why didn't either of them speak?

She jumped when another cry sounded. Louder this time. Slowly, she opened the tin, a whole tin this time, of product she'd bought from Li Bai and selected a pill. Should she or should she not offer it to the boy? Cutting it in half, she rolled it between her fingers into an even smaller pill. At the sink, she pumped out a cup of water and carried it toward the room.

The door, fully closed, for the most part muffled sounds coming from inside the room. The boy must've been fairly loud for her to have heard him.

Rio hesitated, then tapped on the door.

The sounds stopped.

She tapped again. “Win?” she called, her voice low. “Are you all right?”

No reply.

“Beckett?” She tried again. “Win?”

“Come in.” The shaky reply came in the boy’s voice.

She entered. A glance told her this room was as tidy as Beckett had left the kitchen. Every indication of the surgery had been cleaned away. Only the bed where Win lay showed his distress in the rumpled covers. The pillow was mashed flat, as if maybe he’d held it over his face in an attempt to stop his cries from being heard.

As for Win himself, his face and shirtless torso were almost as pale as the sheets. He’d been sick to his stomach as well. Rio well knew pain could take some people that way when it got to be too much. Win’s eyes, as he stared at her, were bloodshot and wet.

“What can I do to help?” she asked. Besides clean him up, she meant, the work of minutes, as practiced as she’d become. That, and try to alleviate his pain.

“I’m cold,” he whispered after she finished. “May I have another blanket?”

“Absolutely.” She rushed to the dresser and pulled out the bottom drawer where an extra blanket lay ready. She kept an extra in every guest room. First plumping his pillow and fitting it behind his head, she flung the blanket over him and tucked it around his shoulders.

Boo, who had followed her in without notice, jumped onto the bed beside the boy and curled at his side.

Win smiled wanly.

“Better?” Rio asked.

He nodded, although she didn't think she'd had helped much.

"Beckett said you might have more of that stuff you gave me earlier. For the pain." Whispering, his voice sounded rough. "Could I have some more, please? It hurts awful bad."

"Yes, certainly. But...have you ever taken opium?"

"Opium?" His eyes big, he shook his head. "No. Beckett says..." He stopped, then said, "Do you have opium?"

"Yes. My father takes it for his cancer pain. I can give you some if you want. Just a little bit. Maybe enough to let you sleep. Sleep helps a body to heal, you know."

"Yes. Please," he said. "It hurts so bad." He grimaced, an expression that for some reason looked... guilty. But guilty of what?

Though not at all sure giving the boy the drug was wise, she took out the small dose she'd prepared, but then hesitated. "Should we wait and ask your brother first? He might not—"

He cut her off. "He's not the one got shot. I did. And it's his fault."

Rio gasped. "It is?"

Win's mouth twisted. "Well, sort of. His job. Not him. His job. We...I...I can't tell you. Just, please, the pill."

She couldn't even say how relieved she was. Not a case of would-be fratricide, at least.

From being cold, Win was sweating now. Not so good, since going from chills to excess heat might portend an infection. Unless, Rio thought, he'd gotten overheated just thinking about giving away Beckett's secrets as he'd apparently come close to doing.

She helped him to sit, handed him the pill, and gave him the mug of water. "Drink all of this."

He struggled, but did, then lay back down and looked up at her. "Does it work fast?"

"I think so. Pretty fast."

"Can your dog stay with me?"

Rio hesitated for a single moment. "Sure. He'll be good company." Something she well knew from experience.

The pill did work quickly. Rio stayed by the boy's side, waiting to make sure the drug didn't cause problems. It didn't. Only a few minutes later Win had closed his eyes, the sweat dried, and the pain lines faded from his face as he dropped into slumber.

He would look just like his brother when he matured, Rio thought, looking down at him. Same dark hair, same dark—though maybe not quite as dark—eyes, same strong build. Good faces, both looking as if a smile was a more common expression than the tense, or in Win's case pained, frowns she'd seen so far. With his face relaxed he looked younger than the fourteen years she'd first thought although he did have a few whiskers sprouted. She wasn't good at guessing a boy's age and she believed he might be tall for his years.

They didn't—Beckett didn't—look like outlaws or killers. Whatever outlaws or killers looked like. She pictured them more with a face like Donaldson's. Or Li Bai's.

"What are you doing in here?"

The sharp, though quietly spoken query had her spinning around. The look on Beckett's face right now changed her mind into thinking he could indeed potentially be a outlaw. He looked angry. Suspicious. And his dark eyes were snapping.

"Tending to your brother. He called out for you, needing help." She put her forefinger to her lips to indicate quiet, and picking up the water cup, she whisked out of the room past him. He followed her into the kitchen where she deposited the mug in the sink. "He didn't seem to know where you were."

Beckett ignored what had come close to being a question and probably not any of her business. "Help with what?"

"First and foremost, he needed a blanket. The poor boy was freezing." Next came the part she needed to confess. "He's in a lot of pain, as well. So I gave him some medicine."

"That herb stuff? It doesn't help much. A little, maybe. I'm surprised he went to sleep."

"Not the herb stuff, which for your information is feverfew and willow bark among other things. I gave him half of one of my father's pills."

The way he grabbed her by the shoulders and pulled her right up into his face scared her. Her eyes widened. And if he didn't let go, she might need the other half of the pill for herself.

"Ow," she said, attempting to shake loose. Unsuccessfully, as her struggle only tightened his hold.

"You gave my brother morphine?" Beckett's teeth ground together.

Which proved he'd heard her father yelling at her to bring his pills this morning. "Let me go." It came out a mere squeak.

"You gave my brother morphine." He shook her.

"I gave him opium. He was in pain. He was crying."

Another shake. "My brother was crying?"

"Ow," she said again, almost ready to cry herself. "Yes."

He cursed, releasing her so suddenly she nearly fell. "Don't do it again. Hear me? Don't give Win drugs."

"Yes. I hear you." Feeling as if she couldn't stand up anymore, Rio staggered to a chair and collapsed onto it. "But the pill did ease his pain. It's letting him sleep. You should be glad of that."

Beckett had a glare that could crack the hull on a walnut. "Maybe so. But it's better he suffer the pain than become addicted."

"I don't believe one half-dose will addict anyone," she said in a small voice.

"Oh. You know these things, do you?"

She had no answer for that. Didn't she see evidence of what drugs could do, the good and the bad, every single day with her father? And there'd been Mrs. Schlinger, who had addicted not only herself but her baby, and finally killed them both. But Win, he would soon heal. A small dose or two, that's all she'd thought to give him, just to see him over the worst.

She opened her mouth to say as much, right up until he pulled out a kitchen chair and sat across from her. She stared at him. He stared back.

"I shouldn't have shaken you. I'm sorry," he said. "I know you were just trying to help."

Silenced, no, flummoxed by the apology, Rio nodded. "I should have asked you. I knew I should. He just...just. I felt so bad for him, in so much pain."

He nodded. "Yeah." He sighed and looked away. "It's killing me. That sonofa..." He stopped, his mouth tightening. "Last night, the rain was pouring down. Lightning was getting real close. Win and I had been leading our horses down some kind of trail, maybe an old deer trail, when we found a spot with shelter and decided to set up camp. I had our packs on the ground and was picketing the horses when a man who'd been standing under a tree out of the rain, shot at us. I don't know why. I didn't even see him at first."

"Did you shoot back?"

Beckett shook his head. "Didn't get the chance. For one thing, my pistol was under my coat where I couldn't get at it in a hurry. The horses, already spooked by the thunder and lightning, jerked away at the sound of gunfire and took off back the way they'd come. But the main thing is that Win got hit right away. All I could do is pick him up and run for it, leaving our belongings behind."

Rio gaped at him. "Shot in our woods? Why on earth would anyone do such a thing? Who..."

"Being a stranger here, I can't tell you. You'd know better than me. I'd sure as hell like to catch the man who did it, I can tell you that." He eyed her as if to find the answer written on her face.

Truth to tell, while Rio couldn't put a name to anybody, she was able to take a guess as to the why. It hadn't escaped her notice Li Bai had presented her with a fresh tin of opium this morning, when two days ago what she bought had been dry and stale looking and in a different container. And he'd counted off the pills she'd bought then in a more careful way as if to make certain not to give too much. In fact, she remembered, he'd tried to short her one pill.

Then there was the so-called deer trail. Could that

be the route the smugglers took to bring Li Bai the drugs, and Beckett and Win had accidentally found and followed it? Which might mean either the smuggler or Li Bai had shot Win and tried to shoot Beckett. But in that case, what was Sheriff Donaldson doing when he came around early this morning looking for strangers? How did he mix in this? How did he even know about it?

And so she put the question—or questions—to Beckett and watched the way his face turned hard and closed against her.

"You've raised some good questions, Miss Salo. Some very good questions. Maybe I'll see if I can find out." Beckett rose and without another word, retreated to the room where Win peacefully slept.

Feeling at a loss for no discernible reason, Rio got up to find her legs still a bit wobbly. Beckett had, just now, fulfilled her earliest impression of him, when she'd opened the door in the night and gotten swept into this...whatever it was. Commanding. Stern. Scary.

Scary in a different way than Thor Donaldson, but every bit as intimidating. And now she thought about it, earlier he'd asked her to procure a few items for him. A shirt, trail food, a bedroll, ammunition for his gun, a horse.

She'd start with the easiest item. A shirt.

Six

A year and a half ago, when Eino decided to go back east and visit an uncle in New York City —his mother's last known living relative, in fact—he'd left most of his belongings behind.

"This old stuff," he'd said, curling his lip at the shirts, snowy white with matching starched collars, Rio had stacked in his dresser drawer. He'd been particular. Anna Golz had always taken great care in laundering his clothing. "I don't need any of it. First thing I'm gonna do when I get there is buy new clothes. I'll need to make a good impression on those Italian fellas Donaldson was telling me about. Maybe I can hitch up with some wop heiress. I hear some of those men make a lot of money and their womenfolk do as they're told."

Elias had laughed. "You're a well-favored man, son. Reminds me of me when I was young. Folks will always look twice at you. You won't need new clothes. I never did."

Eino winked. "From what I hear of the women, I won't need any clothes."

And though Elias had laughed along with his son, he'd sent a quick look at Rio and shook his head. "You're not looking to impress the wrong kind of women, are you?"

"Me?" Eino puffed out his chest. "You're right, Pop. I don't need clothes for that."

Rio had felt herself flushing, and even Elias frowned a little. But to him, this was Eino talking. His precious, perfect son. Elias may have thought she hadn't caught the nuances of that little comment, but she had. Her brother considered himself a ladies' man. She'd been on the losing end of Eino's blather all her life and gotten a whole lot wiser than maybe she should have been. Or more than was considered respectable for young ladies, anyway.

But the result of this particular talk ended with Eino carrying only one smallish carpetbag when he caught the train headed east. He did, however, have a wallet chockablock full of five, ten, and even twenty-dollar bills, along with a substantial letter of credit.

Rio thought her father had lost his mind, sending Eino off with all that money. She figured he'd be broke within a month. Her brother had no idea how to eke out his finances and pay for necessities. If he saw something he wanted, he bought it. Or sometimes, she thought, stole it. And either way Elias paid.

She'd been proven right over the eighteen months Eino had been gone. Elias had wired a thousand dollars to him three times during those months. Three times that she knew of. Very possibly more. But now, they hadn't heard from him for six months. Not one word. And when Elias's cancer was diagnosed and it spread throughout his body, the old man fretted more and more wanting his boy to come home. He wrote to Eino at the last address he had but received no reply.

Just opening the door to Eino's old room brought back these memories. His room was next door to Elias's, so Rio moved as quietly as she knew how when she crossed to the dresser and pulled open the top drawer. The shirts lay untouched all this time, the top one appearing somewhat yellowed and dusty. Setting that one aside, she selected the shirt under it, and laying it on the bed, shook open the folds. As she'd thought, too big for Win, but not, perhaps, too small for Beckett. If he'd lost everything in the woods, he, too, needed a clean shirt. The one he was wearing had the residue of Win's blood on the front though he'd rinsed it out.

She collected enough of Eino's old things to make an entire clean outfit, choosing only the best. The bottom drawer contained a few items Eino had outgrown years ago. From there she pulled clothing for Win and put everything in a basket to carry downstairs.

Apparently, she hadn't been quiet enough, for as she pulled the door shut, Elias's voice came from his room. The bed creaked, as if the old man tried to rise.

"Eino? Eino, is that you? You've come home at last!"

Rio stood as if paralyzed. What to do? Pretend she hadn't heard him? Escape without answering or showing herself? Let her father believe he was imagining things?

In the end, she couldn't leave him thinking Eino had returned. And in truth, though she didn't like seeing the emotion in herself, she felt some gratification in disappointing him.

Setting down the basket—no need for her father to see what she'd taken from Eino's room—she called out,

"Of course not, father. It's just me. I was checking to make sure the windows didn't leak during the storm last night."

She poked her head into his room, knowing from the smell she'd need to change his sheets for the second time that day. And start the boiler in the basement for hot water to wash the ones she'd taken off.

The lie came to her easy as pie, although it occurred to her she should've done exactly that while she was in there.

He beckoned her inside. "I thought it was Eino, finally come home." A wealth of sorrow showed in his tone and on his face. And then he said, "You stay out of his room. You got no business in there. He won't like you poking around."

Anger surged through her so fast it made her dizzy. "Poking around in his things? Even if I had been, I don't know what difference it would make. He evidently doesn't care about this place. What's more, I doubt he's ever coming home again." She barely stopped herself from adding out loud, "And I hope he doesn't."

But the implication was there, and she could see Elias knew it. He must surely have thought the same a time or two but refused to admit it.

"He'll be here," he insisted. "And when he comes, you'd best mind your Ps and Qs. Could be he'll have a wife by now, and she won't tolerate your jealousy. Probably throw you out on your ear. Count on it."

"Huh," she huffed, "and I guess that's just fine with you." Unable to stand his apparent glee at the thought, she spun around, meaning to leave him to his gloating. Why did he hate her like he did? Because her mother had left him all those years ago? Worse, abandoned Rio to his not-so-tender upbringing, a daughter he felt had no value?

Still, she thought fiercely, this was her home and she'd fight for it, whether against Elias, Eino, or Eino's wife. Should any self-respecting woman be fool enough to marry him.

He stopped her before she made it out of the room. "Here. Take this letter." He plucked an envelope from the side table and waved it at her. The envelope had a scribble of untidy handwriting meandering across it. "It's about setting up an allowance to buy my medicine."

He'd remembered. She hadn't thought he would.

"You'd best get it sent off right away," he added and cackled with bitter contempt. "Before it's too late to do you any good."

She snatched the envelope from his hand. "I'll do that."

Pausing to pick up the basket of clothes she'd left in the corridor, she hurried down the stairs. Elias's beginning cries of needing his morphine followed her into the kitchen, and try though she might to ignore him, his increasing volume made her fear he'd awaken Win.

Just what she needed. Her father yammering for attention, when what she needed to do was get out the wringer washer and wash the bedding, always an onerous chore at best. Sighing, she set to work.

Somehow, everything got done.

By five o'clock, exhaustion had set in. Ten—at least ten—trips up-and-down the stairs, plus everything else she'd had to do today made her weary beyond saying. And Donaldson's visit to start her day hadn't helped.

Rio sat at the kitchen table with her head in her

hands, staring down at the letter her father had written in an almost illegible scrawl. Of course she'd opened the envelope. Had he thought she wouldn't? But now, what to do with what she read?

Motion at the doorway made Boo, who'd been napping on her lap, give a short bark. Startled, she scooted around.

Beckett stood there looking a little worried. "You never told me the room rate. Or if you serve meals here."

Rio gaped at him. *Room rate? Meals?* How odd. She hadn't been thinking of Beckett and Win as hotel guests. More as...as what? Invaders? And everyone knew invaders didn't pay for anything.

"Oh," she said. "Oh," and couldn't think what else to say. Then, "Of course. You'll need supper. I...I..."

Unexpectedly, a half-smile crooked. "Yeah. It's been a day for you, hasn't it?"

Wondering how much he'd overheard of Elias's complaints, or Wash's business, or really, even more mortifying, of Donaldson's threats, she nodded. "Maybe even a day and a half."

It made the crooked smile come again. "So, how much do I owe you for the room? And for helping with Win last night? And...about the food?"

She got up, leaning a little on the table for support. "The room is a dollar a night. As for food, well, supper is usually arranged for ahead of time. I charge room guests thirty-five cents. But tonight, I'll throw it in. I'm not really prepared, you see, as the hotel has been closed for six months." She made a helpless gesture. "Since my father became so ill."

He nodded. "Fair enough. I'm not picky. Whatever

you can scare up is fine. And Win, he'll probably be okay with more of that chicken soup."

"Give me an hour and I'll have something ready. The dining room is through there, just down the hall from the lobby." She nodded in the proper direction, thinking she'd best get the soup on to warm.

But Beckett shook his head. "Too much effort for you. If I won't get in your way, I'll eat in the kitchen like I did earlier."

Rio didn't mind at all. Mostly, she was just surprised at his consideration.

And when Beckett drew out a wallet and peeled off two one-dollar bills, she minded even less. It was as he turned to go back to his room that she noticed the outline of the gun he still wore at the back of his britches. It occurred to her maybe he just didn't want lights on in the hotel dining room, an advertisement for any passerby to notice and perhaps question why the place was lit up. Well, she didn't want that either.

"Oh," she said, and he turned. She gestured at a chair where the basket she'd brought down from Eino's room still sat. "Those are for you. You and Win."

"Thank you." He picked it up as though surprised at the weight. "This is more than a shirt."

She shrugged. "Shirts aren't the only things you probably need. I'll require you to sign the register, as well. If you wouldn't mind."

Evidently he did, for he shook his head. "Not now," he said, sounding hard again, and walked out.

Left with the conundrum of fixing a supper suitable for a paying hotel guest with hardly anything on hand, Rio set to work. When she'd made the soup this morning, she'd saved the best parts of the chicken to fry for her own dinner. Now they'd serve for Beckett's supper. That would have to do along with mashed potatoes and gravy. She'd open a jar of her home-canned green beans, and gather some early greens already sprung up in her garden patch.

As for herself, like an invalid, she'd be eating more soup like Win and her father. Not that it mattered. She was used to short rations. A thick slice of bread and butter would serve if that's all there was.

Standing back from the grease spatter of frying chicken, Rio caught the tap at the kitchen door. It sounded like Wash's familiar cadence, although she was surprised at his showing up twice in one day. A shiver ran down her spine, as if the mere thought could only bode evil. Had there been an accident? Loggers and sawmill men were prone to them, what with their saws and axes. Or a tree falling the wrong way. Or even a bad fall.

Putting a lid on the chicken, she, with Boo pattering beside her, went to open the door. Sure enough, Wash stood there, his face sober. More than sober. Worried. And sad.

"What is it?" Rio knew her expression echoed his. When he didn't answer right away, she changed the question. "Who is it?" Holding the door wider, she said, "Come in."

First wiping mud from his boots onto the mat outside, he entered. "I guess it's not hard to tell I've got bad news, is it?"

She shook her head.

"Let's sit." He held a chair for her and took one for himself.

As he scooted it out, Rio heard a door down the hall

open. With the faint sound muffled by the scooting chair, Wash evidently didn't.

"It's Bill Hightower," he said grimly.

The name jumped out at her. They'd talked of him this morning, when Wash told her the timber cruiser hadn't reported on the progress of his work either yesterday or today.

"You've heard from him?"

Wash shook his head. "Not exactly. Li Bai's helper cook, the feller who stays out at the timber camp most of the time, found him. Or his dog did, I should say. Been dead since sometime yesterday, best we can figure."

Rio felt the blood draining from her face. "A fall?" she asked. She didn't believe it, though. Not from the expression on Wash's face.

"Murdered. Shot dead, a bullet in his back, like he never even knew anybody was there."

"Murdered." Her mouth simply formed the word, soundless. "Where?"

Wash's face, already grim, became grimmer. "Out on the north section. He'd wanted to get started marking trees before the storm blew in. You know he was pretty independent with how and when he did his job. Never knew him to be late with the results though, no matter what."

Louder now, she spoke with an odd croak. "Why would anyone murder that poor man? As far as I know, he didn't even carry a gun."

"Sometimes he did. In fact, we found his rifle beside him. It hadn't been fired. Whoever did it shot him down by surprise and in cold blood. But..."

"But?"

Wash's answer came slowly. "It's just I can't figure why anybody would want to murder Bill. He kept to himself, didn't stir up trouble. He still had a little money on him so it wasn't robbery, but anyway, why would anybody be robbing a man just out in the woods doing his job?"

Rio had no answer, but she asked, "Does Sheriff Donaldson know about this?"

"He does. I took the fellow who found him to meet the sheriff right away. But, Rio—Miss Salo—uh..." Wash seemed to lose track of what he wanted, or needed to say, just then, and fixed her with an uneasy stare.

"When did you learn about this? About Mr. Hightower being found dead, I mean. And when did you tell the sheriff?" Wash's uneasiness must be catching, she thought. She'd been nervous and afraid all day, ever since the sheriff had turned up here at the hotel. The odd way he'd talked about strangers, as if he had been forewarned of trouble. Or about Hightower's murder. But Mr. Hightower hadn't even been found yet, so early in the morning.

Then there were the strangers who'd awakened her in the night, one of them with a bullet hole in him. A connection? There had to be.

Goose bumps rose on her arms as Wash talked.

"Chiang finally worked up his nerve to report it to me about noon. We rowed across the lake to tell Donaldson right away. Trouble is, we couldn't find him anywhere around town. The only one in his office was that dull-witted deputy he hired."

A remarkably inept young deputy if what Rio had heard about him was true. One who probably suited Donaldson just fine by doing anything the sheriff told him to do. Regardless of whether it was the right thing, or not. Legal or not.

She stared at Wash. "So what did you do?"

"Do?" Wash looked disgusted. "Not much. I told Klingaard, the deputy, to hire a team and wagon and drive it around to the camp, so that's what he did. Hired a driver to do it, then he had me and Chiang row him over. We took horses into the woods to collect Hightower's body and bring it to the landing. I'd thought I shouldn't move him, you see. In case the sheriff could tell something about who killed him from the way he'd been left." Wash had told Rio once that he read mystery novels, like those written by that British author, Sir Arthur Conan Doyle over in England. She'd laughed at the time, thinking it funny for a logger here in the west.

"And was he?" she asked, skepticism in her arched eyebrow. "Able to tell anything about how Mr. Hightower died?"

He snorted. "For sure Klingaard couldn't. Didn't even look. He seemed to have an aversion to the dead body." Wash blew a puff of air through his lips. "Didn't seem interested. But about the sheriff...well, never mind."

Rio realized the effort it took for his scowl to clear, and wondered what it was he'd stopped himself from saying. Did he think her a child to be kept in the dark?

"I'd best get on back to camp and let the crew know what's been going on," he said. "I'd thought I should let you know first. Afterward, I'll row over to town and put out the word about needing a timber cruiser. I hate to do it this soon. Seems like disrespect to Bill."

Rio liked Wash's consideration of the men who worked for him. All the men, not just those like Bill

Hightower had been. Loggers of any race were a rough bunch, but for the most part, these Chinese did their job well. They all deserved respect.

"Yes. All right." She looked into his clear blue eyes. "Thank you for letting me know about Mr. Hightower. Keep me posted about the funeral. If I can, I should attend in Elias's place."

His smile was a mere twitch of the lips. "Will do." He left then, closing the door behind with a firm hand.

Rio went back to her cooking, catching the frying chicken just before it burned. She turned it in an absentminded kind of way.

Disrespect of Mr. Hightower wasn't on her mind. Danger to whoever applied for his job was.

Seven

Though serving her guest's dinner at the kitchen table instead of the dining room, pride made Rio use a stiffly starched placemat under the restaurant's trademark pottery and silverware, along with a precisely folded napkin. The napkin was shaped like a swan, a clever piece of work her mother had taught her when she'd been as young as five. It was a hallmark of the hotel, along with the special dishes. They'd been ordered way back in her grandfather's day when the hotel first opened under his care. She set up a matching tray for Win, ready for when he awakened.

Satisfied with the result, smoothing her apron, she went to tap on Beckett's door. He opened it as if he'd been expecting her.

"Dinner is ready when you are," she said. He'd cleaned up, she noticed. Washed, shaved with the razor and soap she'd taken from Eino's room, and donned one of her brother's clean shirts.

"Thank you. I'll be there directly."

She looked past him to the boy on the bed. He was stirring, his eyelids fluttering, but not yet truly awake. He didn't seem to be in pain. The drug had done him good. She hoped the effects would stay with him long enough to let him rest after he had something to eat.

"Would you like me to help your brother with his soup while you have your supper?"

He smiled at her. A real smile. "A kind offer, but he's still waking up. I'll do it after I've eaten. He should be truly awake by then. "

Nodding, she went back to the kitchen. For all his demands for her to help him last night, today he seemed determined to keep her away from the boy. All of which served to raise a great many questions in her mind. Most of them didn't sit well with her.

Finally, she had a few moments to read what her father had written to the bank. If he'd thought to keep it secret from her, he'd been mistaken. Steaming open the envelope had been easy, accomplished within seconds. Elias's mouth was often dry, so he'd barely touched the tip of his tongue enough to hold the flap closed.

The writing, faint, because of his weakness, contained only one sentence besides the salutation and the signature. It asked Mr. Masterson to set up an account in Rio's name in the amount of ten dollars per month, effective immediately and payable until rescinded.

For a moment Rio burned. Ten paltry dollars a month? She'd been spending almost that much on his opium every week for the last two months. And what did he mean, *until rescinded*? Did that mean when he got angry enough with her, he'd simply close the account? But her father had slipped up. For one thing, he'd written in pencil. For another, he depended on her to get the letter in the mail. And last, he'd left an opening in which a small correction could easily be made. So Rio made it.

Barely aware of when Beckett entered the kitchen and began to eat, she found a pencil and, with a scrap of the paper she used for shopping lists, practiced turning a one into a four with the slight quiver of her father's hand and getting just the right slant to the shape.

"Light touch," she whispered to herself, which is when she noticed another mistake. This one made her blink. There was no end date, and no mention of who was authorized to do the rescinding.

Only when she'd sealed the envelope again, did she realize how she'd begun shaking. She felt like a thief. Justified? Yes. Definitely justified. But...

She jumped when Beckett said, "Is something wrong, Miss Salo?"

Rio turned, hand on chest to still her racing heart. He was watching her, his dark eyes intent.

"You mean besides my father dying, my half brother missing, a man being murdered on Salo property, and the sheriff nosing around?" She looked away. "Just the usual." But she didn't plan on detailing them. Not to anyone.

"I heard what your timber boss said about the murdered man. Do you trust him? Do you think he's involved in what happened?" Beckett's questions sounded almost casual as he lifted a forkful of mashed spuds into his mouth.

"Trust Washington Ames? Yes. I don't think he had anything to do with what happened to Mr. Hightower. Absolutely not. I trust him, and so does my father." She snorted. "Why else do you suppose he'd be bossing the timber crew? My father won't tolerate a drunken, unreliable, or careless man."

He shrugged. "Just asking, that's all. Does Ames run the sawmill, as well?"

She frowned, wondering how he knew about the sawmill. He hadn't been outside as far as she knew. Not to go very far, at any rate. And wasn't he a stranger here?

"No. Mr. Stokes runs the lumber business. The sawmill is on my father's land, but Mr. Stokes leases it from him. Everything works out. Keeps men working and makes a decent profit most of the time. My father wouldn't allow it otherwise."

"Not that benevolent, eh?"

"I don't think anyone ever called my father benevolent." Her mouth pursed. "But they do call him an honest businessman." Or so she believed.

Smiling down at the design, Beckett shook out the intricately folded napkin and dabbed his mouth. "About the sheriff, do you trust him?" He took a sip of coffee, sat back in his chair and eyed her.

He had, she noticed, eyes dark enough to match his hair. And much darker than her own milk chocolate brown.

Rio twirled the pencil between her fingers, wondering if she'd said too much already. Last night, when Beckett had burst into the hotel carrying his brother and began ordering her around, frightening her really, her first impression had been of an outlaw forcing her into sheltering him and his wounded companion. She'd sort of changed her mind since then. But only sort of. The way he had avoided calling for a doctor still struck her as especially suspect. Then there was the way he made himself scarce when the sheriff and later, Wash came around. He'd somehow managed to keep Win from crying out, as well.

So, he intended to keep his presence a secret. His and Win's. Why? On the other hand, if he distrusted the sheriff, and she distrusted the sheriff, did that make them allies?

"I don't trust the sheriff one bit," she admitted. "I know you heard how he spoke to me. He's a domineering tyrant and I doubt his honesty, as well. I've heard he takes bribes."

He nodded. "So I figured, just by listening to him. His reputation precedes him. I wonder..." He seemed to be lost in thought for several moments, before he looked back at her. "He is a man to avoid."

"Yes. If you can." Just how did Beckett know about Donaldson's reputation? More questions rose in her mind, leaving her to push them down. For the present, she promised herself.

Nodding, Beckett rose from the table, his silverware placed tidily on his plate, the napkin draped beside it. He smiled at her. "Good victuals, Miss. You're a good cook."

He left her with her mouth hanging open. That smile had been something.

As for being a good cook, well, she was a well-taught chef, not just a simple cook. One capable of running a fine restaurant kitchen. If she got the chance when her father died.

THOUGH RIO'S amendment to her father's letter scratched at her and made her sleep restless, when Elias got her up by crying for his morphine a second time during the night, her conscience stopped nagging. At four o'clock in the morning, by the time she finished with him, there was no point in going back to bed.

Boo was waiting for her on the porch when she stepped outside with the letter in her hand. Daylight barely touched the tops of the pine trees surrounding the hotel.

"Want to go for a walk, Boo?" she asked.

The dog spun in circles, his tail wagging furiously. Rio smiled as he bounded ahead of her, diligently chasing into the bushes to bark at birds beginning to flutter about their morning search for food. The RFD mail pick-up box sat on a post a quarter-mile away, where the trail leading to the hotel met with the main road surrounding the lake.

Down at the lakeshore, wind-driven waves broke against the rocky beach, rocking the three rowboats tied to cleats fixed in the wooden dock. Although the hotel sat some distance from the sawmill and cut logs, the scent of fresh-cut timber reached her on the breeze. Unless that was her imagination.

Standing before the mailbox, Rio stared down at the letter she carried, considering its delivery one more time. Then, with an almost savage thrust, she stuffed it in. There. Done, and she refused to think more on it.

At the hotel, she had chickens to feed and eggs to gather, which, with Boo's help, only took a few minutes longer than without his shenanigans. The farmer who lived up the road had already left a bottle of milk on the back porch doorstep, leaving her determined to make milk toast for the wounded boy. He might like that and at least it would be a change from soup. She planned to make a custard for her hotel guests and—it suddenly occurred to her to think of Elias—perhaps milk toast and custard were things he could swallow, as well.

She went into the kitchen, Boo frolicking ahead of her, to find Beckett already there, standing beside the sink with a cup of coffee in his hand. Nice to see he wasn't shy about helping himself, she told herself, the sarcasm hitting a sour note.

Boo, happy to meet his new acquaintance, dashed over to sniff the man who immediately offered his fist and said, "Good morning to you. My brother enjoyed your company yesterday." He looked up at Rio. "Win doesn't know his name but he hopes to have his company today, if you can spare him."

"His name is Boo."

"Hey, Boo." Beckett grinned. "Good name, but he doesn't scare me."

Rio didn't smile back.

His eyebrow quirked. "Something wrong?"

"How long do you intend staying? I mean..." She faltered. There were things she wanted to say to him if he and Win were to take up residence more than a day or two. For instance, she wanted to ask how and why he and Win had turned up at the hotel in the middle of the night. And to say his behavior struck her as suspect. She wanted the details of how Win had gotten shot—and by whom. But she didn't dare.

The kitchen cowbell's jangle and a pitiful cry from her father saved those awkward questions for another time—or perhaps never.

Boo growled at the bell.

“Stay, Boo.” She set her finger over her lips. “Quiet.” And with a quick head shake at Beckett, she fled. Elias was the devil she knew, easier to face perhaps, than the devil she didn’t.

Rio found her father, once again toppled sideways, coughing and gasping for air. Blood splattered the front of his nightshirt, a new symptom, one the doctor had warned her might happen as the cancer progressed throughout his body. Elias’s eyes were watering from the force of the cough. She hurried over to him.

“Hang on,” she said, already piling pillows at his back and pulling him upright. She offered water, helping to hold the mug to his lips. Gradually, the cough eased off and she wiped his face with a damp cloth. He lay back into the pillows, panting worse than Boo when chasing a rabbit.

“Better?”

He managed a nod. And one word. “Eino?”

As if she could produce her brother out of thin air. As if she would if she could.

“Not yet. But the day isn’t over, you know.” As an offering of comfort, it wasn’t much. But then, she didn’t mean it to be.

He pushed her away. “Eino,” he said.

Hands clenching, she shook her head. “He isn’t here. I’ll get the doctor.”

“No use.”

She knew it wasn’t, but then, she didn’t want anybody raising doubts on how he’d died, either. It had occurred to her that some, like Donaldson, provided there might be a profit to him in an accusation, would be all too eager to shanghai her right into prison. Or even the hangman’s noose.

"I'll get the doctor," she said, decision made. Which, if anyone wanted to know, was a worrisome ordeal. She had to risk leaving Elias alone for the hour's labor of rowing back and forth across the lake. God only knows what her father might get up to while she was gone. Less, now, she reminded herself, since he'd become entirely bedridden. Getting the money from his stash yesterday had been the first time he'd stirred from his bed in a week—that she knew about, at any rate. And the effort had taken a toll on him.

The second largest of the hotel boats was gone from its place at the dock. It had been the one Rio had hoped to take, considering she expected to have a passenger coming back. Wash must have taken it, she figured, in his quest to hire a timber cruiser.

She took Boo, who loved riding in a boat no matter what size, with her. The sun, proving almost too warm, shone down on the wind-tossed choppy waves, the tops of which sparkled with diamond glitter. Though rowing against the wind made the passage across to town take longer and proved quite onerous, she knew the return would be faster with it at her back.

Thirty minutes later they landed at the town dock. Rio, well-practiced with the oars, edged her small craft in among the larger ones and tied up. Boo leapt out, barking with glee as he chased a squawking seagull.

Rio took a breath and stretched her back. "Come on," she told the dog, and with him pacing beside her, his tail fluttering like a white flag, they made their way to Main Street where Dr. Clement had his office. An old house freshly painted a gleaming white and reborn into his surgery bore a sign outside announcing his occupation.

The doctor's wife, Molly, served as his receptionist and nurse. Rio found her sitting at a desk in the former front room of the house. A telephone took pride of place on the desk although it rarely rang. As one of only six people hooked to the system, the instrument served mostly as a conversation piece. One patient sat, his knees jiggling impatiently as he waited his turn.

Molly looked to be hard at work on a document, though Rio figured she was drawing. An accomplished artist, the patient may have been serving as a model under Molly's clever fingers. Her graphite pencil made a final mark before she looked up. "Rio Salo," she said on a note of surprise. Then alarm. "Is your father..."

Rio glanced over at the waiting patient. "He'd doing very badly. I hoped the doctor could come to the hotel and take a look at him."

Mrs. Clement immediately stood. "Let me go tell the doctor you're here."

"Me first," the impatient man said. "I am first in line." He had a blood-soaked bandage wrapped around a finger, which he held up in the air.

"Yes," Mrs. Clement said. "Of course, Mr. Ware." Regardless, she went to confer with her husband.

Almost immediately, she returned, and a minute later, the doctor. He ushered a woman with a very large belly out ahead of him. Nodding to Rio, he cocked a mildly disapproving eyebrow at Boo who, in "good boy" mode sat quietly at Rio's feet, and led the man with the bloody finger into a back room.

"Doctor said to tell you he'll be with you shortly," Molly said when they were gone. "He's been expecting a summons any day now." She cleared her throat. "I don't suppose there's been any word from Eino." It wasn't a question. Most folks who'd lived around there for a long time had a clear impression of her half brother.

Rio shook her head. "No. My father wasn't sure of the address the last time he wrote. But he keeps hoping."

"Umm." Molly's muted response may have said more than she intended. "A lost cause, I suspect."

An implication perhaps, that people were aware of Rio's hard life. That she'd been abandoned by her mother, her father hated her, and her brother was an ass. Some of them even thought well enough of her to be polite, despite her relatives.

The row back to the hotel with Dr. Clement made Rio uncomfortable, to say the least. She'd expected the questions the doctor put to her. But for the first time, she confessed to how Elias went beyond the prescribed morphine to ease his pain and relied on added opium.

The doctor tut-tutted. Dragging his hand in the water, he splashed Boo, teasing the dog as he tried to catch it.

"I suppose he has you obtain the drugs for him?" He looked up, his disapproval striking clearly.

"Yes." She sighed. "And every day he begs for more and more. I try to limit him, but he..." She stopped. How could she tell anyone, even the doctor, how her father sometimes wept when he wasn't shouting at her. Cursing her, as if the cancer and his suffering were her fault.

And his ongoing talk of Eino. Always his precious Eino.

"A shame," the doctor said, frowning. "I expect he is

addicted to the morphine along with the opium, you know. Beyond the need for pain relief, the drug itself commands him."

"Yes. I do know." Pulling at the oars took all of Rio's strength. The wind at her back helped, but not enough. It made her realize just how tired she was with the constantly interrupted sleep. The meals with barely enough to eat. The lifting and shifting and the washing and the broken nights. She suffered right along with her father.

The doctor realized it, too. "You've gotten very thin yourself, Miss Salo. You need help around that big place, especially in these last days."

Last days that seemed to go on and on.

Well, she knew where there was money to pay someone now, even if she had to steal it. If she dared to steal it. If you could even call it stealing. Not when she used the money for him. "He won't allow it. He doesn't want anyone to know how ill he is." She shook her head. "The sheriff barged in yesterday, which made him so angry. My father hasn't even allowed Mr. Ames to see him these last two weeks. Just me." And then, faintly, "God only knows why, when he hates me most of all. I guess because he has to have someone around to do as he says, and I always have."

Rio didn't miss the shocked look Dr. Clement bestowed upon her.

"I'm sure he doesn't hate you, Miss Salo. Why on earth should he hate you? You've done nothing but take care of him since he's been ill. And before that. I, and my wife, remember very well that you, from the time you were no more than fifteen years old, are the one who kept the hotel restaurant going, making sure not only the food, but the service was prime. It always amused us to see the way..." He stopped, seeming to ponder something. "But no. I also remember Elias hasn't always treated you well."

Hasn't always? Rio didn't remember a time that her father hadn't had words of blame on his lips.

She kept rowing, bending her back into the labor. As if sensing her distress, Boo left off playing and came to sit with her. She was relieved when they reached the hotel landing in record time.

Dr. Clement, black bag in hand, hurried up the path to the hotel, leaving Rio to tie up the boat. The other boat, the one missing earlier, was back in place. She hoped Wash's search for Mr. Hightower's replacement had been successful.

Leaving Boo to amuse himself chasing squirrels, she went inside. Best, she supposed, to be there with the doctor as he checked her father. Mounting the stairs, she peeked into Elias's room in time to hear Clement, who'd evidently awakened him by placing the bell of his stethoscope on Elias's chest. "Easy," the doctor said. "I'm just listening to your lungs. You're wheezing."

Elias flailed his hands, trying to bat the instrument away until he realized he owed the annoyance to his doctor. "Uh. I thought you were that damned girl, always pestering me for one thing or another." He gasped for breath. "She was in here not five minutes ago, making noise and letting that damn mutt she's taken to feeding tromp on my chest."

Unseen, Rio's teeth gritted together.

"Did she? Do you think so? Elias, those are simply opium dreams. Not real."

"The hell. I'm here to tell you—"

"Don't bother." The doctor lifted Elias high enough to get the stethoscope against his back and listened intently. Shaking his head, he lay the patient down again. "Five minutes ago, your daughter and her dog were rowing me across the lake from town."

Elias's frown puckered his face into a gargoyle's snarl. "So maybe it was earlier."

"I don't think so." Taking out a magnifying glass, Clement lifted Elias's eyelids and studied his eyes. "Miss Salo told me you're coughing a lot and bleeding from the lungs. When did this start."

"Couple days ago. I'm almost done, ain't I, doc? Tell me the truth."

"Soon, I think. It's not for me to say just when."

"You tell her I need my morphine, Clement. When I say I need it, I need it. Right then, not when she says I can have it. She's torturing me on purpose."

"Your daughter is trying to keep you alive, Elias." The doctor spoke quietly. "Don't you know that? You want to see Eino when he comes, don't you? You can't do that if you die of an overdose of morphine. You wouldn't be alive now if it weren't for your daughter."

Elias huffed two big breaths through his nose, a certain sign of his anger when contradicted. This time, it set him to coughing again, a gout of blood followed by pink-tinted foam staining his lips. The doctor wiped it away.

When he'd quieted, Clement had one query that demanded an answer. Glancing over at Rio, who stood as if paralyzed just out of her father's sight, he asked it. "Why do you treat her like this, Elias? As if she's some kind of enemy instead of your own child? She does nothing but work for you. Before you got sick, though barely past childhood herself, she ran this hotel like a trained professional."

"No," Elias said, sharp and stern. "It's my hotel. I run it. Me and Eino."

Dr. Clement, like most of the other regular customers, apparently knew for a fact the only thing Eino ever did for the hotel was eat there and take money from the till. "That's not true and you know it. What do you have against her?"

More of those breathy coughs stopped his speech again, until finally, Elias found words. "Her mother was a whore, that's why. Rio, she looks just like her ma, acts just like her ma, all quiet and...and demure. But that's all a lie. I found out. They stole from me, Juanita and her pa." He snorted. "I guess I took care of her, all right. And I kept the girl too, didn't I, afterward? Just like I told her I would. Somebody had to pay for her sins." He bellowed a laugh, then coughed and coughed.

"What do you mean by that?" Clement demanded. Blood seemed to drain from his face.

Elias didn't reply.

CLOSING HIS MEDICAL BAG, Clement stumbled out of Elias Salo's room. He took hold of Rio, still standing motionless, as he passed, drawing her along with him.

They reached the bottom of the stairs. Jamming a straw hat onto her head, Rio anchored the ribbon ties under her chin hoping the wide brim would hide her telltale face from him.

"He didn't mean it," the doctor said. "It's the opium talking."

Rio looked at him, trying to decide whether he wanted to convince her or himself. Maybe both, if she felt generous.

"It may be the opium talking, but that only makes it more likely he means everything he said." She stopped, thinking the words were all tangled up on her tongue. "Did he mean he killed my mother? And maybe my grandfather? I think he did. I've always wondered..." She stopped.

The doctor swallowed, his Adam's apple moving laboriously. He shook his head, but she could see he wondered too.

Had Elias murdered her mother? Had he buried her somewhere in the forest and trusted her bones would never be found?

"That would explain why he hates me," she said, so matter-of-factly the doctor nodded. "When he says I look like her. I don't know. I barely remember her face now. But I'm not a whore, and she wasn't either." She laughed, cold and harsh. "I don't know when she would've had time. As I remember, she worked every minute of every day. He made sure of that."

"Miss Salo," he said. "Rio...I don't know what to say. Just know this will soon be over. Hang on just a little longer. Can you do that?"

Her chin trembled. "As long as it takes. I remember my mother saying the hotel would be mine one day. Well, I'm going to wait him out. Count on it."

The second trip across the lake was almost silent. The morning wind had died to infrequent gusts, so thankfully, it took less time, too. The doctor clambered out of the boat after only twenty minutes.

"Take care of yourself, Rio. And of your little dog. Eat more, and don't let Elias take you down."

She smiled. A small smile, but still a smile. "I will. I won't." At least with a room occupied at the hotel, she could buy a few necessary groceries before she left town.

Halfway down the dock, Dr. Clement turned around, his face somber. "My advice? If you can get it, let him have all the opium he wants. The more the better. You may call on me when it's time." With that, he turned and stomped away.

Had he really said what she thought he'd said? Rio stared at his retreating back, her mouth half-open in astonishment at the implication.

A NOTE SAT on her kitchen table when Rio got back to the hotel and set a string bag of groceries on the table. Leaving it lay, she hurried down the hall to Win's room, where she heard Boo scratching at the door. Having put him in with the boy to keep him company while she was gone, she made that her first stop. Tapping first, she waited, then went in.

Boo made a dash around her to get outside. Meanwhile, she found Win sleeping with his mouth half-open and snoring peacefully. She went over and laid a hand on his forehead. Finding it cool, she left as silently as she'd come.

Though she dreaded facing her father again, she went upstairs. He, too, to her relief, was snoring, but with a queer, sucking sound like barrels being scooted through mud. Too bad. When the doctor had said to let him have all the opium he wanted, she'd hoped he had left enough morphine within his reach to...

She stopped herself. Clement was a physician, his mission to save lives, not take them. But maybe to make it easy for them to end themselves.

In the kitchen, Rio built up the fire in the cookstove, beat together some eggs, milk, sugar, salt, and vanilla extract for her custard and set it, with a sprinkle of nutmeg on top, to bake in a hot water bath. It wasn't until she started cleaning her workspace that she found the smudged note on the floor, blown off the table, perhaps, by the opening and closing of the door.

Written in Wash's precise hand, it said:

Miss Salo, I've hired a timber cruiser. He's from out of town and will require a place to stay due to special considerations I'll tell you about when we get there. I hope you can provide temporary accommodations. I'll be by late this afternoon and introduce him. Wash

Luck, Rio thought. Wash had been lucky.

The custard had just come out of the oven when upstairs, Elias began hollering. Wordless, but loud. Not surprisingly, it brought on a coughing spree. When that subsided, he began ringing the cowbell, its harsh jangle filling her head. Anger so fierce it almost burned coursed through her.

After what he'd said about her mother, about her, how could he? As if she were nothing. Less than nothing. Not even a tool, to be discarded when he was through with her.

Through tormenting her.

And at this rate, with the racket he was making, he'd soon have Win needing attention, as well. Still, her footsteps dragged as she climbed the stairs, taking her time until she stood in the doorway to his room. "Yes? What is it?"

"Where's my morphine? Did you take it? Steal it from me?" Blood foamed at his mouth. "That's it, ain't it? You stole it. I figure you're taking it for yourself, you ungrateful little witch. Hand it over. I need my medicine." He ranted on until he ran out of breath. Rio hadn't said a word.

At last he stopped. "Well?"

"I heard what you said to Dr. Clement. About my mother. About me." Her chin trembled and she was glad she stood far enough away he probably couldn't see it, since the room's curtains were drawn. "Did you kill her?"

He took a couple snorting breaths. "Kill who. Juanita? Juanita the whore?" He chuckled. "Wouldn't you like to know?" He peered up at her. "Well then, I did, if you think you have to know. And I put her where nobody'll ever find her. Maybe I ought to kill you too. Spawn of the same gypsy blood."

Rio gasped at his ready admission. It struck her that he wanted her to know. To hurt her with the final truth. But gypsy? That was new. "Your kin too, to my shame."

"Never."

At this, a corner of her mouth lifted in a sneer.

"Anyway, I'd like to see you try. You can't even get out of bed. And you may have another problem—not only do you not have the strength, you don't have a gun. I know. I took the .44 you kept in here away days ago, when you first started ranting."

His face changed. "I don't have to do it myself. There are people who will do it for me. Eino will, when he comes home. Bank on it."

"Eino isn't coming home. Someone most probably had the decency to kill him."

She whirled away, shaking so hard she had to brace herself on the wall as she went. Was Elias Salo really her father? Maybe there was truth to his accusation. She found herself hoping so.

An hour later, Elias started in with the cowbell again and Rio took pity on Win, who called out to her in concern.

"I'll take care of him," she assured him and climbed the stairs yet again to answer Elias's demand for help. Her eyes were red from weeping. The last tears, she vowed, that she'd ever shed for the past.

"Morphine." Her father panted out the word. Sweat beads rolled down his face. His blood-splattered nightshirt was wet. His bedclothes tumbled half onto the floor. He spoke to her, impatience in speech so twisted she couldn't make out the words.

A moment passed as she looked at him blankly. What in the world had happened to him in the last hour? Had he had a fit of some kind? After a moment, she decided he'd said, "This is killing me. I need my morphine. Get it for me. Now."

No please help me. No I'm sorry for the things I said. No acknowledgment of his cruelty. A less aware woman might have thought it an aberration of his illness. Rio knew better. The pain he inflicted was calculated.

She reached in her apron pocket and withdrew the tin Li Bai put the opium in. Walking over to the bed, she showed the contents to her father. "This is all that's left. I won't be able to get more until morning when Li Bai is at the cook shack. You'll have to get by with what's here until then. You'll space out the doses if you're wise. And I'll need money for morning."

He grabbed for the tin, fingers unsteady as he tried to open it. His mouth worked. "Just two. I'm strong. I'll make do. No thanks to you."

At least, that's what she thought he said.

He fumbled in the tin, gulping the pills down dry and swallowing convulsively.

Rio didn't offer him water, and he didn't ask. Thrusting a hand under his pillow, he extracted a small leather purse. Shaking fingers poked through the contents. He drew out a bill and gave it to her. "Morphine." His eyes were already turning dull from the opium, which made Rio wonder if the pills had been stronger than usual.

She took the money. Elias hadn't even looked at the bill he'd given her—a twenty. She'd have to find a way to break the money into smaller bills if she didn't want Li Bai to become even greedier than he was already. He'd try to take it all if he got the chance.

Nine

Rio had meant to tell Elias about Bill Hightower's murder and that Wash had hired another timber cruiser, until she realized he was beyond making sense of any business concerns. Which suited her just fine. Elias had only two concerns now. Maybe three if you counted his persecution of her. But even his constant abuse was probably only third in line compared to his need for opium, and his insistence that everything he owned was meant for Eino.

All of which meant she needed to keep her father alive until the money from the new bank account could be set in motion. Three more days, she estimated, although his end seemed very near. His speech had become so jumbled, she was unable to understand him most of the time. And when she did, he hardly made sense.

Even if Elias somehow found out she'd amended his letter and protested, she doubted that if anyone heard him, they could decipher what he was saying. She'd keep the account secret until Eino, if he ever came home, put a stop to it. If he ever even realized she was benefiting. He'd never had to account for the money Elias gave him, and probably still didn't bother. Until then, she, with Wash running things, would keep the men working, the logging operation going, and the hotel running. She would take the profit in cash. And if Eino never came back to claim the inheritance, surely she would be next in line eventually, regardless of Elias's wishes.

She didn't dare even consider what she'd do otherwise, if her half brother returned. She and Boo.

With her father quieted for the moment, Rio went to reassure Win. He'd managed to scoot himself up in the bed, and while he was still pale and weak, he seemed to be on the mend.

"Is he all right?" He cocked a thumb toward the ceiling so she'd know who he meant.

The innocent question made her own anger flare again. Embarrassment mixed into the equation, which didn't help. She couldn't answer and shrugged instead.

"Can I get you anything?" She moved to adjust the blankets. "Are you in pain? Or hungry?"

"Starving. I hurt too. It ain't any fun, gettin' shot." Win's smile, she found, was every bit as engaging as his brother's—when his brother wasn't being intimidating. "But Beck said I wasn't to pester you. He said he'd bring something for me to eat when he got back, but it's taking longer than he said he'd be. He thinks maybe I can have real supper tonight."

His stomach growled as if to tease him.

She forced a smile. "You're not pestering. Did you have any breakfast?"

"No, ma'am." He looked as pathetic as possible.

Guilt took hold of Rio. She'd forgotten her guests, what with rowing back and forth the lake a couple times. Plus dealing with her father. Come to think of it, she hadn't had any breakfast either and here it was past noon.

"I'll make something tasty for supper." Thank goodness she'd bought beef at the butcher in town earlier with some of the money Beckett had given her last night. "But I can scare up some bread and butter for now. Will that help?"

"Yes, ma'am." He grinned.

So it happened she ended up making milk toast after all, only for herself and Win, instead of including her father. She fetched a jar of last fall's applesauce too, doctored with a little sugar and cinnamon, along with a couple slices of yellow cheese the man who brought her milk had talked her into trying last week, when she still had a little money. She'd been saving the cheese for a special occasion. This qualified, she guessed. Piling everything on a tray, she carried it in to share with Win.

He declared it all a feast, licked a last bit of applesauce from his bowl, and sat back. "Miss," he said, and took a breath, looking at her out of the corner of his eyes, "can I ask you something?"

She nodded. Rio figured it would be "what's for supper" or "what's your name" or...well, she didn't know what a boy would question. But he surprised her.

"Who is that man who keeps shoutin' at you? Cussin' and yellin' for his morphine. Is this a hospital? Are you a nurse? Has that man been shot too?"

"Hasn't your brother told you anything?"

Win shook his head. "He don't tell me much. I shouldn't even be with him. I been livin' with an uncle, but he up and died two weeks ago. Beck and I don't have any other relatives, so Beck had to bring me along on the job."

Job? What job?

Maybe she'd find out. Answer Win's questions and ask some herself. "I'm sorry about your uncle. Was he good to you?"

"He was all right. Not mean or nothing. But he... well, he never had anything much to say, except when he said I wasted too much time reading books and such. But all he wanted to do was work, eat, drink a whiskey, and go to sleep."

"You like to read? So do I, when I have time. I have a few books. I'll bring them and you can see if you want to read one."

Win's eyes lit. "Thank you."

"Sure." She drew in a breath. "The man you hear is my father."

Though quiet, she heard his gasp. "Your father? But he—he talks to you like that?" His brow puckered. "He ain't what you'd call good-natured, is he? My uncle Bernard wasn't either, in his last days, but he sure never talked to anybody like that man talks to you."

"He hates me." She said it matter of factly, as if it didn't matter. "Like your uncle, he is in his final days before death. He has cancer, you see, and it's spread throughout his body. He has a great deal of pain." It may have sounded as if she were making excuses.

"But...your father? He hates you? Why?"

She shrugged, trying to appear nonchalant. "I don't know." Except she did, as of today, though the knowing made no sense and made nothing any easier. "As for your other questions, no, this is not a hospital and I am not a nurse. Not a real one, although I've been nursing my father. This is a hotel, although it's closed just now. Except for you and your brother. When my father passes, I'll open to everybody again."

Win nodded. "Will you be sad? When he dies?"

"No."

"Why don't you run away?" He cocked his head. "I would."

Shaking her head, Rio tried to smile. "You're not a girl. It's harder for lone girls, you see. I have no money. And I have nowhere else to go."

"Oh." Win blinked. "Kind of like me, only I have Beck. Leastwise you ain't got shot."

Yet. Only because he needs me to fetch his opium. But Rio didn't say as much out loud.

AS IT HAPPENED, Rio was a better than good cook, when she had anything to cook. She had begun learning from Juanita, her mother, as a tiny tot. Forced by circumstances to work in Elias's hotel, her mother's cooking talent was the reason he married her when he found her food kept patrons coming back to the hotel. Unpaid labor to him. Though a little out of the way, being across the lake from the town proper, most people considered the effort to get there well worth it. Mostly, she came to understand, because the experience was similar to what big city people would expect of a high-class hotel.

In other words, Juanita made money for the hotel and Elias's object in life was making money. Lots of it.

Juanita had learned fine dining from her father,

who'd been a chef in a famous New Orleans restaurant until he lost his job due to excess drink and high stakes gambling. He and his daughter had come west as he fought his demons.

Rio knew her mother had continued to run the hotel and restaurant after Benedict Serrano died. Later, Elias had told her Juanita was obligated to pay Benedict's debt when he lost everything to Elias in a card game. Apparently, Elias had secured her services permanently by marrying her. And then Rio came along, another captive in Elias's fiefdom.

Rio's recipe for beef stew was different from what most folks considered stew around their little town. Her version contained wine, a variety of vegetables, tomatoes, and herbs. She thickened it with a fine butter roux, and even a splash of vinegar. Then came a long slow baking to tenderize the meat.

The sun was sinking behind the western mountains as suppertime approached. The scent of Rio's stew wafted outdoors so that Wash and his companion were salivating as they climbed the path from the worker's barracks to the hotel.

As usual, Wash stopped at the back door and scraped his boots on the mat. His companion did the same. In a show of consideration, Wash knocked before he and whoever belonged to the second set of footsteps entered. Boo, who'd been waiting outside on the porch, pushed in ahead of them.

"It's me," Wash called out, laughing at the dog.

"Come on in." Rio raised her voice only a little, hoping not to rouse Elias. Or Win, for that matter, since his room was closest. She stood at the worktable, shaping balls of dough in preparation of baking rolls to go with the stew. "I've prepared a room and will have supper ready in about an hour." So saying, she turned to face the men, then blinked in quick startlement. Her next thought was to hope Wash didn't notice.

"This here is Beckett Ferris," Wash said, frowning only a little. "He's an experienced timber cruiser who happened into town this morning and saw the notice I stuck up at the general store. So I hired him. He's got good references."

Beckett stood there looking a little sheepish. He carried a small carpetbag in one hand, one she'd be willing to wager contained only the clothes she'd given him. Or maybe even just a crumpled towel or newspaper. Something to fill out the bag's sides in a realistic manner. She had to wonder where he'd gotten the bag.

Boo sat down at Rio's feet.

Ruing the fact she was such a poor actress, Rio knew Wash had noticed her reaction. Managing a smile, she waved floury hands at both men and said, "How do you do, Mr. Ferris." Had she put too much emphasis on *Mr. Ferris*? But why hadn't Beckett warned her? Or had Win warn her? Was he really an experienced timber cruiser?

She guessed they'd find out. Win had said something about him and his brother coming here for the job, but that had been before Wash even knew there'd be an opening. How had Beckett known?

"Ma'am," Beckett said, smooth as butter. "I hope this won't trouble you too much. Mr. Ames said you've been caring for your sick father."

Just as if he hadn't heard what went on here for himself.

"I am," she agreed. "But you'll be no trouble, I'm

sure. Where did you work before, Mr. Ferris, if I may ask?" She put the pan with the bread rolls on the stove's warming shelf to rise with a damp cloth over it.

Beckett's dark eyes flashed a warning at her, though he answered easily enough. "At a company over toward Cle Elum. Western Forester Consolidated, to be exact. The boss wrote me a reference when I left."

She wondered if that were true, or if he'd written a reference for himself.

"I see. Well, I'm sure my father will approve. If Mr. Ames vouches for you, that's good enough for Salo Timber Products."

"Thank you." He glanced at sideways at Wash. "Did I mention that my young brother will be coming to join me tomorrow or the next day? He's been a bit under the weather, but should be well enough to travel real soon."

Rio had to fight back a smile. Under the weather? A grand understatement, to be sure. "No. I didn't know," she said. "I'll look forward to meeting him. How old is he?"

"Thirteen."

"Ah. A half brother?" The question came from her mouth even before Rio had time to regret asking it. For Win's sake, she hoped the Ferris brothers got along better than Eino and herself. They certainly appeared to. Besides, it was none of her business.

But Beckett smiled. "Nope. Guess it just took a while before things clicked with our parents and they gave me a brother."

Taking a last longing whiff of the aroma rising from the oven, Wash turned to go. "I'll be around at six in the morning," he told Beckett. "Be ready to go. We'll have a long day ahead of us while the crew moves camp."

"Aren't you going to stay for supper, Mr. Ames?" Surprise made Rio sharp.

"Can't. Too much to do. Sure does smell good though. Li Bai isn't a bad cook, but he's not in the same league with you."

"Oh. Thank you, I think." Rio smiled, unsure how she felt about being abandoned, then decided maybe his decision was good. It gave her and Beckett time to discuss this turn of events without having to talk around Wash. But serving supper to Beckett as a paying customer instead of whatever he'd been before, just seemed different. As if she were less in control–if she ever had been.

"Will you be coming back to the hotel every night, Mr. Ferris?" Rio pressed for the information. If not, did that make her responsible for Win's recovery?

"If all goes well, I intend to. I doubt we'll be here long."

A relief. "Well, I've put you in room number four just down the hall to your right, if that's satisfactory. When you're ready, you can put your bag in there."

"Thanks. I'll do that." Nodding to Wash, doing his best to act a little unsure and bewildered–but not too much–Beckett went to find his room, and no doubt talk to Win while he was at it.

Wash remained a moment longer before asking quietly, "Did something strike you wrong about Ferris? I thought you looked at him like there was something."

Rio forced a little laugh. "No. Nothing. When I first saw him, I thought I might've seen him before, but then

I decided not. He just reminded me of someone, that's all. Probably a hotel guest at some time or another."

He smiled too. "Sure, that makes sense. Are you satisfied with him? His references are good."

"Hiring crew is your job, Mr. Ames. I leave all of that to you."

Wash's blue eyes flashed and she could see her reliance on his choice pleased him. "See you in the morning."

"In the morning," she agreed. Seeing him out, she watched until he'd gone beyond her sight on the path to the camp barracks.

Looking down at Boo, she took her first full breath since the men had arrived. "You," she said. "It's a wonder Mr. Ames didn't catch on that you already knew Beckett...Mr. Ferris. You should've barked at him. Given him a good going over, not acted like he's already a friend."

WASH DIDN'T KNOW what troubled Rio, but he had an idea. A couple ideas, besides the consideration of old Elias being flat on his back. Or more accurately, on his last legs, from what he gathered. He wasn't wounded by the thought as he'd never cared much for Elias. The last time he'd met with the man had been two weeks ago, with Elias propped up by a half-dozen pillows in his bed. Papers had been scattered on the bedcovers, as if he'd been interrupted at work, but it had seemed to Wash his boss's mind wandered. Elias lost track a couple times when he was speaking. Rio had taken up the thread and finished the meeting.

Wash didn't mind admitting he'd been astonished when Elias let her. Normally he treated his daughter as if she were a half-witted servant of some kind.

And Elias always had, Wash reflected, ever since he'd gone to work for Salo three years ago. It was pitiful. And puzzling. And wholly untrue.

In these last two weeks, Wash had met with Rio in the hotel kitchen. She said the written instructions she gave him came from Elias, but sometimes he wondered. Once last week he'd heard Elias upstairs berating her and crying for morphine, then yesterday it had been even worse after Thor Donaldson made his appearance. He didn't know how Rio stood it—or why. And if Eino ever showed up, she'd be treated even worse. People around there still talked of how her brother had always acted as if she were less than the dirt under his feet.

Wash broke out of the woods to find Li Bai and Chiang unloading a supply wagon and getting packs ready to take out to the logging camp. He gestured to Li Bai and cocked his head to the cook shack, where he could smell food cooking. The scent came nowhere near comparing to whatever Rio had in her oven.

Scowling at the interruption, Li Bai trotted over, shouting rapid instructions in Chinese at his helper over his shoulder. It sounded as if they were fighting, but Wash didn't think they were.

"What you want?" Li Bai asked. "I busy. Got this..." He indicated the packs. "And get supper on table now. Men be here in ten minutes."

As would Wash, since he ate with his men.

Plates and utensils were already on the table waiting for the men to pick them up, Wash noted. All the Chinaman needed to do was set out the food, a matter of two minutes. And he'd probably order his helper to do it. Didn't take a genius to gather Li Bai would rather avoid him.

"I won't keep you long. Tell me, how much opium are you selling Miss Salo for her father?"

Li Bai's already narrow eyes turned into slits. "Not your business, boss. She buys, I sell."

"Yes, and I'm not asking how much you're making off of her, though I suspect it's plenty. More, I'd guess, than you're telling the supplier about. They might be a little crabbed if they found out how much you're keeping for yourself." By the way Li Bai's lips tightened, Wash figured he was on the right track. The man was not the inscrutable Oriental writers liked to depict in books. "Seems to me you'd be better off talking to me if you don't want to talk to them."

Li Bai avoided looking at him. "What you want to know?"

So. He'd guessed right. Wash sat down at his usual spot at the table and crossed his legs. "I want to know where you get the opium. How it gets here, how often. I want to know how often Miss Salo is buying it and how much. I told you, Not," he said quickly as Li Bai grunted a protest, "how much she pays. How many pills or spills or whatever you call them. The quantity."

These questions would do as a point to work from. Or the ones about how often and the method of transport. The other ones, the personal ones, came more from curiosity. There'd be nothing he could do about it. He just hoped Rio never had to visit the little den on the edge of town he knew Li Bai not only supplied but owned. Painter's Bay was a small town, short of workers, so most of the laborers thereabouts were Chinese.

Many had arrived with the railroad twenty years previously and had never been able to return to China. Some ran laundries. A few more had jobs at the railroad roundhouse, not many miles up the road. All seemed to visit the den when their work was done. And they weren't the only ones. Plenty of whites did the same.

Internally, Wash snorted. The Chinese cook would soon be as rich as Elias Salo himself if this kept up. Except he'd heard there was a lot of fuss over on the coast with the Women's Temperance League trying to shut the opium trade down.

Li Bai avoided giving out too many details. "I do not see the boss man. Hear him sometimes. He don't want me to know. Is a white man, that I tell you. So is man from coast, from Canada. All whites. You watch out, Mr. Ames. They dangerous."

About that, Wash didn't figure Li Bai exaggerated.

He was halfway to his cabin when it occurred to him Li Bai had been very careful in what he said. *I do not see the boss man*, he'd said, yet the indication had been clear. He knew the boss man's identity.

And that boss man was not only dangerous to Li Bai, but also to Wash.

Ten

As it turned out, while Boo wolfed down meat scraps, Rio dined on her fine beef stew at the kitchen table by herself that night. She'd had no choice when Beckett poked his head into the kitchen and asked for his and his brother's meal to be served in their room.

Of course, they had a good excuse what with Win not being well enough to come to the table. And of course he wanted his brother's company. But it left Rio with a whole lot of questions she needed, and intended, to get answers to.

But not, apparently, that particular night.

Oddly enough, she felt as though she'd been set adrift without a raft after this day's events and slept only fitfully when she went to bed. Even Boo nestling against her back didn't ease her into relaxing like it usually did. Once, when Elias made an unintelligible cry during the night and she got up to check on him, he only mumbled and when she offered, swallowed his opium pills with difficulty.

In the morning, he was silent, barely managing to turn his head away when she brought his breakfast and tolerated only a single swallow of coffee. She changed the sheets and bathed the sweat from his body as he moaned softly. Slipping a single opium pill onto his tongue, she held his mouth closed until it melted and he swallowed. By then the tin was empty and she, with Boo's company, went to get more.

Li Bai didn't speak to her, not even to ask for more money than the usual. Rio didn't speak either, once she'd voiced her—or rather, her father's—needs. Turning away and calling to Boo, she hurried back to the hotel, hoping this had been her last purchase.

Beckett joined Wash while she concerned herself with Elias, so that she didn't manage a word with either one.

In late morning, Elias dropped into a coma.

At first, Rio thought he was dead, he lay so still. But as she moved to the bed she saw his chest rising a fraction every so often. A fraction only, and not in any regular rhythm.

"You stay alive," she whispered fiercely. "One more day, that's all I ask. It's the least you can do for me." Her chest felt heavy with the weight of her thoughts. And with guilt over her greed. But it wasn't greed. Not really. Didn't she deserve to live some kind of life? Hadn't she served his interests, and only his interests, for long enough?

And her mother. He said he'd killed her. Murdered her. What about that?

His eyelids never flickered. He didn't move. If he heard anything he was beyond any response.

She covered him and tucked him in against the

chilly evening. There was nothing more she could do. He'd either live tonight or die.

He made no sound during the night but when Rio crept down the hall to check on him come daylight, he was still alive into the third day since sending the letter.

As birds began their morning song and sunlight shone in the east window, his breath stuttered. The intervals between them took longer and longer.

When Rio heard Beckett stirring, she dressed and went downstairs, Boo on her heels, to build up the fire and make coffee.

Her guest looked surprised to see her. His mouth curling into a smile, he said, "Good morning. I didn't hear your father last night and thought you might sleep in."

"I'm out of the habit of sleeping more than a couple hours at a stretch." She set a frying pan on the stove to heat. "Maybe tomorrow. I expect my father will die today."

He sent a startled look at her. "Today?" He looked surprised at how dispassionate she sounded.

Rio shrugged. "Possibly. I don't really know. I'll row across the lake to town and get the doctor. He should be able to tell me. Is it all right to leave your brother on his own? Now that he's better, he needs attention and gets restless."

His dark eyes followed her as she got eggs and bacon from the icebox and sliced bread for toast. "I know," he said. "He doesn't need constant attention though. Leaving him is fine. He's healing fast. Besides, I don't think nursing is part of a hotelkeeper's job."

"It's not. On the other hand, I wouldn't want to see him suffering from neglect."

She lay strips of bacon in the hot cast iron skillet. "How do you prefer your eggs?" Rio barely heard what he answered as she was busy trying to form her first question so it would get an answer. She didn't know if what she came up with would, but she asked it anyway.

"How did Win happen to get shot? Do you know who shot him?"

With a little sigh, he sat down at the table. "I thought we'd get to this at some time or another. I'm surprised you've waited so long to ask."

She shot him a glance out of the corner of her eyes. What could she say? That he'd frightened her into silence? Or because he always seemed to be on the move to somewhere? Both were true. The night when he forced his way into the hotel with his bleeding brother and demanded her help, he'd been so terribly fierce. She'd certainly felt threatened. At the same time, there'd been her father to consider, to keep from being disturbed, which kept her from making a fuss.

Not that it mattered now. After the way Elias had treated her, her concern for him struck her as ridiculous. Think of the way he said he'd killed her mother.

Fiercely, she forced the memory away, but looking down, she saw her hands were shaking again and she wasn't quite sure why.

The coffee perked, squirting a dollop of coffee out to sputter into droplets on the stove lid. She drew the pot back to where the heat was less intense to finish perking and fixed her gaze on Beckett again after getting a plate from the shelf. "Are you going to tell me?"

Without being asked, Beckett got up and found a mug, drawing a little water out of the faucet to pour in the coffee pot's spout to stop the cooking and settle the grounds before he poured. He waved a mug toward Rio and she nodded.

"I'll tell you what I can," Beckett said. "First, the simple explanation is that Win and I were in the wrong place at the wrong time. We were on our way to town when..." He stopped, taking his time as if remembering. "The shot came out of the woods. I had time to see a man moving but it was dark and the rain was heavy. I couldn't identify the man. I moved fast as I could to pull Win to shelter behind a log and didn't have time to get off a shot at him. Otherwise, believe me, I would have."

Rio heard the grim purpose in his explanation as he went on.

"I'll be looking for him. I don't intend on letting him get by with shooting an unarmed kid just minding his own business."

She nodded. "I understand. Sounds like you're lucky both of you got away alive. Did he follow you?"

"Yes. Tried to, anyhow, for a while. I could hear him blundering through the underbrush. Whoever he is, he's not at ease in the woods." Beck made a little scoffing noise.

Rio believed his story. So far. But she had more questions. For instance, why weren't he and Win on the road leading directly to town? Why were they traveling through the Salo woods in the first place?

So she asked. "How did it come about?"

His answers were slick. Something about unloading their horses when the train stopped at a water tower and, since they wanted to see the countryside, taking off on horseback. She didn't believe that part. Or she did, some of it anyway, about them doing that. Just not the reason why.

He sat down, slurping his coffee and watching her crack eggs into the bacon fat. She put a lid over the eggs and turned. Her next question seemed to surprise him.

"Did you find Mr. Hightower's body? You and Win?" She guessed right away that they had. His narrowed eyes and clamped jaw admitted as much. "Did you shoot him?"

"No." An explosive denial. "No. Why would I?"

"Then—"

"Where'd you get an idea like that?"

Rio snorted. "Maybe because of the way you turned up here, Win with a bullet in him." Her temper flared. "Maybe because I can tell you're lying about most everything. Who are you really? What are you doing here? A man is dead. Somebody should care."

"I do care. As for you, stay out of it." He stared at her, his dark eyes hard, his mouth set.

"I will, just as soon as you tell me the truth."

At this Beckett sat back and seemed to be thinking. Suddenly, he relaxed. "Maybe I owe you that. Some of it, anyway. Sit down."

"I...the eggs."

He made a motion, which she took to mean to tend the eggs first. Rio dumped them unceremoniously on a plate and set it in front of him. Certainly not her regular standard of service.

"Now," she said.

His lips tightened. "It was after dark, raining hard. We didn't spot the firelight up ahead until after we—Win and I—had picketed our horses. I was carrying a pack and a rifle; Win had our bedrolls. Then we heard a shot. I decided to check it out, and Win came with me. As we got closer, we could see a man lying sprawled on the ground. Win rushed ahead. I called to stop him but he didn't hear. He'd just knelt by the man when a shot took him down. I yelled, making the biggest ruckus I could and ran forward to pull him out of sight. I guess the shooter decided he'd better not stick around. He shot at me but missed."

Rio's eyes widened.

Beck stared at her. "Win was bleeding bad and unconscious. I carried him deeper into the woods opposite the direction I'd noticed the shooter go. He emptied his rifle at me as he ran off, managing to spray bullets around but shooting blind. Anyhow, I abandoned our things and carried Win until he woke up and could walk a little on his own. After a while I found a path. We followed it to the lakeshore, then we found the hotel and you." He shrugged. "That's it."

Rio had doubts. His story seemed...sparse. Still, it might be best not to pursue. "Are you really a timber cruiser?"

His mouth quirked up again. "I know how to do the job. Don't worry. I can use the tools and figure the math. Pure luck I came along, seems to me. But I'd rather none of this—what happened to Win—is talked about."

Rio felt certain he'd left a whole lot out and glossed over the parts he'd mentioned. She was a bit surprised he'd said as much as he had. Now if only any of it was true.

The eggs had overcooked a tad although Beckett didn't seem to mind. He'd just passed Boo the last inch of his bacon when Wash tapped on the door jamb and poked his head inside.

"Ready to go?" he asked Beck, and smiled at Rio.

Her own smile quivered back at him. What if Wash was in danger? He might be what with an apparently mad shooter on the loose?

But even Beckett didn't appear too concerned. He got up, pulled on a shabby jacket he'd acquired from somewhere, and turning, said to her, "Good breakfast, Miss Salo. Thank you."

All Rio could do is nod.

RIO TOOK WIN HIS BREAKFAST, oatmeal and cream with apples cooked in the oats, and leaving Boo to keep the boy company, hurried down to the dock. Wanting to be first at Dr. Clement's office, she untied the boat, and pulling hard on the oars, rowed across the lake to fetch him. The water was smooth today, the usual breeze still. She got across to the town pier in record time.

Earlier, Elias's breathing hadn't changed much from the last time she'd looked in on him. It had only grown a little slower, a little less deep. He didn't seem to be in pain. Her intention now was to have a witness to Elias being alive on this day. That's all. She didn't think the doctor could do anything for him. His life had become a waiting game.

A woman already sat in the otherwise empty doctor's waiting room when Rio stepped inside. To Rio's eyes, the woman didn't appear very sick. Indeed, Molly Clement had abandoned her desk and left the woman by herself. Molly came bustling through from their private quarters as the bell above the door pealed on a cheerful note.

"Miss Salo," she said, with a glance at the other woman, "you're here very early. Has your father passed?"

"Not yet." Rio forced her features into what she believed to be a suitably sad expression. "Soon, I think."

The other woman perked up at this, happy, no doubt, to have news to impart to her neighbors. Especially news about a man as important in the county as Elias Salo.

"I hoped the doctor could come take a look," she said. "Maybe there's something he can do." Double-edged words. They didn't mean she hoped he could.

"I'll let the doctor know you're here." Molly went through into a back room, voices murmured, and seconds later she returned. "Mrs. Marshall arrived before you." She nodded toward the woman. "He'll be with you when their business is finished."

The other woman, presumably Mrs. Marshall, smiled. "That's very accommodating," she said as if surprised.

When Molly returned after shepherding the Marshall woman into the doctor's treatment room, she beckoned Rio closer. "James told me about your father, Miss Salo. About Mr. Salo pretty much admitting that he killed your mother. Do you believe he did? Would he do such a dreadful thing?"

Rio swallowed. The sympathy in Molly Clement's voice left her almost undone. "Yes. Yes to both questions. I guess...I guess I've always thought he did something to her. If she ran away, she wouldn't have left me behind." Her little speech faltered. "She made a lot of money for him, cooking and running the hotel but I remember he was never good to her. Always yelling at her when no one was around. Hitting her when he was in a temper. I don't know why he'd kill her, but I don't think he'd say he did, if he didn't."

Molly nodded. "I remember Juanita very well. Such a lovely woman. Always so kind to everyone. She'd have been a great beauty if she hadn't been so work-worn." Molly studied Rio a moment with a discerning eye. "You take after her, you know. Right up to the work-worn part. Where was Juanita from? Do you know?"

Rio shook her head under this barrage of information and questions. "She never told me. Or just that her father had been a chef in a New Orleans restaurant."

Molly smiled. "Ah. From New Orleans then. Such a romantic city—or so I hear."

Rio didn't think there'd been anything romantic about her mother's life. Not ever. More like hard work and pain. Decidedly not when her husband had felt free to murder her.

Changing the conversation to some of the food preparation techniques Juanita had learned from her father and passed on to Rio, it was a relief when the doctor ushered his patient out of the treatment room. He already had his medical bag in hand and wore his coat.

Nodding goodbye to the woman, he turned to Rio, saying, "I'm ready." And to Molly he said, "I probably won't be long. Tell folks to come back this afternoon."

Rio couldn't help being nervous when two men, one of them the banker who had been charged with setting up the arrangement for her to withdraw money every month, stopped them on the way to the boat landing.

"I understand Elias is unwell," Nels Masterson said to the doctor, shifting his gaze and eyeing Rio. "Miss Salo. When I see you with the doctor this early in the morning, I wonder if I should be concerned."

She didn't understand why he should be. He and her father weren't great friends as far as she knew. It was money that brought them together. "Concerned? I don't know," she said. "Should you?"

And she wasn't wrong, as his next words indicated.

"He's our biggest single depositor, as I'm sure you must know. He's been kind enough to set up a monthly allowance for you. It went into effect this morning, as a matter of fact, so you can draw on it immediately."

Kind. Rio barely contained her snort. But she was relieved to hear her bit of forgery had gone undetected. She took a step, impatient with the delay.

Masterson had already lost interest in her, going on to question the doctor. Dr. Clement, with a side glance at her, admitted that indeed, Elias was unwell. That his death could come at any time. Very possibly today. That Miss Salo's concern was the reason she'd rowed to town to pick him—the doctor—up and take him to the hotel to see if there was anything he could do. And no, there really wasn't.

"Cancer?" the man with the banker asked. Rio didn't recognize him.

"Yes." Clement nodded, sounding as doleful as a man whose house has burned to the ground. "Spread throughout his body, I fear."

The men exchanged glances. "Nothing catching, then."

"Oh, no." The doctor shook his head. "Not catching. Excuse me, gentlemen, I must be on my way. I can see Miss Salo is in a hurry to get back to her father."

They were in the boat and away from the town pier before he spoke any further. "Elias set up a monthly allowance, did he? After what he said the other day, I'll admit to being surprised. Not that you haven't earned it. He's worked you like one of his Chinese crew from the time your mother...disappeared."

"Died, you mean." Rio was rowing fast, sweating, breathing hard. The hard work did nothing to assuage her anger. "He set up the account at the bank so I could pay for his opium." There were halts between every few words. "He didn't set it up for me. But I'll take it." What she wouldn't do, not even to the doctor who might possibly applaud the action, was tell him she'd altered the amount.

The doctor grinned. "Serves the old devil right."

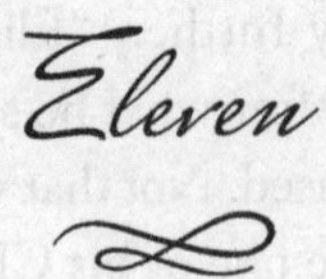

Eleven

Dr. Clement, well-acquainted with the hotel layout by now, headed up the stairs without waiting for Rio.

She told him she needed to release her dog from the room where he'd been penned. And she did, though mainly the object was to check on Win. She found him up and dressed and reading from the book he'd selected from her small collection. *Call of the Wild* by Jack London.

He stuck his finger in the book to keep his place and grinned up at her. "Good book. I heard somebody talking about it once but never got to read it before."

"I'm glad it pleases you. Has my father made any sound?" she asked.

He shook his head. "No. Silent as a tomb up there. I haven't heard anything but Boo panting and your chickens out there clucking."

She gasped. "Gracious. I forgot to gather the eggs this morning." Then she shrugged. "I brought the doctor, so please don't call out until I say it's safe."

Win opened his book. "I know to check first. Beckett told me not to let anyone know I'm here. Told me several times, as a matter of fact." He scowled. "Sometimes I think he thinks I'm stupid."

Startled, Rio said, "Oh no. Not at all. He's just afraid you'll get hurt."

"I already got hurt."

Well, there was nothing she could say to that.

Boo safely shooed outside, Rio climbed the stairs, her feet dragging. She'd still have another round trip across the lake with the doctor when he finished here, and she was already tired to the bone.

Dr. Clement had his finger on Elias's wrist when she entered the room. He shook his head and shifted his finger to the side of his patient's neck.

Rio stared at him, her dark eyes wide. "Is he..."

"Not yet." Placing his stethoscope over Elias's heart, he listened, moving the instrument here and there on his chest, then back to the heart.

If he has a heart. In Rio's opinion he did not. An observation which, as a habit formed over the years, she kept to herself.

The doctor checked Elias's body for bedsores without finding any. He looked at the sheets Rio hadn't yet had a chance to wash and, finding a small, dark-colored urine stain, declared it a sign Elias's kidneys had to all purposes shut down. Lastly, patting Rio on the shoulder, he predicted that indeed, this was her father's final day on earth.

Rio glanced at her father. His face looked waxy under the short growth of whiskers. His beard had stopped growing days ago, she realized. "Can he hear us?"

The doctor shook his head. "I don't know. It's possible. He may sense we're here."

"Huh."

They walked out of the room together.

"Don't worry," Dr. Clement said. "You've kept him clean and as pain-free as possible." His wink showed he knew the method but wouldn't speak of it. "Also, kept him alive longer than I thought possible considering how quickly his cancer spread. A combination of your good care and his own stubborn will to see Eino return home, I believe." He cocked a bushy gray eyebrow at her. "Have you heard from him, Eino, by any chance?"

"No. Not for months and months."

"Ah. Well, no one could've done more. Most wouldn't have done as much."

She couldn't speak. Once in the boat, in rowing the doctor across the lake she remained for the most part, silent. Until she thought to ask what came next.

Dr. Clement had been straightening his medical bag while Rio plied the oars. He closed it. "After he dies, you mean?"

"Yes."

"Send someone for the undertaker. He'll let you know the process and arrange for the funeral, the burial, and the church. With your help, of course. Your father's bank account may be frozen except for his final expenses and anything he's preauthorized. I'd say you're very fortunate to have whatever funds the banker referred to. I hope it's enough to keep you."

She frowned. "I have plans beyond *being kept*."

"You do?" He looked surprised.

"I do. But I don't know about the logging operation," she added. "I hope it can continue. Both for Mr. Ames's sake and for the crew."

He shrugged. "Good point. Perhaps, in the interest of the men who worked for him, the judge will allow Mr. Ames to continue running the business."

"And the hotel? What about it?" She did her best to keep the anxiety and the eagerness out of her voice. "I have nowhere else to live. I can open the rooms and the restaurant for business again now that my father won't be bothered by the commotion." She had a thought. "In fact, I already have a tenant. The timber cruiser Mr. Ames hired when Mr. Hightower was killed has taken a room."

The doctor shrugged again. "I don't know about these things, Miss Salo. Perhaps Mr. Masterson can help you. And whoever Elias designated as his executor." A thought shadowed his face. "Provided he had a will and an executor. He was—is—a stubborn old cuss with old-fashioned ways. Check with Hal Majors. He's the only attorney in town. I imagine he'll know."

He'd been dragging his hand in the water, but suddenly sat up straight and pointed a finger at her. "Don't do any of these things regarding the property until Elias is dead and buried. Hear me, Miss Salo? You're all alone here with him, and if Eino ever does return, well, you don't want any misunderstandings. Not on anybody's part. Do you understand what I'm saying?"

At his first sentence Rio had stopped rowing and let the boat drift. Oh, yes. She believed she understood. "You mean people might think I...I killed him? Because of the way he treats me? Has always treated me. And because of my mother. I don't know how many people he may have told about giving everything to Eino." She smiled ruefully. "Probably everybody."

"I don't know either. He and I were never friends and he didn't speak to me of such things." The doctor's mouth set grimly. "But he wasn't shy in speaking of his son and his wishes for him. Folks haven't missed seeing the way he treated you. For instance, I expect that dress you're wearing has been washed a good fifty times. He was not a generous man, or only to his son."

An oar slipped out of her hand. "Oh." The word was a mortified whisper, even as Rio regained control of the boat and started rowing again. If the doctor had noticed her shabby attire, what about others? What about Washington Ames? Or Beckett Ferris? Or even the farmer who supplied her with milk?

Reaching the pier, she didn't bother to tie up. She merely held the boat steady against the sloshing waves while the doctor disembarked, both his feet barely on the dock before immediately turning around to row back.

At the hotel, she found Win asleep again with *Call of the Wild* open on his chest. She put a marker in the book to save his place, laid it on the bedside table, and tiptoed out without disturbing him.

Upstairs, Elias Salo still lived. He hadn't moved. The blanket covering him lay as perfectly smooth as it had when she left with the doctor. She stood still a few moments, looking down at him and counting the seconds between breaths. Once she got up to twenty-three. The next only fifteen, then twenty-two. Each period seemed like more.

Her eyes filled with tears. Not sad tears. Angry tears. "I hope you go straight to hell," she said to him, and praying, for all Dr. Clement's doubts, that he heard.

The day dragged on. The morning chores finally got finished. She found a stick for Boo to chase and catch and spent some time with the dog in an attempt to teach him hand signals and some obedience. He was young. He preferred to play.

Taking time at noon to eat a slice of bread and plan the evening dinner, after some thought she went back down to the dock and dropped a hook baited with a fat wiggly worm into the lake. Crisply fried trout, potatoes with a sour cream sauce, carrots glazed with honey and lemon juice, were now on the menu plus the custards. Not nearly as fancy as her previous usual restaurant cuisine, but she was out of practice, as well as being low on foodstuffs. This would have to do for the two hotel guests tonight. She'd just have to make sure everything was beautifully prepared.

Even the weather seemed heavy, as if another storm were brewing somewhere over the mountains. Clouds rolled in, dark and low. The fish, at least, seemed to like the atmosphere. They snatched at her bait and filled her supper needs in less than a half an hour. Most of all, the slow activity gave her time to think as she gutted the fish. It all suited Rio's mood, possibly wearing on her because of Dr. Clement's comment about her dress.

The Lord knows she couldn't think when she last had anything new. Sometime when the hotel was booming, she supposed. It had to be before Elias got so sick, although the seeds of his illness had been starting to show. Back then even Elias had known his daughter had to present an appearance of prosperity in order to keep customers coming through the door. And because, like it or not, she belonged to him, and it slighted his reputation should she look like a poor servant girl.

Aloud, she snorted. What else was she but a poor serving girl?

The noise made Boo bark at her.

"Well, I am," she told him. "Or I was. That is going to change, my lad. Count on it."

Boo set a paw on the skirt. Once, she realized, she would have chided him. Not this time. Maybe because she noticed the skirt's hem had frayed to shreds, the stitching completely worn away from the thin fabric. What did a small dog's paw print matter?

All of which made her think of funeral clothes. She would need funeral clothes. Soon.

Oddly, almost like being uttered by a ghost voice, a conversation came back to her—or not a conversation. An order. From when she'd been eight years old, and she'd awakened one morning to find her mother gone, never to be seen again.

Elias had been clutching her arm so tightly her fingers went numb. He'd dragged her into the bedroom he and her mother had shared—when he so desired. Most times Juanita slept with Rio.

He'd pointed toward the cupboard that held Juanita's clothing. "Get a box to put your mother's stuff in," he'd said. "There might be a trunk in the attic. Gather it all, from the dresser too, and get rid of it."

She looked up at him, trying to keep her tears from overflowing. "Get rid of it? But why? When Mama comes back, she will need her things."

"The bitch ain't never coming back. I've done with her. Hurry up now. Shouldn't take you long. Get Harry to take the trunk up to the attic when you're done. Or, hell, burn it for all I care. Just as long as it's gone and out of my sight." He'd pushed her away and shouted. "Now, girl. I said now."

"No, Father..." she'd tried to argue, but he wasn't listening. He slapped her instead. Slapped her hard and said, "Get busy before I give you a real whipping."

His whippings, as she was well aware of back then, hurt. How had she managed to forget that episode for all these years. Because it had been safer?

Rio hated the attic. She'd hated it then and she hated it now. But she remembered the trunk had contained the gown Juanita had worn to her own father's funeral six months before she disappeared.

Dr. Clement had mentioned how much Rio resembled her mother. Well, she did, in size as well as in looks—except for inheriting her father's light-colored hair. If the moths hadn't gotten to the dress in the years since her grandpapa's death, that's what she'd wear to Elias's funeral. It seemed only fitting. Anyway, she didn't want to waste funds on a black funeral dress she hoped never to wear again.

The fish cleaned and in the icebox to keep cold, Rio went to stare up the back staircase. Dust like gray velvet coated the steps. She'd been neglecting maintaining the hotel for several weeks. Without guests to poke around where they didn't actually belong, what did it matter?

Leaving Boo at the bottom of the almost vertical stairway into the attic, Rio no longer worried about disturbing her father. She'd peeked in his room before continuing up to the attic and, almost as if he were frozen in place, saw him as immobile as before. She heard one breath before she closed the door again.

She held on to the handrail as she climbed, a barn lantern swinging in one hand. Once into the attic, the pool of light only reached a short distance, but it was enough to see dust covered everything in a thick layer. Some old furniture dating from the first days of the hotel's existence had been pushed back against the walls. A few boxes she was sure contained junk better discarded before it fed a fire were stacked on top. All stuff that should've been thrown out. But the trunk sat right in the middle of the floor where Bill had left it that awful day.

She hadn't really had time to fold her mother's things neatly, instead sort of just shoving them in. Scooping things from the dresser, she had put those in a separate wooden crate. Where had Harry put that? Looking into the dark corners of the attic, it crossed her mind to wonder why she'd never looked at these things before.

The answer came. Because her father didn't want her to. And as always, she'd done just as he wished. A sort of rage rose, burning in her chest.

Those days were finished. She was done with being small and helpless. Done with cowardice. And if Eino ever returned, she'd prove it.

Swinging the lantern about, she spotted the crate she sought only a few feet from the attic entrance, just where Harry had dropped it. He'd been eager to get out of there too, though not as badly as she. From the looks of things, nobody had been to the attic since, almost fourteen years ago.

For a lone woman to hoist a medium-sized trunk

and a largish crate down those steep stairs proved no easy task. After some thought, she simply tied a rope onto the trunk's handle, stood at the top of the stairs and allowed the trunk to bump its way down. Though noisy and a bit unpredictable as to direction, she did the same with the crate.

The rest of the junk in the attic could remain for another day.

Elias, she found, had been undisturbed by the noise. Watching, she saw the blanket over his chest rise and fall, a movement slight enough she barely caught it.

Stowing the items in her small bedroom, she dusted herself off and went downstairs.

AT DARK, Beckett showed up after his first day in the woods. Wash accompanied him. Both appeared pleased with themselves.

Boo, happy to see them both, cavorted around the men as if hoping for a playmate. Wash accommodated him briefly.

Beckett, glancing coolly at Rio, said, "A good day of work," and passed on inside, headed for his room.

Rio stared after him.

Wash left off playing with the dog, stomped his boots free of dried mud, and entered the kitchen.

"Was it?" she said. "A good day of work?"

He grinned. "You bet. Ferris had to borrow Hightower's tree scale and diameter tape, but if anything, his math is better and faster than Hightower's. Bill always had to take his time. Ferris and I got along fine. I trust him to go on his own tomorrow."

Rio let out a breath she didn't know she'd been holding. "So you'll be moving camp tomorrow?"

"Yes. Or the next day. Depends." Wash's grin faded. "I should look in on Elias this evening, if that's all right with you."

She didn't know why he should or why he thought she'd care but decided not to ask. "He's in a coma, Wash, and can't speak to you. I don't know if he hears anything or not. Dr. Clement was here again today. He says...he says..." She didn't know how to tell him the doctor's prognosis without sounding as if Elias's death didn't matter to her.

As it didn't. Not to her, or not in the way he meant, but it might to Wash.

"Go on up," she finished. "You'll see."

"Come with me?" His eyes fixed on her in a kind of questioning sort of way.

She shook her head and bent over the potatoes she was paring, their spiral skins coming off thin and precise. "Not this time. My guest will be wanting his supper." She'd almost said *guests*.

Down the hall, she heard the bathroom door open and close. Beckett, cleaning up from his day in the woods. She hoped he was aware of Wash going upstairs instead of leaving for the camp.

Within five minutes, Wash stopped in the kitchen doorway. His face set. "Why didn't you tell me? I could've done more to help."

"You've kept the men working, the business going. And he couldn't have asked for anything more." Rio looked up from seasoning the trout and smiled at him, unaware of the pale tendrils of hair escaping from the mass gathered at the nape of her neck. Or that she looked tired half to death.

"I could've helped you." His emphasis came down hard on *you*.

"Thank you, Wash. I've managed." Her gaze went upward as if seeing through the ceiling into her father's room. "Not much longer now, as I'm sure you've guessed. Dr. Clement thinks tonight. Or maybe at dawn. He says for some reason many people die at dawn." I'm chattering, she thought.

He studied her. "What happens then?"

Rio shrugged, a dismissal of his concern. "I guess we'll see when the time comes." She knew what she wanted to happen. Making it happen was something else entirely.

"At least you won't have to deal with Li Bai again. I think you'll be relieved. "

Her smile returned. "That's true. I won't miss my meetings with him at all. It will be a relief." A minor one compared to all the others whirling through her mind just now. She wished she could tell Wash what her father had said about her mother. Pour out some of the rage, the fear, the hopelessness she felt. Wished she had someone to share all this with. Impossible.

Wash turned to leave. "I'll go then, Miss Salo. Call on me if I can do anything."

"Thank you, Mr. Ames. I will."

He stopped. Turned back. "You called me Wash a minute ago."

"I did?" Her eyes opened wide.

"You did. I like it. I hope you'll do it all the time. I find it easier to answer to Wash than Mr. Ames." He seemed serious.

Her heart began beating faster. "All right. If you'll call me Rio."

Wash nodded. "I will. Good night, Rio. I'll see you in the morning. Sooner if necessary."

With that, he was gone, striding away into the gathering dark. Rio didn't know if he even heard her say, "Good night, Wash."

Twelve

Beckett and Win ate their supper in Rio's kitchen that night. She kept the settings as if they were in the hotel dining room, but neither guest wanted to put her to the trouble of lighting the lanterns in there and carrying the food that far.

"Besides," Win stated, "it's cold outside the kitchen. I know. I walked through the hotel while you were gone this afternoon. Walked around the ground floor, I mean. I didn't go upstairs."

"Blast it, Win. What if you'd passed out?" Beckett glared at his brother. "When Miss Salo finally found you, she couldn't have gotten you back to your room by herself. She's too small. Think before you do these things."

Rio flapped her hands. "I'm stronger than you think, Mr. Ferris. Anyway, Boo would've told me something was amiss. He came and got me one day when my father collapsed out in the yard, even though Elias had kicked him just that morning. He's a good dog."

The men were able to agree on Boo and his good-natured intelligence, while frowning over anyone mistreating such a fine dog. They also agreed about enjoying the trout and the potatoes in sour cream sauce, something neither brother had ever tasted.

Rio, flushed with pleasure, started the washing up and pretended not to hear them talking. In the hotel business, staff did a lot of pretending. Not to hear, not to see. Not to speak unless spoken to. To become invisible. Tonight she was staff, nothing more.

When the Ferris brothers had finished eating, Win pleaded boredom having been stuck in bed for three days and talked his brother into escorting him on a short walk in the dark.

Rio gobbled her own supper and finished her chores as quickly as possible. Anxious to go through her mother's things, she found herself curious about Juanita as she'd never been before. And there was the funeral dress to consider. She'd probably have to do some adjusting on the fit before she could wear the dress, provided it was wearable at all.

She heard Beckett and Win come in as she went up the stairs, going directly to look in on Elias before she started on the trunk. He clung to life. His heart still beat, and his lungs still drew air.

"Stubborn, aren't you?" she whispered to him. "You should just let go. Be on your way to hell. And good riddance to you."

It felt good to say that to him and not shiver with fear. It felt bad to say that to him and not feel guilt. He was her father. Why had he never, ever cared for her?

Turning, she left the room. It did no good to ponder the question when it was too late to receive an answer.

In her own room, she'd barely wiped the dust off the

trunk lid—what hadn't shaken off during its tumble down from the attic—when the bell above her bed began jangling. For a moment her heart nearly failed her. Had Elias awakened somehow? Had he heard what she said and determined on retribution?

Then she identified which bell was ringing, discovering it to be the one to the locked hotel door. Once again, someone had ignored the closed sign and appeared to be dead set on entrance. Hurrying downstairs and through the lobby, she heard Beckett's door open, then his voice. He was telling Win to stay out of sight.

When she was sure they were settled, she opened the door.

Thor Donaldson stood there. Her heart sank.

"Where's Ferris?" he demanded without preamble. "That feller Wash Ames hired to take Hightower's place. I heard he's staying here. That means this here hotel is open for business and you can't keep me out. What room is he in. I need to talk with him."

He shoved past her, making sure to touch her as he went past. Unable to stop herself, she shrank aside.

"Well?" he demanded. "Which room? And light a lamp, for God's sake. It's darker than Satan's cellar in here."

Clearly, the sheriff planned to intimidate. His normal method of communication, apparently. And, even as Rio's resentment grew, the intimidation worked.

She opened her mouth to speak, but Beckett's intervention stopped her.

"I'm here," he said. "I heard the commotion. Thought for a second the place must be ablaze and the fire brigade on hand. Who, may I ask, are you, and why are you cursing at Miss Salo? Have you no manners or decency?"

Rio's innards gave a lurch. "This is Sheriff Thor Donaldson," she said. She meant it as a warning.

Beckett glanced at her. "I don't care who he is. He has no business speaking to you like that. Or to any lady."

"See here," Donaldson said, rough and loud as usual. "I'll have a word with you in private, mister. We'll go to your room. Don't figure you want some bird-brained little woman listening in on a man's business."

He turned to Rio. "You wait in the kitchen. I'll be talking to you when I'm done with Ferris."

Rio looked at Beckett. He winked as if whatever Donaldson wanted didn't concern him in the slightest. And maybe it didn't, though the idea of her being alone with the sheriff gave her the willies.

Meanwhile, Beckett couldn't host the sheriff in his room with Win there. "We can talk right here."

Donaldson grunted and turned to Rio. "Scat. I'll call you when I'm done with him."

Folding his arms across his chest, Beckett nodded to Rio. "I'm sure it's nothing, Miss Salo." Then to the sheriff, he said, "Make it short. I've had a long day and I'm tired."

As much as she would've liked to stay and hear what the sheriff thought so important, Rio marched off toward the kitchen, just as Donaldson had ordered. Doing her best to keep her head up and spine straight tried her strength, but she thought she managed pretty well.

The sheriff began talking before she reached her destination, and truthfully, she wasn't much inclined to obey his orders. This was her home, her hotel—or soon would be if things went right—and she had the say on what went on here. And that, she figured, included listening in on Thor Donaldson's talk with the hotel guest.

Just inside the doorway, she stopped and shrank against the wall. Their voices carried fairly well, especially Donaldson's since he didn't bother to lower the volume.

"How'd you hear about the cruiser job?" he demanded.

"No skullduggery, sheriff, if that's what you're implying. I saw a notice posted in the general store. I've got experience at the job and figured to apply. I did. Ames hired me. Simple as that."

"Yeah? Stranger in town, ain't you? How'd you happen to stop in here?"

Beckett's answer was quiet, calm, assured. "Pure luck. Right place at the right time."

The sheriff apparently didn't think much of the explanation. "Did anybody tell you it could be real dangerous, working in this part of the woods? Working for Salo?"

Beckett sounded almost amused. "Dangerous? In what way?"

"Did Ames tell you Hightower, the previous man, got himself killed?"

"He told me. Him and at least two other people. They told me he was murdered, but I need the job. And I may not be so easy to kill Mr. Hightower."

The bald warning in Beckett's reply stopped even Donaldson—for an extra beat of the heart. Then he said, "Nobody can watch every minute, out there in the woods by yourself. Could be in your best interest to quit while you're ahead."

"You're worried about me?"

"Hell, no. Not worried. Just giving you a warning concerning your good health." A pause. "You're a stranger hereabouts. Folks, meaning Wash Ames, wouldn't find it surprising if you decided the job didn't suit."

Beckett didn't say anything but Donaldson wasn't giving up his argument.

"Elias Salo is a very sick man who will be dead real soon. When he's gone, his holdings will fall apart. Looks like the old man's son has croaked too, since he ain't been heard from in a year or better. That chit of a girl is nothing. Not too bright from what I can tell. Ames won't need much persuasion to move on. Not when his job peters out."

Rio's hands clenched into fists. The nerve of the man. The...the...she couldn't think of anything bad enough right off.

"You seem mighty sure of how this might play out. What's your interest in it?" Beckett's question reclaimed her attention.

"Me? My business is none of yours, Ferris, though you can take it that I plan on picking up the pieces. But I'm warning you. Stick your nose in and you'll regret you ever heard of this place. Understand me?"

"Oh, I think I do, Sheriff. Yes, I do. See yourself out."

Beckett's footsteps headed her way. Not wishing to be seen eavesdropping, Rio whisked herself into the kitchen and was standing in front of the stove as Beckett passed the door on the way to his room. She waited there but didn't hear the hotel door close. Nor Beckett's, for that matter. Had Donaldson left the front open to the night?

No choice. She had to look. She got back to the lobby in time to see the sheriff on his way up the stairs. Anger rushed over her.

"Sheriff," she called, hurrying after him. "Sheriff Donaldson. I'm talking to you. Where are you going? You have no business up there. Come down."

It was as if she were both silent and invisible. He reached the landing and headed toward Elias's room.

Rio followed as fast as her legs would carry her. She caught up with him as he leaned over her father's bed. He sniffed, no doubt smelling the odors of impending death. Undefinable, perhaps, but there, even though she'd kept her father clean.

Elias lay unmoving, unaware—uncaring.

"Elias," Donaldson half-shouted. "You alive?"

There was no reaction, no sound, no movement. He lay as still as ever.

Rio huffed. "He's in a coma, as anyone with a half a brain can tell. Leave him be."

"You." He turned to look at her. "Watch your mouth, girl. I ain't so sure you're not helping him along. One thing for sure, he ain't gonna last much longer."

"He'll pass in his own time and not before. Get out." She knew her temper was overwhelming her good sense, talking to him like that, but she couldn't stop herself.

He grinned—or maybe sneered—at her. "When I'm ready." He looked around the room as if inventorying the furniture, then pawed through the few things on the bedside table. There wasn't much to see. Just a thin roll of bills and a few coins from the stash Rio had seen her father retrieve from the armoire a few days ago.

Donaldson touched the wad with a look toward Rio that made her think he would've pocketed it if she hadn't been watching. "Enough here for his funeral?" he said.

"I wouldn't know." And she didn't. A sense of propriety had kept her curiosity at bay. She would take nothing from her father that he didn't hand to her. Not while he lived.

She took a breath. "Not your business and not your problem. I would appreciate it if you'd leave now."

"I don't like your tone, young woman. Remember that, later." His jowly face had turned red and she thought if he hadn't known Beckett was in the hotel and within call, he would've said more. Done more.

Rather to her surprise, he did leave, although once again he made sure to jostle her on the way down the stairs. The expression he wore told her he would've just as soon set an elbow in her ribs and sent her flying.

RIO HAD BEEN asleep for a few hours. Deeply asleep, so that when something awakened her, she sat upright disoriented and groggy. It was either very early in the morning, or very late at night. Boo, who had been lying against her, sat alert with his ears pricked.

"What is it?" she whispered.

He jumped off the bed and went to the door, his toenails making tiny clicks on the plank floor. Moonlight shining through the open window let her see him look back at her as if waiting for her to follow. Sighing, she got up, shoved her feet into slippers and her arms into an old flannel robe long past its respectable days. The spring night carried a chill.

"Your move," she told the dog as she opened the door.

He didn't hesitate but headed down the hall. Rio's heart sank as she followed him. They went straight to Elias's room.

The bright moonlight flooded her father's room, drowning any color into various shades of black to gray with his bedcover showing almost blue. His face shone white as paper.

The first thing Rio noticed was that although he remained in that same position on his back, his eyes were slitted open, the lids relaxed as if the muscles that controlled them had given up.

"Father?" Tentatively, as if she feared retribution, she touched his hand. Cold. Set two fingers on his face. Also cold. No pulse in his neck. Drawing back the cover, she lay her head against his chest, her ear pressed close. Nothing, though she listened for more than a minute by a second by second count.

So. He was gone, dead at last. Oddly, she felt nothing. Not even the relief she'd thought she would. Collecting his pocket watch from the bedside table, set there and meticulously wound every morning of the week, she took it over to the window where the light was best and found the time. 3:52 in the morning.

Beckett Ferris would soon be up, ready to get an early start on his day. And Wash would probably stop in as well before they set off into the timber. She'd be glad to hear a living voice. Strange how alone she felt now, how helpless when she'd believed herself ready for this moment. More than ready.

Maybe either Wash or Beckett could go for the undertaker per Dr. Clement's advice. She should have written the steps he'd told her about down on paper since they all seemed to have flown from her head. Why hadn't she been thinking?

Stumbling on the dark stairs, she made her way down to the kitchen and let Boo out the back. Rio stood a moment on the back porch, watched the scruffy little dog dart about his morning business as the sky changed from slate gray to a mild blue-gray streaked with pink. The sound of waves lapping against the dock footings came clearly, the boats rocking gently with the motion. Her breath went in and out, keeping time with the waves. A sense of peace stole over her to be replaced with a shiver. Apprehension, this time. What came next?

Beckett's question came from behind her. "Your father. Is he gone?"

She jumped. "Yes."

"I'm sorry," he said.

"Don't be. He's free from pain now." There were other things she might have said. She said none of them. Inhaling deeply, she let it out. "I'm trying to think what I should do first. I can't seem to remember what the doctor told me. Maybe I am bird-brained, just like Sheriff Donaldson said."

"Pay Donaldson no mind. He's mean and he's stupid." He paused. "Seems I remember when my mother passed, the first thing we did was send for the undertaker. Is there one in town?"

"Yes. Thank you. That's exactly what the doctor

said to do." Rio's relief was so great she had to keep herself from hugging him. But then she wondered what it would be like, to hug a man. Would he embrace her back? Or would he push her away?

She folded her arms around herself, aware suddenly of her ugly old robe and her unbrushed hair.

"Boo," she called sharply and as the dog came running, turned around to go inside to build up the fire.

"I guess there's no hurry. I'll get the coffee boiling," she said and, head averted, set about her chores. She had a responsibility to her guests that came before her duty to her father this day. He was dead and they were alive. A responsibility she'd have to handle if she planned on surviving past this time.

Thirteen

Rio prepared a breakfast of oatmeal and eggs, toast and jam for her guests and got it on the table for Beckett and on a tray for Win, still sequestered in their hotel room. If all went well, the charade of Win openly arriving would take place today, his presence lost, perhaps, in the turmoil of Elias's passing. A game made easier to play.

Wash arrived on time as usual, taking the news in stride. It wasn't as if it were unexpected. He held her hand for as long it took to say his condolences. Then he snatched his away as if he'd been too forward. She could see he wanted to say, or do more, but had trouble coming up with either adequate words or the right gesture. She wished he had, or tried, anyway. What might she have done if he'd hugged her? Would she have liked it?

What was she thinking? Hugs? First with Beckett and then with Wash? What kind of woman was she to think of such things at a time like this?

At any rate, no hugs were forthcoming. Not from anyone.

Wash set off to row across the lake and arrange for the undertaker, a certain Mr. Meadows, to attend to Elias's body. When he'd gone, Beckett called Win from their room and cautioned him on how to act when he finally made an appearance. Seen maybe, but not heard.

"Be darn careful how you answer any questions, little brother. Wait until Miss Salo gives you the word it's safe to make yourself known. You hear me? Lord only knows what might happen if that sheriff learns you've been here all the time. He's stupid, but wily, and he has a suspicious mind."

Win set his jaw, increasing the resemblance to his brother. "You told me already. Several times. I know what to do. I won't cause Miss Salo any trouble. Seems as if she's got enough."

Rio smiled doubtfully at him. "What are you planning to do."

"Come train time, I'll go through the woods and over to the depot. I'll hang around out of sight until I can make a point of going through town like I just got off the train. Then I'll walk around asking folks how to reach this hotel and tell them about meeting my brother here."

"Are you sure you're strong enough to do all that? It's only been a few days since you lost a lot of blood."

Win nodded, grinning. "Well, I might not be as pert as I usually am, but see, when I tell everybody I've been sick it'll explain why I didn't get here the same time as Beck. If I look kinda puny, it'll all make sense." He sobered. "We're hoping whoever killed that man won't put Beck and me together as the ones he shot at that night."

Rio's gaze flew to Beckett. "You think that'll work?" She thought their whole act a bit iffy.

"Best we can do," he said, and that was that. "I wanted to wait a few more days, but with Donaldson already looking around here and with your father passing on, it's too dangerous to put it off."

"Yeah," Win said, "and I'm sick of hiding out and worrying about somebody seeing me."

For the life of her, Rio didn't know why Win thought he'd be better out in plain sight.

After a few more orders to his brother, Beck gathered his gear and left. He knew the way to the section he'd been assigned to work and didn't need Wash as a guide. She wondered about his quick knowledge of the woods and also whether his concern lay in discovering if his measurements would prove the section profitable, or if he had another kind of job in mind. She had her own suspicions. Between the two brothers, everything they'd said seem to indicate an enterprise more dangerous than a simple timber cruising job. She just couldn't figure out what it was.

But those were questions she had to drop for now. Getting her father buried and taking control of the situation were her first and only order of business.

The morning passed in a blur.

Wash returned, reported in, then went on to work.

The mortician eventually appeared, having driven the trail around the lake to pick up Elias's corpse. An assistant who sat alongside him on the exposed bench seat held tightly to the rails to keep from being bounced off in the rutted road. By then, Win, careful not to be seen, had slipped off through the woods to attend to his playacting. Also by then, others in the business community had received the news of Elias's death and come, by boat or by road, to poke their noses through the hotel door.

Most, to Rio's relief, were content to gather on the hotel's front porch where benches provided a place to sit and talk. Seemingly bent on plaguing Rio, they continually bombarded her with questions. Most of those questions she had no answers for, or, if she did, had no intention of sharing with them. No intention of allowing them upstairs to view the body either, as one man asked to do. A ghoul, for sure.

Excusing herself to the latest arrival, Rio met Mr. Meadows at the hearse and led him up to her father's room. The assistant made short work of bundling the body into a canvas shroud for transport and by mid-morning they were ready to take him away.

Meadows, she found, proved a sympathetic and kind man. "Don't you worry about them." He cocked a thumb toward the hotel lobby where the men had gathered. "There's always a few who congregate at times like these. Some are even well-meaning and want to help."

Rio's eyes got big. "How will I know which ones? They all seem rather..." She hesitated, searching for the right word.

"Vulture-like?" The assistant, a thin, white-haired man, supplied one for her. Meadows hushed him, but it was true.

Rio nodded. Meanwhile, she was very aware that no women accompanied the men. Even now it was as if she barely existed, unseen, unimportant and undeserving of sympathy or support.

The crowd had followed the mortician and his assistant as they carried their burden out to the workaday hearse he'd brought, and watched as they loaded Elias inside. Mr. Meadows beckoned Rio around to the front for a private word.

"I'll have Mr. Salo all fixed up by tonight. Don't look like it'll be much of a job. It's not as if he was in a gunfight or got felled by a tree, after all. If you'll come around early tomorrow morning, we can figure out the casket, the burial plot, and the time for the funeral. That suit you?"

He'd turned brusque and businesslike, which surprised Rio a little. But then she figured that he must think her stiff and uncaring since she hadn't shed a tear. Why should she weep over the man who had murdered her mother?

With the body gone, the gathering lost its focus and the men left.

Rio blessed the quiet—until she sat down on the now empty bench and discovered not only an awful ache, but thoughts that whirled like a myriad of dust devils inside her head. All through the long ordeal of Elias's last days, she'd thought of what she'd do when he was gone. Start up the hotel business again. Do what she liked. Sleep soundly at night without having to listen for his call. But she hadn't prepared for this yawning emptiness.

What next? She didn't know. A minute ticked by as a silence so profound she could hear the surrounding pine trees whispering, their susurrant sound like ghostly voices. She breathed in time with the whispers.

What else had she planned? Her lips twitched. Avoid Li Bai for a start. She distrusted that man. Another plus, Boo could have the run of the place. Jumping to her feet, Rio dashed into the hotel, up the stairs and to her room. Opening the door, she found Boo stretched out to twice his size and sleeping peacefully on her bed. Just where she'd left him when all those visitors began appearing. He lifted his head and looked at her.

"We can do as we please now," she said. "You can come and go whenever you want." She thought a moment, then went on. "Within reason. You can bark a little, if you like. Run up and down the stairs."

The dog got up and shook himself, head to tail and back again, floppy ears waving. Rio thought he was smiling.

Another thought occurred to her. A chore she'd had to delay until *he* was gone. "You can even come with me into that room," she told the dog. "If you're not afraid." He'd shied away from her father's room previously right up until the early hours of this morning. Boo hadn't liked Elias any better than Elias liked him.

Boo turned fearless with him gone. Padding along beside her, they went into the room together. The dog stopped in the doorway, his nose wriggling. He sneezed, shaking his whole body.

"Yes. It stinks, doesn't it?" Taking long strides, Rio crossed to the window, pulled back the curtains and threw up the sash, hoping to let the miasma escape.

The bed, which previously had been almost smooth with Elias's shrunken frame barely mussing the covers, was rumpled now, the blanket pulled to the foot and tossed askew. The pillows had been thrown on the floor.

Apparently, the undertaker's assistant had not been particularly tidy as he wrapped Elias in the shroud.

Though she'd told Elias she'd taken his .44 Smith and Wesson revolver away days ago, stains from the oils used to clean it lay at the head of the bed where he always kept it, an oily spot permanently marring the white of the sheet. Having been unable to turn or twist his body for weeks now, he hadn't been aware.

Stripping everything from the bed, she bundled everything together, ready to be taken downstairs to the porch where the laundry tubs awaited. When the hotel opened for business again, she planned to ask Mrs. Golz to return and tend to those kinds of chores. But first she needed to have money to pay the woman.

Which brought her to the table where the money Donaldson had eyed so greedily still awaited. Her money now, she guessed. No one else could claim it. And she still had most of what Elias had tossed at her to buy his last batch of drugs.

Twenty-one dollars and thirty-seven cents. She counted the money aloud.

"Look, Boo."

The dog sniffed at the money in Rio's hand.

"This is enough to buy supplies to start up the hotel kitchen again. Not a broad menu, but enough for a few courses." Then she frowned. "Although...I wonder how much it will cost to bury my father. More than I have on hand, I expect." And that's when she blinked and her line of sight landed on the armoire. "Unless—" She was already on her way across the room, Boo pattering on her heels.

Flinging open the armoire's double doors, she peered inside. Her father's good suit hung there. The one he wore for other people's funerals and business meetings he considered important.

Dressing well, she'd heard him say more than once, declared a man's worth to the world. Utter nonsense to Rio's mind. For instance, she doubted Wash Ames owned a suit like this one, and she knew he was worth a dozen of Eino, who'd owned a half-dozen or more.

Rio's mouth twisted. Could be Elias's comment was what had turned Eino into a dandy, always concerned with looking his best, although to Rio's mind, acting his best would've been a more worthy undertaking.

She had to wonder if Elias's premise about declaring worth went for women. Maybe, because she had noticed he always paid more attention to a richly gowned woman. If she could get the hotel making money again, she'd have to try the idea and see. A promise she made herself.

Anyway, Elias would need these garments for his last public appearance. She took them out and placed them on the bed along with a white and blue striped shirt with its stiff white collar, and a bold tie. A memory of the last time he'd worn the suit flashed through her mind.

He'd attended a dinner in town celebrating the retirement of old Mr. Blankenship, the owner of the biggest sawmill in this part of the state. Or not just a single sawmill, but several, each one placed in a small town close to the big timber. He'd contracted with other privately owned mills, as well. Elias sat on the executive board as one of the directors of the consortium, and the person who leased the Salo mill was also connected to the Blankenship enterprise.

She remembered when Mr. Blankenship the

younger had taken over from his father, Elias had bragged about Eino being in the same position when it came time for Elias to retire.

Or die. He hadn't planned on that. But he had begun showing signs of his illness shortly afterward and Eino had already been gone a year at the time.

On impulse, she went through the suit's pockets. An inner pocket contained one twenty-dollar gold coin, two letters, and one scrawled note. One letter, she found, had come from Eino's relatives—but not hers as they were from his mother's side—with a date post-marked a couple weeks before the retirement party. The other letter, received the day before the party, bore a return address from Elias's lawyer.

Rio remembered her father had been angry for weeks around that time. Would these letters have anything to do with his mood?

She set them aside to read later and put the coin in her apron pocket. A smile twisted her lips. Elias would hate it, that she planned to read those letters.

With the armoire emptied and in direct line of the sunlight pouring in through the window, she had a much better view of the interior. Elias had procured money from here. He hadn't opened the drawer that made up the lowest component of the piece, so it hadn't come from there. Which meant the bottom piece of the closet part must be a secret compartment.

She'd opened the door hundreds of times as she put her father's clothing away. Never, ever, had she suspected there was anything out of the ordinary in there. He'd had the piece custom built, she remembered, of the finest oak with a cedar veneer lining. He'd been proud of that. Given Elias's propensity toward secrecy, it made sense he'd put in a false bottom.

Now she just had to figure out how to open it.

It had to be fairly simple. From where she'd watched from the doorway, it had appeared he'd simply passed his hand over the outer edge and a hatch had popped open. From the distance of her view, the piece that sprang up had been cabinet wide and maybe three inches in depth. Enough to get one's fingers in, but certainly not particularly large or deep.

Slowly, carefully, Rio let her fingers drift over a narrow band that finished the edge and provided backing for the doors. *There.* Was that an indentation? She made another pass. Definitely an indentation, and not one, she thought, that came from wear and tear. It was too smooth, almost invisible, and seemed to her deliberate.

First she tried pressing on the piece.

Nothing happened.

She tried lifting.

Nothing. Not a surprise as she didn't think her father's stiff fingers would've fit under the slight lip. Stubbornly, she started pressing on the edge, working from left to right. Nothing. But had she felt a sort of give there in the center? When she peered closely, the finish on the wood seemed a tad more worn in that particular spot.

She pressed again.

Nothing.

Impatient, now, she pressed and pressed again. A double tap.

Like magic, the whole edge flipped upward, the

hinges that held it snug showing underneath the wood, and fitted so expertly it was undetectable from above.

"Found it, Boo!"

The dog barked as Rio's feet did a little dance, her heart thudding with excitement. She'd done it. Discovered the secret to the old man's hideaway.

She found a bank book, where the balance made her gasp. She found some women's expensive jewelry. Nothing too formal or ostentatious, but certainly valuable. Juanita had never worn this jewelry, so Rio figured it must've belonged to her father's first wife. There were some papers.

And there was money. A lot of money. Two thick stacks bound with twine. Two small bags filled with coins. Three envelopes with bills stuffed inside. She'd count it later, she decided.

Rio didn't know whether to shout with glee or to weep.

Where had all this money come from?

She didn't want to know. Or did she?

Guilt, a black, crawling sensation crept over her, and without another thought, she replaced everything and without looking further, closed the compartment and the armoire and bolted from the room.

Fourteen

Elias died on a Monday. The following Saturday, his funeral cortege formed a line and followed his casket from the church at the edge of town to the small, but growing graveyard a few hundred yards behind the building. Edith, Elias's first wife was already there with a large and important marker at her head. They placed him beside her.

Rio viewed the whole process with resentment. Edith, apparently so precious. Juanita, murdered, God only knowing where her bones lie. Probably scattered in the woods somewhere, never to be found.

At least this part of the ceremony wasn't taking too long, unlike the sermon at the church. Rio hadn't listened to a word. Just clenched her fingers in the lacy black mitts that had been stored with Juanita's old-fashioned black dress and endured.

The way to the cemetery was even more miserable. Wind blew the pouring rain from trees overhead into their faces. Few women were in attendance, and even the men showed signs they'd rather be sitting in the saloon with a stiff drink in front of them.

Wash stood beside her at the gravesite. It turned out he did have a suit. Not bad, just not one tailored to fit. At the thought, Rio smothered a wry little smile. For all its cost, Elias's hadn't fit him, either. Not at the end.

She gripped the umbrella she was trying to hold steady over both her and Wash's heads and chided herself for being petty. This was her father's funeral, no matter how he'd treated her.

A gust of wind took hold of the umbrella, nearly tearing it out of her grasp.

"Hang on," Wash murmured. "This won't last much longer. Even Reverend Müller can't drone on forever."

"Seems like he can," Rio murmured back.

Wash had the right of it. No more than a minute later, the reverend finished his prayer with an "Amen" and stepped away from the coffin. Most of the others didn't bother with amens. They just turned and left, hastening back toward town and shelter from the rain.

Dr. Clement was the only one who paused beside Rio, worry creasing his brow.

"How are you holding up, Miss Salo? Mr. Ames?" He made a gesture toward the people hurrying away. He wore a wide-brimmed hat and an oiled slicker. "The weather. Not a good day for a funeral." His lips twitched. "Not that any day is."

Rio might have argued that if she hadn't been so cold and wet. And getting wetter every moment. She smiled at him, though she felt her lips quivering. "No. And probably not the send-off my father expected."

He looked at her and blinked. "I hadn't thought of

that, but you may be right. Mr. Salo always managed to be the center of attention wherever he went. Even at company meetings of the Blankenship consortium."

"Yes. Especially after the meetings when the poker games started." As it turned out, she'd discovered the source of some of the money hidden in the armoire's secret compartment. A scrawled note in one of the envelopes had explained. Apparently, Elias had been a superlative poker player and the money was from bets he'd won. She didn't exactly know how to handle one note's message, and was afraid to discuss it with Wash. Not his problem. But the note had come from Thor Donaldson and she was sure he'd like it destroyed.

Wash took her elbow and started her away from the gravesite. She noticed he gave his head a slight shake at her words.

The doctor walked with them. "You know about those? The poker games?"

"Yes." And she told a little fib. "They weren't as secret as some folks may have thought." Including the good doctor, going by the look on his face.

He seemed a bit uncomfortable with that. "Have you mentioned the games to anyone else, Rio?"

She thought he was unaware that he'd used her first name. "No. I don't consider it any of my business when grown men get together over a friendly card game."

"As long as they stay friendly," he said, and she had to wonder about the comment.

"As I suppose they were. Not that it makes any difference now," she said, shrugging.

She heard him exhale. Relief? Apparently, Dr. Clement had been one of the card players. She wondered if Molly knew. Possibly not, judging by the doctor's reaction.

They had reached the church, sliding a little on the wet grass. She released the umbrella and gathered it closed. The parson had gotten there before them—funny how the tall, thin man had galloped past them at one point—and was drying his face with a towel. As soon as he spotted her, he came forward, proffering a slip of paper with some numbers visible on it.

"I'm sorry, Miss Salo," he said, "but there is a charge—call it a requested donation—for the burial plot where your father lays. No rush, of course, as long as it's paid within the month."

"No rush?" Wash's voice sounded more like a dog growling. "Then I don't think this has to be done right at this moment. My God, man, give the lady a break. She's just lost her father."

Dr. Clement glared displeasure as well. He turned to Rio. "If you don't have—"

"No worries." She smiled at him. He'd been going to offer payment, but she'd already looked at the number on the paper. It seemed fair. "I have it right here." She opened the small purse dangling from her wrist and withdrew a ten-dollar bill. She held it out. "And witnesses to show the bill is paid. I believe a receipt will be necessary. At your convenience."

The doctor's eyes seemed to pop. Wash sent her a sideways glance.

"Really, Miss Salo..." The parson didn't seem able to finish the sentence. Finally, he settled with, "That's fine. Thank you. Oh, and I assume we will see you at church tomorrow. I can have the receipt ready then."

Rio, who'd already turned and popped open her

umbrella again, spoke over her shoulder. "I wouldn't." She didn't look back.

"Wouldn't what?" Reverend Müller called after her as if puzzled.

"Assume." She walked on.

Wash hurried after her, his blue eyes glinting with laughter.

When he'd picked her up from the hotel that morning, he was driving the small, two-passenger buggy that had been stored in the barn a few hundred yards beyond the hotel. It hadn't been used since Elias had gotten so terribly sick. He'd demanded men come to him, rather than the other way around. And they, for the most part, always complied. Those who didn't, simply talked to Wash instead.

Rio would've preferred the boat for transportation, except the lake was exceptionally choppy today. Plus, she was wearing the black dress she'd found in the trunk and its narrow top made rowing impossible. Made doing anything much impossible, in fact. She'd be glad to get home and change into her workaday clothes, even if they were nearly worn to shreds.

Wash didn't speak as he helped her onto the buggy seat and went to loosen the horse from the rail. He tossed the hostler a coin for allowing him to park the rig in the shed out of the rain. At least the seat wasn't wet. They were out of town heading back around the lake at a fair clip before he let the reins slacken.

He turned to face her as the horse plodded on. "What was that between you and the reverend? Something, plain as the nose on your face." He grimaced. "Something besides showing his penny-pinching."

"He made a consolation call on Wednesday. Let's

just say he was a bit overly zealous in demonstrating his consolation and leave it there. But I was glad young Mr. Win Ferris happened out of his room just then. Who knew so young of a boy could be so forbidding."

Wash chortled. "Must take after his brother. Beckett doesn't seem anybody to mess with, either. I figure that's good after what happened to Bill Hightower."

"Did you—" Rio had it mind to ask if he ever wondered how Beckett and Win had just happened to be so johnny-on-the-spot after Hightower's death, then changed her mind.

"Did I what?"

"Oh, nothing. Forgot what I was going to say." But she hadn't really. If he found out about the Ferrises being in the woods the night of Hightower's murder—and Win also being shot—who knows what might happen. The idea of Wash looking into Beckett's motives might not be safe for him and she wouldn't put him in danger for the world. Because if it wasn't Beckett Ferris he'd have to look out for, it was Sheriff Donaldson.

Sheriff Thor Donaldson hadn't, as far as she could tell, looked into anything more to do with Hightower's murder. He had put it about town, loudly and often, that he even doubted the man had been murdered. "Suicide. That's what my investigation shows now. Or maybe just a bad accident. Tripped in the brush and his gun went off."

And yet, she distinctly remembered Wash saying that the rifle laying beside Hightower's body had not been fired. And that the man had been shot in the back.

All of which made Rio think Donaldson may have

had a hand in the killing. And she wouldn't say anything to put Wash in the sheriff's crosshairs. Not even the tiniest hint.

Soaked to the skin by the blowing rain, Wash urged the horse into a trot the rest of the way to the hotel. He jumped down to help her from the buggy. Hands warm on her waist, he stood looking down at her. "You going to be all right? Do you need money to see you through until you get the hotel going again? I've got some saved. I can help."

Rio gulped, holding back a gurgle of laughter. She did let a smile shine through. In fact, with him still so close, she couldn't resist. On tiptoe and leaning forward, she kissed him right smack dab on the lips, drawing back before he had a chance to respond. His hands tightened.

"Mmm. Nice. What was that for?" His eyes looked to have grown darker.

She could feel her face glowing hot. "For being such a good friend. For showing up today and escorting me to the funeral. For offering to help. Thank you, Wash."

"Well—" he started but she stopped him.

"I'm fine. My father had some money in his wallet. It was enough pay the preacher and to buy some supplies. I'll get the restaurant running by the end of this week and ask at the local newspapers if they'll announce the hotel is open again. People may not care about me but they've always liked the meals I served."

Wash hadn't let her go. "You sure? It's a lot of work."

Didn't he know she'd had charge of the hotel for years, from the time she'd turned sixteen and Elias had said she was old enough to earn her keep? Probably not.

Few had known the scope of her responsibilities, which included most of the cooking.

"I'm used to work," she said, and though she could've stood here all day with his hands on her waist and that look in his eyes, she couldn't stop a long shiver as the wind billowed the skirt of the black dress.

Wash noticed the shiver right away. "You're cold." He chuckled. "So am I. You'd best scoot along inside. Wouldn't want you to catch a cold when you've got all these plans."

He didn't let go of her though. Not yet. Instead, he pulled her closer. Right up until their bodies touched. His head dipped. Rio's tilted up.

"I've been wanting to do this for a very long time," he said and set his mouth on hers.

It was quite a kiss, she discovered. Long, hard, and deep.

Fire curled in Rio's belly—or thereabouts. She wanted to smile but her lips were too busy doing different things. Should she tell him she'd wanted him to kiss her? Also for a very long time?

Maybe not.

Besides, he let her go and her eyes opened, though she hadn't been aware of closing them.

"Wash..." she said, breathless.

He smiled and stepped back. He really did have a delicious smile. "I'll be here in the morning for our meeting," he said and went to the horse's head to lead him to the barn.

Rio stood outside a moment longer watching him. On the other side of the kitchen door, she heard toenails scratching frantically. Boo, knowing she was out there, but ignoring him when he craved attention. The sound seemed to wake her from a sort of dream.

The rest of the day was spent making up new menus for the restaurant and listing the supplies she'd need. Or would as long as people showed up for dinner like they had before Elias got sick. The lists, she found, were long and expensive. Then there was the other work. Wash the restaurant dishes and cutlery. Pull out the pans. Check the tablecloths and napkins. Order in ice for the big restaurant icebox.

And there was the cleaning. She might manage that herself to begin with, but at the least she would have to hire at least one housemaid, a waitress or two, ask to rehire Mrs. Golz for the laundry if her eldest son approved, and find someone to take care of the guest's animals in-between rowing people across the bay to the hotel.

So much to do.

Rio tried not to think of how different her position was today. Different from the aftermath of most funerals, when neighbors swarmed to bring comfort to the family. They brought food, offered help, offered sympathy, offered consolation.

Only two people knocked on her door that afternoon.

One of them was Sheriff Thor Donaldson.

WASH, in making his way back to his cabin at the lakeshore, couldn't stop thinking about that kiss. About both of them. The one she'd planted on him, and then the one he'd settled on her.

Rio was an innocent. He could sure enough tell that. She hadn't drawn a breath either time, and thinking about that made him laugh just a little. And she hadn't known to close her eyes at first either. He knew, because he'd looked. But when he looked again, she had, the fan of her long black lashes fluttering almost to her cheekbones. And her lips, soft as...as rose petals. Hadn't he read a description like that somewhere once? He might never have gone around kissing rose petals to see if the description was accurate but the idea sounded pretty.

What he did know was that she was in a precarious position there alone in the hotel. God only knows who might turn up asking for a room—or something more personal. Before, when the hotel was open, she'd had her father for protection.

Wash didn't like her being alone. He'd been worried when he foisted Beckett Ferris and his young brother on her, although he'd thought a little income would help her out. At least there hadn't been any complaints. Not from either side.

He knew Rio was ambitious too, with plans to bring the hotel back to what it had been before Elias got sick. He admired a lady with ambition—and the sense to follow through on her plans. If she got the chance.

He could handle the logging aspects of the business. After all, he'd been doing it for the last few months. The crew and even the buying and selling part. Rio might not know, but Elias hadn't been totally besotted with his son. In his heart, he'd known Eino would never make a good manager, so he trained Wash in all parts of the business with the idea of keeping him on as a general supervisor. But Wash didn't know what would happen if Eino never came back. Or for that matter, what would happen if he did. It all depended on the terms of Elias's will, he supposed. Or whether Eino would want to get out from under Wash's influence. If Eino took it into his head to fire Wash, well, Wash would survive just fine. There was nothing certain he'd want to work around Eino. Wash'd had a good many job offers in the last few years. Excellent offers. The reason he'd stayed here was his liking for the autonomous control Elias gave him, along with the training. And Rio.

Eino. Wash's brows drew together. Eino resented Rio. Wash had never understood the reason, though he'd seen the way Elias treated her and figured it was a case of like father, like son. What would happen to her? Had any provision been made for her well-being? He doubted it.

Cold and wet, Wash ceased his pondering as he entered the clearing back at headquarters. Smoke issued from the cook shack chimney in a dark gray cloud, an indication he might find hot coffee and hot food there. The sawmill was quiet, as Saturday was a half-day and the men had either holed up in the barracks or, if they were locals, gone home. He'd given the logging crew the whole day off in respect for the boss, though none of them had attended Elias's funeral. Not surprising. The Chinese wouldn't have been welcome there.

Not even Li Bai, he realized, though he'd had status. Not that the Chinaman would've been welcomed in Reverend Müller's church. He wouldn't have. Plus, Wash knew the man frightened Rio, although she tried to hide the fear. Thinking about it, he didn't believe it was the cook's foreignness that frightened her. Or even the opium, although early on he'd guessed her distaste—no, her dread—at having to meet with him to purchase the drug for her father. And to his mind, that left only one thing.

Could be he'd best have a little talk with the Celestial. Now, while no one else was around.

At the cook shack, he paused to scrape mud off his boots before thrusting open the door. He found the room dark. Dark, but not empty. Motion caught his eye, and the gleam of light on metal. Enough light from the open door to send him lurching to the side just as a shot thundered through the room. For just a flash, he thought he'd been hit.

"What the hell?" His shout, lost in the gun's report, went unanswered. He saw the gun being raised again. He leaped forward, diving into the legs of the man holding the gun. He managed to wrap his arms around the knees, one of which banged his cheekbone hard, and twisted as they fell.

Wash landed mostly on top, though the man didn't stop squirming even as he yelled and collapsed beneath Wash's greater weight. Grabbing at the hand holding the gun, Wash wrested it away.

Only then did he identify his assailant. "Li Bai. What the hell?"

Li Bai went slack, breathing hard. After a moment he said, "Boss man. Boss man. I no see who you are. I sorry. I sorry."

Wash, breathing plenty damn hard himself, narrowed his eyes. "Who did you think I was? And why did you try to shoot him?"

"I sorry," Li Bai said again—repeatedly. "I sorry." His English devolved into broken half-sentences.

But Wash, regaining his feet and putting some distance between them, read a whole lot of insincerity in this avowal. He tucked the revolver, a new-looking Iver Johnson .32 in his waistband.

"Is that right?" he said. Then, "Get up and light the lamp. Meanwhile, you can tell me why it's dark in here and where you got this gun."

It only occurred to him later, when he was back in his own pokey little cabin, that he never did get around to telling Li Bại he'd best show utmost respect to Miss Salo.

Fifteen

Not long after Wash left, Rio heard tapping at the hotel's front door. Deep in the linen closet where the hotel bed linens, towels, tablecloths and such were stored, she was counting what was there and whether it would serve upon reopening. Thankfully, it appeared the moths and rodents had been kept at bay.

Busy counting off on a full fifteen sets of sheets, or two sets for each bed less the set on the bed in the Ferris's room, she probably wouldn't have heard the visitor at all had it not been for Boo jumping up and down and emitting soft barks.

She cocked her head. "I hear it. Good boy, Boo." At first she thought it might be Wash, back again for some reason or another, until she reminded herself he never came to the front of the hotel, but always slipped in through the back.

Pushing aside a lock of her hair that had come undone from the twist at the back of her head, she hurried toward the front, determined to have someone

—probably Wash—drill a small hole in the door so she could peer outside without having to open up.

Rio didn't know the man who stood there, but she seemed to remember him sitting at the back of the church during the eulogy this morning. But not at the graveside. He probably hadn't wanted to get wet or chance the mud. Tall, thin, with iron gray hair and a full mustache, the gentleman wore a fitted suit—better perhaps, than even Elias's best—and shoes gleaming with polish under the fresh mud. He'd removed a fine bowler hat and stood with it held against his chest.

The rain, she saw now, had finally stopped. A horse she identified as belonging to the livery in town was hitched to the rail.

A slight frown drew brows barely darker than his hair together. "Miss," he said. "Is Miss Salo available? I hesitate to disturb her on the day of her father's funeral, but I must catch the next train to town and wish to speak with her as soon as possible."

Rio sighed. She supposed she did look like the hired help. If there'd been such a thing as hired help after the hotel closed. As it was, there was just her. He probably didn't recognize her from the funeral this morning. The mourning hat she'd worn had been draped with a concealing veil.

"I am Miss Salo," she said. "What can I do for you."

A slight expression of disbelief crossed his face so fast she almost missed it before he said, "You're Miss Salo? Miss Rio Salo?"

"I am." Boo pawed at her skirt. She reached down and put her hand on his head. "What can I do for you?" she repeated.

He peered beyond her into the dark hotel, the lobby

hollow and not very inviting having been closed up for the past seven months.

"May I come in?" he asked.

"I—" she began, but he cut her off.

"But where are my manners," he exclaimed with a rueful half-smile. "I am Mr. George Brackman, your grandfather's...er, Benedict Serrano's...attorney. You may not have heard of me. Or remember if you have."

"No, sir," she said slowly, thinking there was nothing wrong with her memory. "I have not. But how can you be my grandfather's attorney? He passed away thirteen...no...fourteen years ago. I can barely remember him." She'd never heard this man's name before. Who could possibly forget a last name like Brackman? The only attorney she'd heard of was her father's, a local man who worked through the bank. She supposed she'd have to contact with *him* at some time or another quite soon and didn't look forward to it.

Brackman glanced around as if standing on the hotel porch in the open air made him uncomfortable. "Please, may I come in, Miss Salo. Truly, I mean you no harm. To the contrary, as you will find. Perhaps your brother, if he's anywhere around, should attend to hear what I have to say."

More and more puzzling. "My brother went to Chicago to visit relatives almost two years ago and hasn't returned," she said. "So no. He won't be attending."

Mr. Brackman raised his brows. "He's gone? Well... well."

While he seemed surprised, Rio noted, he didn't seem heartbroken over the news. Perhaps that was the reason she opened the door wider. "Come in. We can go to the office to talk. I'm afraid the hotel lobby is closed for now."

Brackman looked around as he entered. "A small enterprise still, I see. But nicer than when I was here last. It was still quite rough then but with potential. And the restaurant was extraordinary for such an out-of-the-way location. I knew your grandfather and mother had a lot of plans for the place. And of course, Mr. Salo was very grateful to them."

Rio's eyes opened wide as she tried to digest what he'd said. "Grateful?" she croaked. "My father grateful to my grandfather and my mother?"

"Why yes, as well he should've been. His own endeavors here would've failed if not for your grandfather. And your mother too, of course." Brackman stared at her. "You're trembling, my dear. Shall we find a place to sit? Perhaps call for some coffee or tea?"

Her father's endeavors here would've failed if not for Grandpapa and her mother. That's what this man had said. What did that mean? Elias, and Eino too, later, had always made them seem like hangers-on he supported out of the goodness of his heart, with Rio the greatest hanger-on of all. Never mind she was his daughter. Then Elias came right out and said he'd murdered her mother. And yet this man—

Her heartbeat didn't seem quite right. Blood surged in her ears like waves coming in off the lake, only louder than those waves could ever be.

Rio didn't make it across the lobby. Fortunately for her, a wing chair, bearing a dust cover due to the hotel's long closure, stood handy. She collapsed onto it. Boo, ever helpful, bounded into her lap and she put her arms around him.

"Miss Salo?" Mr. Brackman's voice rose. "Are you—"

But it was Beckett who spoke first. "What's going on? Miss Salo, are you all right?"

Rio shook her head. No, she wasn't all right.

"Sir, what have you said to her? It's clear you've upset her, and Miss Salo doesn't upset that easily. I think you should leave." Beckett strode toward them.

"No." Her throat feeling choked, she swallowed. "It's all right, Mr. Ferris. I just...I just...it's a shock, is all. What Mr. Brackman just told me."

Beckett's eyes narrowed. "And what was that?"

Oddly enough, considering Beckett both looked and sounded very much in charge, Mr. Brackman, in his fine city suit, appeared undisturbed. "Unless I'm badly mistaken, sir, my business is with Miss Salo, and Miss Salo alone. Only she has the authority to speak to you. I do not. And I won't."

"Is that right?" Beckett looked toward her.

"I don't know." Even to herself Rio sounded a weak soul. "What he said, it comes as a surprise. I'm all right. I came over shaky for a minute is all. It's passed."

Kneeling by her chair, Beckett helped her up. "Then let's get you into the kitchen where it's warm and there's light. Do you want me to send my brother for Wash?" He glanced at Brackman. "Mr. Ames?"

Brackman stood with his hands behind his back, rocking on his heels. "Excellent plan. And tea. Tea is called for, I believe, with plenty of sugar. Truly, I had no idea you weren't aware of the terms of the arrangement between..." He glanced at Beckett before continuing, "between the two entities."

Entities? Is that what they were? Or did he say enemies?

Rio took a deep breath and straightened her spine, forcing herself to smile at Beckett. "All is well, Mr. Ferris. Thank you. But I believe I could use a cup of tea. And possibly Mr. Brackman could as well. It will be a chilly ride back to the depot from here."

Beckett glance back and forth between her and the man. "You're sure?"

"Yes." *No, but I'll manage.*

From the kitchen, Beckett went on down the hall to his room. She heard Win greet him, then the door as it closed. Gesturing at a chair, she went to the stove. "Tea for you, Mr. Brackman, or coffee?"

"Coffee, please. I believe after meeting that young man I need something stronger than tea." His chuckle belied any concern he'd felt. "Who is he?"

"A guest at the hotel. He and his brother."

Rio had made cookies yesterday, mostly for Win's pleasure as he was still a bit thin and weak. She placed some on a nice china plate and set it on the table, and poured coffee into two matching cups. "By stronger, do you mean you'd enjoy a touch of whiskey in your coffee?"

He looked surprised, then settled back. "I believe I would."

Leaving the bottle on the table for him to help himself, Rio sat across from him and folded her hands on her lap.

"Obviously," the attorney began as he uncorked the bottle and poured a dab into his coffee. Selecting a cookie, he took a bite. "I fear this has all come as a very big surprise to you. I'm sorry. I would've thought your father would've at least mentioned the legal arrangements of your legacy."

"*My* legacy?"

"Let me enlighten you, my dear."

"Please do. You said my father should've been grateful to Grandfather and my mother. That they had plans for the hotel. That his endeavors would've failed without them. That's what you said. I have no idea what you mean."

"I can see you don't." He shook his head. "You father didn't speak to you of this? But it's almost an entire year past your twenty-first birthday. I certainly thought the terms would've all been explained to you. In plain English, by preference."

This man, Rio thought, was as enigmatic as a poem written in Japanese.

She shook her head. "Why don't you tell me? Tell me everything, start to finish."

Frowning a little, Brackman extracted his watch from his vest pocket and noted the time. "I'll have to speak quickly," he said, "but here are the basics."

Rio sat on the edge of her chair and forgot to drink her coffee as he began. Boo sat on her feet, keeping his big brown eyes fixed on George Brackman the whole time.

"Your father's first wife brought a nice sum of money to the marriage. Did you know that? He bought land here and started the logging enterprise. Your father was a decent manager, better than decent, truly, although the panic of 1893 found him short of cash. But before that, this hotel," Brackman glanced around the room, "was originally begun as housing for the workers. When his wife—I believe her name was Edith, Edith

White—complained about living next to these uncouth fellows, he built barracks for them a short distance away and turned this into a hotel. Then she died, and with her death, the money for Elias to expand dried up. Her father, you see, had bankrolled a good deal of the business. Times were bad and getting worse."

Rio nodded. She knew some of this, having many a time heard Elias rail against his previous father-in-law. Well, both his deceased fathers-in-law, actually.

"Did you, perhaps, know your father liked to gamble? Horse races, cards, even boxing matches."

"I discovered as much just lately," she said.

"Poker. A high stakes poker game. That's how he met Benedict Serrano, your grandfather. They were both excellent card players. And wise gamblers. In fact, you father won his first tract of timber here in a horse race and owned it free and clear. Now I'm not sure of this next part, but from what I've pieced together, your grandfather also had an extreme run of luck when he was chef at a rather famous restaurant in New Orleans."

"I've heard about the restaurant," Rio said and bent to pet Boo. Her hand trembled in his curly fur.

"Serrano was accused of cheating at cards and had to run, bringing his daughter Juanita along with him. Somehow, when he and Elias first met, a short while after Edith passed, he still had most of those funds. They made plans to expand and open up the hotel with a restaurant which he and Juanita would run. In return, he would bankroll the logging and sawmill."

Rio's heart started up that unsteady pounding again. She straightened. "Did he?"

Brackman arched a brow. "Did who what?"

"Did my grandfather Benedict Serrano cheat at cards?" She rolled the double r in his name, as he had done. She remembered that much about him.

"I'm sure I don't know." The attorney smiled a little. "Does it matter after all this time?"

Rio shrugged. "I guess not." But in a way, it did. Her father a liar, a cheat, a murderer. Her grandfather, a potential cheater at cards. Was this the legacy she had inherited? "Please, go on."

"After five years, if all went well for them both, Benedict Serrano and his daughter Juanita would own this hotel, and Elias Salo and his son Eino would own Salo Timber Products. And it did go well. Longer than the five years. After nine years, Benedict died and Juanita inherited. The last time I saw her, only four days before she ran away and disappeared, she made a will naming you as her heir, along with certain other provision."

He explained those provisions succinctly, leaving Rio astounded and barely able to think.

He finished up by saying, "She also named a certain Mrs. Raymond Serrano as your guardian."

"Who?"

"Mrs. Raymond Serrano. An aunt, I believe. I only just found out she passed away a few years ago, as well." He studied her white face. "From your reaction, I see all this is a surprise to you. So you never connected with her."

Rio shook her head. "No."

Brackman added an extra dollop of whiskey to his cup and tilted it into his mouth. "I see."

They both went silent for a long moment. Both rigid in their chairs, until Rio burst out, "She didn't simply disappear. My mother. My father murdered her. And I've never in my life heard of a Mrs. Raymond Serrano."

Rio went cold, thinking. None of this had happened, what Mr. Brackman had said. She had been relegated to a servant, and Elias had taken everything.

"What?" His question was explosive. "Murdered? No. Surely not." A blank expression came over his face. "Although," he said slowly, "that would explain why she made this will and when she made it. If she suspected—" He stopped. "How do you know?"

"He said so, only a few days ago before he died. Bragged of it." She found her fingers were so tightly clenched she was barely able to force them open. "All these years he—"

Right now Rio wished Elias were alive so she could watch him die again, only this time without the aid of opium. And maybe she'd drive a stake through his heart besides. Eino's, as well. He, who'd been pampered and pandered to, who had never worked hard but been given everything.

And the man who brought her this news? Who was he really? What was his stake in this? Questions and distrust threatened to overcome her.

After a moment, she sat up straight again. "So, Mr. Brackman, where have you been all these years? My father wanted everything and he took it. Typical of him and his son. Believe me, I know this very well. But what is your stake in all this? There must be more to the story."

He studied her. "You don't trust me. I understand. We've both been hoodwinked, you see. And you're right, I wouldn't be here now if I hadn't been retiring and clearing out old papers. I wish..." He looked at his watch again. "I must go or I'll miss the train. Miss Salo, please rest easy. I mean you no harm. Indeed, I wish to make amends. I have an important meeting scheduled for Monday morning to prepare for, but afterward I'll get all the paperwork together and be back here either Wednesday or Thursday, if that is convenient for you. You'll understand everything then."

Rio wasn't so sure, but she nodded. What he'd told her so far explained a lot of things. Just not the one question that burned her heart and always had. Why hadn't her father cared for her? Not love. She hadn't asked for that. Even as a child she'd seen it would be no use. But cared enough for his own flesh and blood to at least treat her decently?

When George Brackman had gone, saying "hup, hup," to the horse as it took off at a plod, she went up to her bedroom and wept. Wept until her eyes felt like balls of fire—and looked like it too, when she caught a glimpse of their reddened state in the small mirror hung over her washstand. Boo sat on the bed watching her, looking as if he'd cry too if it would help.

Which it wouldn't, Rio knew, so she washed her face in cold water, straightened her spine, and went back downstairs to complete the linen inventory and plan the dinner menu for her two hotel guests.

THE COOK SHACK'S APPEARANCE, once the lamps were lit, raised Wash's eyebrows. A quick glance around was enough to see he wasn't the first person to visit Li Bai here today. Within the last few minutes, in fact, if he was any judge.

"Who did this?" His gesture took in overturned chairs—one with a broken leg—foodstuffs spilled on the floor, and the stove door hanging open where he could see flames just now licking at a papier mâché box. The box had been painted blue with intricate designs, and whatever was in it smoldered, the cause of the dark smoke Wash had noticed from outside. The stench of opium was almost overpowering in the room.

Li Bai went mute. He lay on the floor and glared up at Wash. His lips were bleeding, and a bruise already forming on his cheekbone. Their tussle hadn't been the cause.

The Celestial had not done the damage to the room, Wash knew. Li Bai's dedication to cleanliness was one of the reasons Wash kept him on. That, and the fact his food was better than average and served on time and within the allowance Wash made for it. Guaranteed, it wasn't because of his winning personality. Or his second business of selling opium, an addiction Wash abhorred. He plain didn't like the man and felt sure the feeling was mutual.

"Are you all right? Hurt?" Wash stepped back.

Li Bai shook his head. "No, boss."

Could've fooled me, Wash thought, but he said, "Then get up. I'll help put the place in order." He offered his hand. Li Bai took it and lunged to his feet. He didn't say anything about the pistol, though Wash had no intention of letting the subject drop. The Chinese in town were prohibited from owning firearms, yet the one Li Bai had tried to use on Wash appeared to be a fine new weapon. Smaller in size, but better than the one Wash owned. He relied more on the carbine he kept in a saddle scabbard to contend with predators and seldom bothered to carry the revolver. Could be he'd best start.

Silent, Li Bai got the broom and began sweeping the debris on the floor into a pile, while Wash moved the table into its accustomed position in the center of the room and got the serviceable chairs replaced around it. A couple had been disabled, with one beyond repair.

As Li Bai went past the stove, he slammed the door shut on the blue box, burning with fury now. From the sideways glance he threw at Wash, he hoped Wash hadn't seen.

Too late, Wash thought. "Who did this?" he demanded. "And why did they do it?"

"Do not know." Li Bai lied, then lapsed in the gibberish he spoke, but which was totally incomprehensible to Wash. Then finally the truth. "I not tell. He kill Hightower. He kill me."

"Who killed Hightower. Who will kill you?"

Li Bai shook his head hard enough his pigtail flipped from side-to-side.

Wash had a good idea what had been in the blue box. "Is this because of the damn opium? Why burn it?"

Slowly, Li Bai nodded. "He kill me, I tell," he repeated.

"Why kill Hightower?" he persisted and something in his look drew an answer from Li Bai.

"Hightower, he sees. He in the way."

Wash figured it would take a worse beating than he was prepared to give before the man would actually say the name. Maybe he could go at it from a different angle. "Where did you get the gun? None of the storekeepers around here would sell it to you. So who gave it to you?"

"I buy," Li Bai said. After that, his mouth closed tighter than a clam.

And there it stood.

What now? Wash wondered. Except first thing Monday morning he intended to start looking for a new cook.

The recent law taxing the legal opium coming down out of Canada had incited a lucrative smuggling operation across Washington and the whole West Coast. With the cook connected to it, Wash didn't want him around, no matter what his food tasted like. If there was anything Salo Timber Products didn't need, especially with Elias dead, was Sheriff Donaldson poking around.

Especially, Wash thought, when he didn't know which side Donaldson was working for.

Sixteen

The second of Rio's post-funeral visitors that afternoon turned out to be both less and more disturbing than George Brackman. Less, because the life-changing information this second one had to impart came as no great surprise. More, because he out-and-out terrified her. And when she was afraid, she couldn't think straight. Of course, her anger had something to do with that.

She'd just doused two beef chuck steaks in a marinade of olive oil, wine, garlic, and various herbs, and put them in the icebox. Hoping to tenderize what she knew had been a tough old steer, the technique was something her grandfather, the famous Louisiana chef, had taught her when she used to help him in the kitchen. Mrs. Golz's husband had raised the beef and generously given Rio a price reduced from what the butcher charged. She hoped the Ferris brothers would find them edible. The hotel could use a good word from a patron.

Washing the residue from her fingers, a loud hammering on the hotel door made her head jerk up.

"Who do you suppose that is?" She aimed her question at the dog.

Boo, still sitting at attention hoping for more scraps, ignored the insistent pounding and showed no interest in answering.

Whoever it was, the way he—she had no doubt it was a man—attacked the door, Rio couldn't think he intended a condolence call. She hesitated to open but then, not only had she always had an inordinate amount of curiosity, she'd been trained to answer a summons.

Seeing her visitor, Rio's first inclination was to slam the door closed and lock it. Too late. Sheriff Thor Donaldson had his foot smack dab on the threshold, blocking the half-formed action.

She stared at him, silent. Boo spoke for her, his growl shaking his small body.

"I need to talk to you, missy. I think you might be in some trouble." He pushed on the door, knocking it out of her hand and bullying his way into the lobby.

Rio couldn't help the frisson that chilled her, but she thought she sounded quite calm as she stood her ground. "In trouble? What on earth do you mean?"

He grinned, which struck her as not at all pleasant. "Seems as if you might be squatting here where you ain't entitled. Depends on what Eino's got to say when he gets here. Bet you can guess, can't you?"

Thoughts like a flurry of black snow swirled through her head. "Eino?" she repeated.

"Yeah. You know. Eino, your brother? If he actually is your brother. Seems there's some discussion about that." His leer made the implication plain enough.

Her eyes narrowed. "He's alive? You've heard from him?"

"I've heard from him." Donaldson was peering around the lobby as if he'd never seen it before. "You will too, in the next few days, I expect. If I was you, I'd pack up my things and make myself scarce before he gets here. Now his pa is gone, he ain't apt to be so forgiving about having you around."

Rio hadn't moved from the doorway. She stood with the door open, allowing a shaft of welcome sunlight to burst in through the opening. Out on the lake, she could hear gulls squabbling.

The sheriff turned to face her, which meant he turned toward the light, and that gave her the opportunity to see behind him. Beckett stood there with his arms folded, listening to every word. Somehow, he presence was...comforting. She guessed—hoped—that was the correct word.

"Why should I believe you?" She looked back at Donaldson. "About Eino, I mean."

Donaldson's chest puffed out. "Because I just said so and I'm the sheriff. And he's given me the authority to see you depart the premises afore he gets here."

For the life of her, Rio couldn't imagine why the sheriff seemed to hate her and treated her like dirt under his feet. Did he treat all women this way? Why would their husbands vote him in as sheriff if he sneered at their wives? She didn't believe they would. Some maybe, but not enough to win an election.

But why was she even thinking of this? Not now, when he'd just said he'd heard from Eino. When he'd said Eino was on his way here.

"I don't believe you." She amazed herself with how calm she sounded.

He stared at her, eyes bulging. "What did you say?"

"I said I don't believe you. And even if you're telling the truth about him being on his way, I'm certainly not leaving my home. Not for you and not for him." She didn't know where the courage came from because inside, her innards were shaking around like beans in a pot of boiling water.

The sheriff's hand raised. Rio knew in that instant he intended to strike her and set herself for the pain. Boo, however, had a different idea. As the sheriff began a downward sweep toward her face, the little dog charged him, biting through his trouser leg and into his calf.

Donaldson yelped. His blow shifted, heading instead for the dog.

Rio screamed. At the same time, she lunged at him, shoving him with all her might. The blow missed Boo, striking her in the hip but losing a great deal of force on the way.

"Sonofabitch!" Staggering from Rio's onslaught, the sheriff clawed for the revolver slung around his broad waist. "I'm gonna kill—"

He had the gun half out of the holster before Beckett reached him. Beckett wrested the sheriff's face against the wall and forced his arm up behind his back. Donaldson, Rio was glad to see, hadn't even seen Beckett coming and probably couldn't see him now.

The revolver sat cockamamie in the holster and Beckett shoved it down. "You're not shooting that pistol off in this hotel. And you're not killing anything today, mister, whether woman or dog. What you're going to do is get yourself back on that horse I see out front and go. Right now. Before I get real mad. I've witnessed enough to curdle my blood already."

"You let me go, you..." The name Donaldson called him shocked Rio. "I'm the sheriff. And you're under arrest. You and her. You're both under arrest."

Beckett didn't act particularly alarmed. "You're not arresting anybody here either. *Sheriff*. If that's who you are. You ought to be ashamed of yourself, trying to slap a young lady around. And kill her dog that's determined to protect her? Nope. Not now and not ever. Got that?"

He didn't speak loudly, but there was enough menace that even Donaldson was smart enough to sense it.

"Who are you? And get your hands off me." Donaldson shook like a horse dislodging flies, trying, Rio thought, to get a better look at Beckett, but when he turned, Beckett turned with him, staying just out of his sight.

"I'm nobody you want to know, Donaldson. Depend on it. Leave, and don't come back here." With that, Beckett pushed the sheriff, pushed him hard, right out the door onto the porch.

Quick as she could move, Rio slammed the door shut, grazing the sheriff's behind as he fell, and flipped the bolt. He was out—for now. But his shout carried.

"You wait. I'll get you for this. You just wait."

Trembling, Rio turned to face Beckett. "He means it."

"I know he does." Beckett shook his head. "You got a good dog, even if he is too little to do much." Then he added, "But you'd better watch out for him. Watch him close."

"I know. I will." She picked up the dog who was panting beside her with a self-satisfied air. "I'm sorry you felt called to intervene. If he finds out who you are, he'll go after you. Make your life miserable—if you stay. Maybe it would've been better if he hit me. Let him think he had the upper hand."

Beckett scowled and folded his arms across his chest. "Miss Salo, if he'd struck you, he would've had the upper hand. What kind of a man would I be if I allowed a woman to be beaten and her dog killed while I watched and did nothing?"

Rio knew such things went on all the time, though not so often to decent women. And she considered herself a decent woman. "Ordinary," she said, which made him grimace. "And prudent."

"You don't think I'm ordinary? Or prudent?"

She thought a moment, back to the night he and Win arrived. The way they'd stayed out of sight until Beckett took a dead man's job; the way he showed no fear of the sheriff. And she shook her head. "No. I do not."

WASH WAS HALFWAY BACK to the hotel when he spotted someone on the path moving toward him. Glimpsed through the woods, he knew the someone was definitely not female and Rio was just about the only person other than himself who ever came this way.

He'd thought twice before deciding to tell her about the vandalism at the cook shack. Or about Li Bai. After he left the cook to finish cleaning up, he'd gone down to the trail that wended around the lake. He found recent horse tracks there, formed since the morning rain. The tracks pointed toward the hotel. Still, it was hard to read anything in particular about a set of hoofprints, except he knew the horse needed shoeing. Its front left hoof had overgrown the shoe. Careless of somebody, for sure. Still, he deemed it unlikely he'd ever discover who the neglected horse belonged to.

After scouting around a bit more and finding nothing, he went to his cabin to change clothes. His suit scratched and constricted him under the arms as he'd discovered with his tussle with Li Bai. Once there, he downed a dram of whiskey and tried to think of the best thing to do. Head back to the hotel and let Rio know about this latest development, he decided. A bad feeling about Li Bai and just who that horse belonged to worried him. He'd warn Rio to be careful. Tell her he intended to send Li Bai packing. He was tired of the surly fellow, and now Elias was dead and didn't need opium, he wanted him far away from Rio.

Leery of meeting anyone here in the woods, Wash slipped behind the trunk of a grand old pine whose branches dipped most of the way to the ground. Toeing a couple of pine cones, he moved them aside. Better if he avoided stepping on them. He didn't want their crunch providing a warning to whoever it was. He'd identify the person before stepping out. Cautious as he'd never been before, he pulled Li Bai's small revolver from the waist of his britches and waited.

"Ames?" The other man had stopped. "Is that you? It's Beckett Ferris. I've come looking for you."

Surprised he'd been seen, Wash stayed behind the tree. "Is there trouble? Has something happened?"

Beckett raised his hands into plain view. Nothing there but bones and flesh. Wash breathed a little easier.

"It's about Miss Salo," Beckett said.

Still carrying the pistol, Wash moved into full sight. "Is she all right? Did someone..." He couldn't finish. What if someone had attacked her? Violated her? He always worried about her in the big rambling hotel on her own, its location on this side of the lake too isolated for him to breathe easy.

"Came close." Beckett picked up on the unsaid part of his question. "I think if I hadn't showed myself to him, she might've been hurt. Her and her dog both."

Wash felt like exploding. "Who?"

"None other than the sheriff. The things he said to her, Ames, makes me think she's in serious trouble. Not because she did anything wrong. Because of who she is."

"Donaldson." Wash shoved the .32 back in his waistband. "That fat SOB. Too bad whoever murdered a good man like Hightower didn't kill Donaldson instead."

He barely noticed the odd look Beckett sent him. Or that Beckett's gaze centered on the .32. A look that stayed for a good long time.

Wash was thinking hard and coming up empty. "What does that mean, about who she is?"

Beckett shook his head. "You should talk to her. Are you headed back to the hotel? I think Miss Salo can use some trusted company about now."

Wash had taken a step before he stopped again. "I was headed that way to warn her. I don't like what's going on around here. Worse, I don't know who all is involved."

"Warn her about what? Why now? Why right now, I mean. Has something happened at the camp?"

This man, Wash thought, must be some kind of

mind reader. Either that, or he already knew more about things than a newcomer ought. But he'd been out in the woods tending to his job. Hadn't he?

"Something has," he said. "When I got back from the funeral, I found Li Bai, our cook, beat up and the cook shack wrecked. Knowing him, I figure opium smugglers are at the bottom of it. Worse thing is, I can't help thinking that one way or another Donaldson is in it up to his eyeballs." He started walking, thinking the sheriff was just the kind of man to neglect a horse. He was a little surprised when Beckett fell into step beside him.

"Li Bai, eh? But this strikes me as being something different. I think you're going to be surprised," Beckett said. "But it's up to Miss Salo to tell you why."

They were silent the rest of the way.

RIO'S HEAD felt light on her body, almost as if it were about to float away. This whole day had been more than anybody should have to bear. First the funeral and the insulting minister. Next, Mr. George Brackman, a real surprise. Could she believe anything he'd told her? Then Sheriff Thor Donaldson with his anger like that of a raging bull. Why should she be his target? If it hadn't been for Beckett Ferris, she didn't know what would've happened. What if he hadn't come to her defense?

And then there was Wash and the kiss.

Sighing, she looked down at Boo, prancing along beside her as they crossed the lobby as if he, by himself, had thwarted the villain.

In the kitchen, she turned the meat in its marinade and started on the rest of the meal by slicing potatoes into thin strips and drying them with a towel. She'd deep fry them in good fat just before serving. Men, and women too, always enjoyed their potatoes when she cooked them this way. But as she worked, another thought occurred to her.

What if the sheriff came back and forcibly ransacked the hotel? Elias's room, anyhow. Would he be smart—or lucky—enough to find her father's stash of money? The way he'd looked around when he'd seen her father the last time not only indicated he suspected a cache, but that he wouldn't be above taking it. That and, perhaps more importantly, the IOU she'd found with his name on it. Maybe he even knew there should be money stashed away somewhere.

And Eino. Was he truly alive after all and on his way to Painter's Bay? If so, did Eino know about the hidden compartment? She thought he might. Knowledge handed down from father to his favored son. Which meant—

She dropped the knife she was using beside the half-prepared potatoes on the cutting board. "Come with me, Boo," she told the dog. "We're going upstairs and we're going to do a little search. Then we're going to count some money. You can keep a lookout for me."

The little pooch looked up at her, his head tilted to the side as if to ask, "Now?"

"Right now." Rio rinsed her hands, swishing them through the warm water in a basin with the angry motions. "If Sheriff Donaldson wasn't lying, this might be our best chance. Win is outside somewhere, so there's just you and me."

She had cleaned and remade Elias's bed and opened the bedroom windows to the weather for most of two days. She'd dusted and mopped and even washed down walls. The room was as fresh and clean as she could make it. What she hadn't done was search for other hiding places. As for the secret compartment, she had thought the money was probably safer there than anyplace else.

But that was until Donaldson spoke of Eino.

Since she'd turned the mattress before changing the bed, she could eliminate that from the search. But she hadn't looked behind the headboard. Now she did. Nothing. Removing the pineapple-shaped toppers on the bedposts, she found the cavities empty, although there were signs they'd been used to hide things before. Bits of paper, cotton fluff, ink stains. Oddly, a marble.

The drawer in the washstand was a minor bonanza. An envelope had been stuck to the underside of the washstand's drawer. It contained a little money. "Success." Grinning at Boo, she put it in her pocket.

She looked under the chairs, upending both the armchair Elias had used when he was still able to get out of bed and the straight chair under his desk. Nothing.

The desk itself held a great many papers. Papers she knew she'd have to go through. She put them in a box she found on top of the armoire and took the box to her own little room.

"Midnight reading material," she told Boo.

That left only the armoire. But first she went to each of the windows and looked out. The hotel grounds were empty. From up on the second floor, she could see the barn and corrals where the two buggy horses, and four riding horses were kept for the hotel guests' pleasure. Win was out there, patting the sorrel mare on her neck.

The chicken coop was there too, where she saw her golden Buff Orpingtons pecking at the ground inside their pen and devouring worms. The other window showed a view over the lake. The waves had calmed after the earlier rain and wind, but the water was still a little murky after being churned up by the storm. There were no boats visible on the lake. Just the gulls on the beach pecking at whatever they could find to eat.

"This is it," she said, and Boo replied with a "rrf."

She took the letters and the money, leaving Edith's jewelry where she found it. If Eino came looking for the cache, he'd find his mother's belongings and he was welcome to them.

Smiling, she put the rest, money and the papers, in her apron and took it all to her room where she tucked everything into the box that held her menstrual necessities. Most any man she'd ever heard of would avoid those as if they carried the plague.

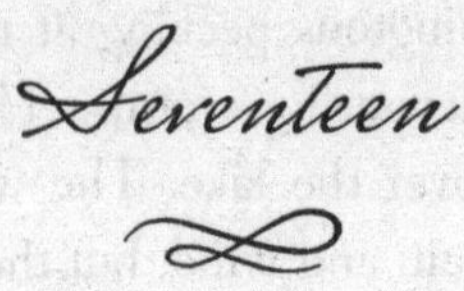

Seventeen

As if the day hadn't already sprung enough in the way of surprises—shock, dismay, and just about everything else she could think of—when Wash and Beckett walked in through the back of the hotel together, Rio felt another bolt of anxiety. She didn't think she'd ever before seen such a serious look on Wash's face.

Had Beckett told Wash about her visitors? She eyed Beckett, but almost as if she asked the question out loud, he shook his head.

"Got a few minutes to talk?" Wash asked.

If she was reading him right, he had some of that same anxiety riding on his shoulders.

At least she'd gotten the potatoes prepared. The rest of her planned dinner wouldn't take long.

She nodded toward the table. "Shall we sit? Coffee?"

"Sure," Wash said. Beckett nodded.

Rio only noticed the revolver Wash was carrying at the small of his back when it made a clunking sound as he sat and leaned against the chair slats. She frowned. She'd seen his old revolver before, when he'd given her a lesson on shooting a gun one day. He'd always been concerned with her safety at the hotel when it was just her and her invalid father.

This revolver wasn't the same one. This was newer, smaller. The barrel shorter and bluer.

But when they all settled down with coffee in front of them, neither man seemed to want to take the lead. Rio guessed it was up to her.

"I had two men call on me this afternoon after you left, Wash." When she looked at him, Rio couldn't help thinking of that kiss. Both kisses. She figured that gave her license to call him by his given name. Just as she was going to insist he do the same with hers.

Wash sent Beckett a quick look.

Beckett nodded.

Wrapping her hands around the warm cup, she stared into the dark well of liquid. "The first was a gentleman named George Brackman. An attorney from Spokane, as it turned out. He'd read about my father's death in the newspaper. Elias's name reminded him of a will he'd written up for a client about fourteen years ago and set him to wondering whatever became of the heir."

She went silent again until Wash said, "You mean there's an older will than the one Hal Majors has been talking about?"

Hal Majors had been her father's attorney and Rio didn't know he'd been talking at all. "This wasn't Elias's will. It was my grandfather's and then my mother's."

Wash's dark-blue eyes went wide. "Your mother had a will?"

She shrugged. "Apparently so."

He waited, brow arched.

"Wash, Mr. Brackman says I own this hotel. That my grandfather paid off Elias's debts on the timberland and sawmill in exchange for the hotel. My mother then inherited the hotel and land it stands on and she left it to me."

He jumped from his chair so fast it overturned. "Rio! That's just fine. It's what you wanted." But then he paused when her enthusiasm failed to match his. "Isn't it?"

Her voice came out a little unsteady. "Seems so, doesn't it? But will I be able to hang on to it? That's the question. Because my second visitor was the sheriff."

"Donaldson."

Rio caught the men's exchange of glances and knew whatever they had come to tell her meant nothing good and that it concerned Donaldson.

"Yes, Donaldson," she said. "Scattered among his other threats, he told me Eino is on his way to Painter's Bay and that he intends on evicting me and taking over the hotel. Taking over everything, really. The whole operation, sawmill, logging, and hotel."

"Sonofa..." Wash turned to Beckett. "You heard him?"

Beckett nodded. "Some of it." He took a sip of his coffee, then another. "But that's not all. If I hadn't stepped in and stopped him on time, he not only intended on more than just threatening Miss Salo. He planned on shooting little Boo."

Hearing his name, the dog got up from where he sat at Rio's feet and jumped into her lap.

"Shoot Boo? Why?"

"Boo bit him, protecting me." Rio kissed the dog on top the head.

Beckett's lips twitched into a grin before sobering as he continued. "Looks as if he intends on receiving a piece of this pie somehow. I just haven't figured where he fits in yet."

Reclaiming his chair, the pistol at Wash's back thudded again. "I've got an idea."

"Yeah?" Beckett asked. "Gonna let us in on it?"

"You aren't the only one Donaldson visited today." Wash reached toward Rio, then backed away. "By the time he left, Li Bai ended up with a bloody lip, a black eye, and a bruised cheekbone. Also the chore of cleaning up the cook shack after his attacker threw supplies all around. He broke a couple chairs, ruined the men's supper."

"Donaldson did that?" Beckett said.

Rio's eyes widened. "He beat Li Bai? Why?"

"Yes, Donaldson, although it took some persuading for Li Bai to come right out and say so. Apparently, the sheriff intends to take over the opium smuggling operation."

"Not shutting it down?" Beckett said.

Wash shook his head. "I didn't get that impression."

"The sheriff is the greedy sort, along with his other...attributes," Rio started. But then she gasped. "He did it."

Both men stared at her, and even Boo stood up. "Did what" Wash asked.

"Killed Mr. Hightower."

"What makes you think so?" Beckett stared at her. But not in disbelief, she noticed.

"The night when..." She cut herself off before she

told the circumstances of Beckett and Win's arrival. "That day after the big storm when he barged in here demanding to search the place. When he said Mr. Hightower was dead. But how could he have known? Mr. Hightower hadn't been found yet then."

Beckett's dark eyes had narrowed. Slowly, he nodded, as if another thought had just occurred to him. "Ah. That fits. Good thinking, Miss Salo."

Wash's expression had frozen. "What can we do about him? He can't be left in charge of this county."

Rio sniffed. "If women had the vote, I can guarantee he'd never have been elected in the first place. I don't know one single woman who isn't afraid of him."

At this, Wash almost—almost—smiled. "I can see that. Too bad he ran without opposition."

Beckett had the last word. "I wonder why."

It took Rio a moment before she understood. Then she did. Beckett was using sarcasm. Somehow, Donaldson had either frightened, or paid, to eliminate any opponents. Scum of the earth. That's what he was.

The little meeting broke up soon afterward. Beckett and Wash made plans to ride out to where Hightower had been murdered—and where Win had been shot—the next morning.

"Just to see if anything is left to prove your theory, Miss Salo," Beckett tried to reassure her. "If so, it'll give us grounds to go to a judge and start the process of removing him from office. And hopefully, seeing him in prison."

Frankly, Rio had doubts about the local judge's integrity—and said so. "He puts everyone the sheriff accuses in jail. Or gives them a big fine."

Wash simply shrugged. "We've got to start somewhere."

And Beckett agreed.

THE WEEKLY NEWSPAPER came out on Thursday, and Rio planned to advertise the restaurant's reopening on the front page—if the editor would allow it. And though she didn't expect many folks would be in need of hotel rooms just yet, she'd advertise that, as well. Then, if all went as planned, customers would arrive in the numbers before Elias's illness had shut down the restaurant.

That evening, Rio served her two guests their meal in the hotel dining room, viewing it as an opportunity to check everything was in place for Friday, the day she'd chosen to reopen to the public. The starting menu, she thought with satisfaction, had been decided upon. All that remained was to stock up on foodstuffs and make sure the big ice box was serviced.

Later, as she washed the supper dishes, she allowed the excitement to surge up in her. But not, unfortunately, to the point of pushing Donaldson's threats from her consciousness. Enough to bury them a little deeper perhaps. His talk of her half brother. Had he been telling the truth? How would he even know about Eino? Had her brother kept in touch with him, but not with his father? It didn't make sense.

So maybe it wasn't excitement she felt. Apprehension may have been a better word. Was Eino truly on his way home?

"I hope not," she said aloud, removing the stopper

from the sink and allowing the water to drain away. Boo, thinking she was speaking to him, barked.

Rio smiled down at him. "Sorry, boy. I've been ignoring you."

She hadn't had time to throw his favorite stick for him today and was feeling guilty about it, especially since he'd risked his life in helping her against the sheriff.

Night was drawing in, making it already too dark to play fetch. But not too dark, she decided, for a short stroll along the lakeshore. Boo liked to get his feet wet, as long as he didn't get too deeply into the water. She fetched an old jacket and put it on against the evening chill, and the two of them slipped outside and crossed the road separating the hotel from the shore. Boo bounded ahead. At the beach, Rio's footsteps crunched in the sand.

Any wind had stilled, allowing the rhythmic lap of water against the shore to soothe her senses. Over at the inlet, a multitude of frogs had begun a conversation. Crickets had already arrived for the season and begun their evening "infernal racket" as Elias used to call their nocturnal song. Personally, Rio rather liked it.

Together with Boo, she walked out on the dock where she checked the security of the three rowboats. All were tied securely against any stray breezes. She'd learned the proper knots to use as a child and since the hotel came under her management, had never lost a craft to carelessness.

"C'mon, boy," she told Boo, who pattered along at her side. "Time to go in."

His toenails clicked on the wood, almost in time with the lapping of waves.

Toenails clicking.

There was just enough time for a single thought to pass through her head. The night had gone silent.

No frogs. No crickets! Why did they stop?

Before she could take another step, the echoing report of a shot split the night. The plank in front of her splintered. Boo cried out and spun, nipping at his side but trying to reach his shoulder.

"Boo!"

Before he could splash into the lake, she snatched him up and ran. Ran faster than she knew she could run, ignoring the dog's wriggling and crying. Another shot sounded, another miss, whizzing past her right shoulder this time and thudding into one of the posts anchoring the dock into the lake bed behind her. Luck. She'd zigged just then. A sort of frantic reflex.

Though it seemed like it took forever, Rio reached the shelter of the trees, spotting a muzzle flash from yet a third—or maybe a fourth—shot. She dropped to the ground and wriggled behind the largest tree she could find. Boo whimpered beneath her.

"Hush, hush," she whispered to the dog.

She had to try for the hotel. Here she had no way to defend herself. Once inside, she could lock the door and barricade herself in. She had Elias's pistol and a shotgun in a rack on the porch. Elias had used it to shoot varmints back before he got too sick. She'd fired it a couple times to scare coyotes away from her chickens.

But no matter how many times Rio told herself safety lay just a hundred yards away, terror held her in place. Another shot split the night, rattling the branches over her head.

She jumped when a different gun fired. One with a

sharper, lighter sound. It came from the porch, she thought. And this time, it wasn't aimed at her.

Beckett.

"Stay low," he called, his voice quiet and barely reaching her. "Wait where you are and be still. I'll come to you."

Stay still? Rio had already found she couldn't move even though she tried. She lay immobile, taking in air with shallow little puffs. Boo had gone quiet too, as if he understood that he must. Unless...dear Lord, he wasn't dead, was he?

"Please no, please no." She whispered it over and over under her breath until Boo whimpered softly.

Over to her right, she spotted movement in the trees where she'd seen the muzzle flash. The shooter fired again. But not at her this time. At the man on the porch.

Beckett fired two shots in rapid succession, aiming into the trees. A man cried out. The brush where he was hiding thrashed wildly, and then he was gone, running through the sand along the shore, then up the bank toward the trail.

He was staggering, but still moving fast. From what she could see in the growing dark, it appeared as though Beckett might at least have winged him.

Beckett let him go. He jumped off the porch and hurried toward her. By then, Rio had discovered she could move again, and was already rising to her feet, Boo safely in her arms.

"You all right?" Beckett was staring down at her, seeming almost as shaken as she.

"Yes," she said, though her voice trembled. "But Boo is not. He's bleeding. We've got to help him." Rio could feel the blood, hot and wet against her cold hand.

"We'll take care of him. Just get inside. Quick now." He still held the revolver ready as he hustled her ahead of him and into the hotel.

They found Win waiting just inside the door, his face pale in the dim light. He had a carbine in his hands, and Rio wondered where he'd gotten it. Neither of the brothers had shown the weapon when they arrived that stormy night. Most likely, Beckett had bought it the minute he got to town.

Win slammed the door shut behind them. "He get away?"

"Yes." Beckett took Boo from Rio and carried him into the kitchen where a lantern hung over the work-table. "Got some towels? I need to lay him down where I can get a better look."

Rio stood, gone stupid with shock. "In the dresser." She thought she looked toward it but wasn't sure.

"Fetch a couple," Beckett told Win, who moved quickly to do so.

"Sit down," Beckett told Rio. "You're in shock."

"He shot Boo. He tried to shoot me."

"I know. I saw. But Boo isn't shot. He's got a splinter in his shoulder. I just need to get it out clean and he'll be all right."

Win, finding the towels, spread a couple on the tabletop. Laying Boo on his side, Beckett took a minute to examine the thick splinter sticking out of the dog's shoulder and turned to Rio. "Got pliers?"

"Yes." The need to help urged her out of the strange paralysis that had held her, and as soon as she handed them to Beckett, she took hold of the dog and held him still. She was leaking tears all the way down her chin by the time the stubborn splinter came free and the dog quit crying.

This had been a day like no other and at the end of it, when Rio finally scattered the money from one of the envelopes found in Elias's hidden compartment on the bed, she had to count it twice to be sure.

"That old..."

$2626.00

No. The decimal point was not in the wrong spot.

Yet he'd fixed it to make her pay for his cursed opium out of her savings.

Two thousand, six hundred and twenty-six dollars.

And that was just one envelope. She'd look at the rest another day. This was enough to leave her feeling faint.

Eighteen

Most of the Chinese logging crew spent their day off at a tightly shuttered little house that had been abandoned, then refurbished and put back into use as the local opium den. A supposed secret that everyone in town knew about. The few white men on the crew were gone as well, scattered to their various homes for the night. That left Wash and Li Bai as the only ones left in the deserted camp.

Before setting off to join Beckett Ferris at the hotel, Wash looked in on Li Bai. He found the cook asleep on his cot in the bunkhouse. Even in the dim light, Li Bai's blackened eye and bruised cheekbone were obvious, but he seemed to be breathing fine, even through a badly swollen nose. Wash backed away, leaving the man to his slumbers.

Figuring Li Bai could look after himself when he awakened, Wash took the path to the hotel. He and Beckett, for better or worse, were joining forces in searching out Bill Hightower's killer. Which, the more

Wash thought about it, raised a good many questions in his mind. It struck him as odd that a stranger to town, and one who was most likely to move on to another job as soon as he finished cruising the half-section of timberland, would be so dead set on solving this particular crime.

Unless he thought the same thing might happen to him.

Unlike yesterday, this morning proved fine, the sunrise having promised a clear day. Wash couldn't help thinking there was something appropriate about a rainy day when it came to funerals, but the sun today would make their ride into the heavy timber easier, maybe more productive. Birds were already frolicking about, and as he looked through the woods to the lake, he saw the water was calm.

Approaching the hotel from the back as he usually did, he was surprised to find two of the horses he recognized as belonging to the hotel standing at the rail already saddled. Two, plus his own dun that he kept stabled at the hotel barn. Did that mean Beckett's young brother felt up to coming along? The kid still looked kind of peaky from whatever had ailed him and made the boy late getting to town last week.

But it wasn't Beckett and Win who saw him coming and stepped out on the porch to greet him. It was Rio and Beckett. And Boo, the dog sporting a rather bulky, blood-stained bandage wrapped around his shoulder, who came limping to him.

"Look at you." He bent to pet the little dog. "What happened? A bobcat tear into you? Maybe one of those nasty raccoons?"

Considering Boo lacked the proper vocal cords, Rio

elected to tell his story. Their story. By the time she finished, Wash was hissing with anger, his jaw set granite hard. He looked toward Beckett. "Any guesses as to who did the shooting?"

"Too dark. Which was, I guess, both a good thing and a bad thing. Good, because he didn't hit anything. Bad, because neither did I."

"Maybe you did," Rio said. "He yelped and ran off moving slow and awkward like...you remember old Billy Eubanks, Wash? Like Billy used to do."

Wash did remember. Eubanks had been a hunchback with a half-crippled left arm.

"Except I only found a few traces of blood," Beckett cautioned. "Might've winged him, is all. Enough to scare him off, but not put him down."

Rio's eyebrows had drawn together. "I glimpsed him once. When I think back, I remember he was a bulky sort of fellow, and he was wearing a bowler hat with a high crown." She looked directly at Wash. "Sound like anyone you might know?"

Put the two things together in a sentence and yes, it did sound like someone he knew. He nodded. "But it's not enough to hang him."

"I know. He'd only deny being here and folks would pretend to believe him." Rio stepped off the porch and picked Boo up. "You, little guy, are going to keep Win company today. You be good, yes?"

She disappeared into the hotel with the dog and a minute later came out toting a basket, which she proceeded to tie behind the saddle on the smallish paint she always favored. Or had in the days she had the opportunity to ride.

"Lunch," she said in reply to his inquiry. "In case we get peckish."

Whatever she and Beckett had cooked up between them—and he didn't mean over a hot stove—seemed settled. She obviously intended to be part of this expedition. And why not? She had a right to the truth. Aside from the fact it was her land. Her family's land, anyway.

Sighing a little, he said, "Mount up. The day is getting away from us."

Wash took the lead, winding through parts of the forest that had been logged off earlier. Elias, a progressive in his own way, had taken care over the years to pay attention to selective logging as introduced by the Forest Service in the last few years, cutting the mature trees and leaving the best of the younger ones to grow. The same area would be ready to log again in five to seven years. And while Elias owned the section they were logging now, he'd acquired options on some of the vast Federal Reserve lands right next door.

Too many loggers, in both his and Wash's opinion, had scalped the land, rendering it useless for years to come. Since this part of the mountains was fairly steep, the land was unsuitable for anything else. Including roads. There were none, though trails had been cut through that weren't on any map. Wash elected to guide them to where Hightower had been killed through the back way. Although he doubted there'd be anybody in the woods on this Sunday, he preferred no one see them.

They came upon the remains of Hightower's campfire in less than two hours. A ring of stones marked where his body had been found. Hightower had pitched a small tent with his bedroll inside beneath a massive pine. A canvas food bag had been hung in the tree and left for squirrels to plunder. Both items had been abandoned when they recovered his body. Other than that, there wasn't much to see.

It seemed a little incongruous that the nearby stream chuckled merrily as it tumbled on its way down the hillside. Wash remembered folks saying there was good fishing for cutthroat and brown trout hereabouts, where the stream flattened out and made pools. The place was handy too, not far off the trail the three of them had come in on.

Beckett dismounted and hitched his horse to a tree branch. "I'm gonna look around."

Wash nodded, and seeing Rio already dismounted, he figured he might as well too.

Slipping her paint's bit, Rio tied him off and went toward the fire pit. "Where, exactly, did you find Mr. Hightower, Wash?" She said his name shyly, as if testing it on her tongue.

Wash had been one of the retrieval party, and the layout was all too fresh in his mind. He came to stand beside her and pointed down at the ground. "A couple steps to your right. Looked like he'd finished work for the day and was sitting there drinking coffee and totaling up his paperwork."

Most of the blood had been washed into the ground in the most recent rain, but Rio gave a little skip to the side, as if somehow she sensed just where the body had lain.

"His paperwork?"

He nodded. "Whoever shot him evidently threw it into the fire. There were bits and pieces left, all scorched beyond use. Nothing worth recovering. Ferris has had to start all over."

When she looked up at him, there were tears in her dark eyes. "Poor Mr. Hightower. I can't understand why anyone would do such a thing."

Wash had some ideas but he didn't think he'd share them just yet. "Whoever it was probably shot from over there." He pointed into the woods where the trail curved past a tall outcropping of boulders. Part of the rocks had fallen away fairly recently, making for good cover to shoot from. "At least that's what we guessed, given the way he was laying and the...how his wound looked. It was quick. I know that. I doubt he knew what hit him. His rifle lay next to him. It hadn't been fired."

The relief on her face made him glad for the lie. Oh, not about Bill's unfired rifle. About the hunch his death probably hadn't been all that quick. It always took a while to bleed out from a wound like he'd suffered, and from the bullet in the man's spine, he would've been paralyzed, unable to move. In fact, Wash had an idea Bill had seen his killer, and had possibly known him.

Wash took her hand and drew her away from the small circle of stones. Hightower had crumbled forward into the fire as he died. He'd been burned as well as shot. It wasn't anything he wanted to think about, and he'd for sure never tell Rio.

Instead, he drew her into his arms, thinking he needed her closeness just then as much as she needed his. His lips touched hair, but he didn't think she realized.

After a moment, she gave a shiver and stepped away, her smile shaky. "Thank you. This..." She waved her hand. "It's so sad and makes me so angry."

He nodded, and although he'd just as soon held her a while longer—she made a nice armful—he couldn't help wondering where Beckett had gone. It seemed odd to him the man had taken off and gotten out of sight so quickly.

"Did you see where Ferris went?" he asked Rio.

She turned toward the creek. "That way, I think. Shall I call for him?"

"No. I think I'll amble that way too." Wash scrambled for something to say that would keep her here. In case Beckett was up to something, he didn't want Rio getting in the way if there was trouble. "Maybe you can unpack lunch."

She looked at him as if he were a little crazy. "Lunch? It's not lunchtime, Wash." A tide of pink rose in her cheeks. "But I'll wait here for you. Take your time."

Wash blinked, understanding what she thought he'd meant, and laughed inwardly. It served well enough. Nodding, he strode in the direction Beckett had taken.

RIO WAITED UNTIL WASH, as he looked down at the ground before jumping across the creek at a narrow spot, disappeared into the forest on the other side. Just as Beckett had done before him.

Satisfied she was alone, she headed off toward the ruined outcropping.

Something about the place struck a chord in her. Elias had been talking to someone, a stranger, one day not long before he became pretty much housebound. He'd met with the man on the back porch late last fall, and they'd talked about an outcropping along the trail where there'd been a recent rock fall. The description of the area had been quite graphic. About the creek. About the placement of fallen boat-shaped stone and a lightning-struck tree with the top broken off. Might, in fact, have been describing this very spot. And while she wouldn't have called the rock with a dip in the middle boat-shaped, another by stretching his imagination might. And the lightning blasted tree was obvious.

Loud and clear, she'd heard the man say, "Bones. According to the skull, human."

Elias had cursed and said, "Forget what you saw. I'll have the Chinaman see to them. They'd best be covered back up."

That had been that. Neither man had known she'd been returning from the chicken coop with eggs and she'd remained silent. Totally silent.

As far as she knew, Elias had never spoken to anyone about the bones.

Just before she reached the first of the rock fall, Rio looked all around. The outcropping stood about fifty yards off the curve of the trail, which as far as she could tell, looked as if it had seen quite a bit of traffic lately. More than a retrieval of Hightower's body seemed to warrant.

Odd, she thought, for what should be nothing more than a game trail through the Salo property. Certainly not a public access. Then she thought of the smugglers and that Li Bai must know about this trail. She would take a gun and ask him, she vowed, as soon as she got back to the hotel. Maybe Wash would come with her.

When she turned back toward the campfire, she saw a way clear of trees right to where Wash had said the timber cruiser's body had been found. *A perfect sight line.* Had anyone, meaning the sheriff, even looked for where the shot that killed Hightower had come from? How could anyone, for even a moment, have thought the timber cruiser's death a suicide?

But there could be more to find there. Elias and the stranger had spoken of bones and an outcropping long before Hightower's murder.

Skirting the tumble of boulders at the bottom of the fall, Rio picked her way up the slope to where she stood beside the large boat boulder. It had broken a smaller one into rough fragments when it fell. Even yet, the wall of granite above seemed a bit unstable, and she moved cautiously, worried a stumble might start another slide.

The bones she'd heard spoken about could've been covered up, depending on when the latest fall had occurred. In fact, though she was light and walked with care, the way was steep here and small gravel moved under her feet. Seeing nothing, she was ready to give up. She didn't like it there. The whole place gave her the willies.

She turned away, only to have some gravel roll under her foot. Struggling for balance, she fell, landing on her behind. A good deal of skin scraped off the palm of her hand in the process of breaking her downward skid.

Crying out, and maybe cursing just a little along with it, she bent to look at her hand. But as she bent, her eye caught the glimpse of an opening into what appeared to be a small cave concealed behind the boulder. And the flash of something that looked remarkably like bones.

Looked like? No. What she knew were bones.

"Wash?" Her cry seemed to get lost in the forest of trees and rock. "Wash? Beckett Ferris? Where are you?"

Neither man answered, although just for a moment she thought she heard someone moving on the trail.

"Washington Ames! Beckett Ferris! I need you."

Rio had forgotten about her hand. Leaving a streak of blood, she pulled at what must've been a forty-pound rock blocking the mouth of the cave and finally sent it tumbling down the hill. The removal let sunshine into the little cave, which was, she saw now, more of a simple indentation in what had been a cliff than a real cave. It also let her see that indeed, these were bones. Human bones. The skull made that much obvious.

The person had been small. Either a boy or a woman. *Woman.* She knew it. Hidden here for the flesh to molder away and leave only bones behind.

"Wash!" Rio flat-out yelled this time, a rush of anger stirring. Where was he? Where was Beckett? Men! Never around when they were needed most. Always underfoot when they weren't.

Coming over a little dizzy of a sudden, she put her head in her hands and tried to think. A piece of her wanted to delve right in and search these bones. A second piece of her wanted just the opposite. But then she knew she couldn't wait. She had to know.

Squirming through dirt and rock shards, Rio pushed into the cave. It didn't take her long. There wasn't a whole lot to see.

She'd just opened her mouth to bawl out the men's names again when she spotted Wash jumping back across the stream and looking around for her. Rio got to her feet and waved her hands over her head. "Up here."

Even from a distance she knew he was scowling. Too bad. She'd bet her discovery trumped his curiosity about Beckett. Anyway, hearing movement behind her, she spotted Beckett approaching from the trail. How he'd managed to circle around the campsite so quickly—and why he had—was to wonder about. But later, not now.

The two men met at the bottom of the scree. Each eyed the other with a certain amount of distrust. At the moment, Rio had no patience with either one.

"Come up," she called to them. "Be careful. All these loose rocks are treacherous." Meaningfully, she held her hand palm out to show the blood.

"You're hurt." Wash, climbing faster than he should, was only a few yards from reaching her.

Beckett, climbing right behind Wash, winked. "Don't cry."

For some reason, the wink made her feel better, though she huffed. "Do you see me crying?"

By then they'd both reached her. "No," they said together.

"So what happened? If you're not hurt, why are you yelling?" Wash asked.

"Anyone for miles around could hear you," Beckett added. "Probably scared away all the game in the forest."

They were trying to jolly her out of the panic they'd noted in her voice. Rio knew that much. Truthfully, she was a little ashamed of it now. After all, dry bones couldn't hurt a living person.

Even so... "Because of that." She pointed.

"What? I don't...oh." Beckett nearly knocked Wash in the head as they both squatted and followed her pointing finger.

Wash stood up. "Well," he said. And again. "Well."

To Rio's annoyance, the men looked at each other, and Beckett said to Wash, "What do you want to do?"

Anyone could see that wasn't a decision Wash wanted to make. Or was up to him to make. "Bones probably belong to a native and this is his burial spot. Could be we shouldn't disturb him. The Indians, they're a bit testy when their dead folks get bothered."

Beckett nodded and glanced inside again. "It's a possibility, I suppose," he said through his frown, though Rio heard doubt. The same kind of doubt she felt. No. That she knew.

"Wash," Rio said, "you're being stupid. First, this isn't a he or him. It's a she. And second, it isn't a native."

Wash's blue eyes narrowed. "What makes you think so?"

"Look closer. She is wearing a gold wedding ring and earbobs set with little pearls and sapphires. And there's a bit of fabric from the dress she was wearing caught under one of the larger stones. You can still see the pattern. I can describe the dress if you like."

"You can?" Beckett's eyes widened. "Wait, Rio. Do you know who this is? Was?"

She nodded. "I think so. I'm almost sure." She hesitated, then, fighting the emotion gripping her, said, "I am sure."

"Who is it?" Wash did the asking.

"My mother."

One thing she'd learned in the last few minutes. Dry bones were able to hurt the living after all. Even if in some ways the discovery was a sort of relief. Of a vindication. Her mother had never been a wayward wife who abandoned her own daughter. She'd been murdered, just like her father had said.

Nineteen

Struck silent, Wash stood looking down at Rio with pity in his blue eyes. Beckett folded his arms across his chest, then unfolded them, his expression copying Wash's. Well, Rio didn't want their pity. Her reaction headed more in the direction of revenge.

Beckett's head jerked up. Rocks scrabbling beneath his boots, he swiveled, eyes scanning into the forest around them and paying quick attention to the road, barely visible from this high viewpoint.

"Did you hear that?" he asked in a low voice.

Wash shook his head, but Rio said, "Yes. Or I heard something."

"A bird?" Wash scoffed.

"Not a bird," she said, "something heavy," and Beckett nodded.

"I don't see anybody," he added slowly. "But I don't see any animal either that might've been moving through the brush."

Rio shivered a little, as if brushed by feathers.

They stood silent, listening, looking. There was nothing, and at last, impatient, she moved from the cave entrance and Beckett eased his stance. His hand, Rio noticed, moved from behind his back where he still carried his revolver.

Wash finally found his voice as he bent for a last look into the cave. "So you think this is your mother? You believe this is Juanita?"

"I know this is Juanita. This is my mother. The wedding ring will prove it. I remember the earrings too. She'd told me I could have them when I turned ten." There was absolutely no doubt in Rio's affirmation.

Just like everyone around Painter's Bay, Wash knew the story about how Rio's mother had run away all those years ago. It was common knowledge around town and spoken of often when Elias Salo did something to make himself particularly obnoxious. Then the story would come up again with a good many folks saying they didn't blame her.

Only that they faulted her for leaving her daughter behind.

But Juanita hadn't. Or not because she wanted to. But because she'd been murdered. The bullet hole in her skull made that clear.

Looking pained, Wash couldn't seem to think of anything to say that might refute Rio's certainty. Beckett appeared curious, but he had nothing to add. Both eyed her as if expecting fireworks. Or maybe the waterworks of a crying woman. But Rio didn't cry. She didn't quite know how she was feeling. Except for the rage like a white-hot flame burning in her guts.

After a minute or so, Wash shook himself like Boo

after a dunk in the lake. "I suppose we ought to call Donaldson out to take a look and gather the remains."

"I doubt if there's anything left to show how she got here, but I expect you're right," Beckett agreed.

"No." Rio almost shouted the word and Wash blinked.

"Never," she said more calmly. "That lout has always been in my father's pocket. I wouldn't be surprised but what he helped cover up her murder when it happened."

"Was he sheriff at the time?" Beckett asked.

"No. He worked for my father back then. Dad had just bought this section, and Donaldson was surveying it. A survey, I might add, that was so off in its parameters the state had to redo the property lines later on. It caused a bit of a stink and bad blood between them. Bad enough my father had to fire him. But then Elias helped get Mr. Donaldson elected sheriff, which has always puzzled me."

"I was just a kid then, but I remember," Wash said.

Beckett didn't fuss. He only looked thoughtful. "You think he...Donaldson...buried her?"

"I think he and my father together. When Elias said he killed her before he died, I wondered if he was simply trying to torment me." She went silent, then added, "But I guess not."

"Elias told you?" Incredulous, Wash's blue eyes turned hard.

"He said he killed her. Yes. Just a few days before he died."

"And still you took care of him." Beckett sounded disapproving.

Rio looked down at her wounded palm where the

bleeding, though not the sting, had stopped. "I didn't think I had a choice. I knew he'd be dead soon and I've been trying to hang on to my place here. Why wouldn't I stay? I have no money and no place else to go." There. It was said. Although it wasn't entirely true. Or not anymore.

She drew a breath. "Mr. Brackman has told me he has in his possession a will written by my mother leaving me the hotel. She had inherited it from her father only six months before. Evidently no one knew about this except the attorney and my father. And he kept it secret all these years, assuming, I suppose, no one, meaning me, would ever find out."

Beckett grimaced. "Could be the reason you're still alive."

Rio nodded. "Yes. I always figured to stick it out and now, even if Eino does come back like Donaldson says he's going to do, he won't be able to take the hotel away from me. Not with the paperwork Mr. Brackman has."

Muttering under his breath, Wash raised an eyebrow.

"Mr. Brackman not only has my mother's will and is ready to produce it, but he has the original papers between my mother and my father in which Elias agreed to relinquish any claim to the hotel in my favor. An unusual provision which the attorney felt meant my grandfather didn't trust Elias to deal fairly with me. He said he can bring my case to probate right away. Before, since we didn't know if my mother was still alive somewhere, there would've been controversy and counterclaims. But now we've found her, along with proof of her death. I'm her heir. Mr. Brackman said she deliberately explained the...the *exclusion* of Elias and Eino from the will at the time."

The woods around them seemed to be listening. Even the swirling waters of the creek were subdued until the harsh cry of a magpie split their silence. They all jerked. The earlier scare must still be on the men's minds, Rio supposed, just as it was her own.

Beckett's face had drawn into a narrow-eyed mask as he thought. "So what do you want to do, Miss Salo?"

For a moment, Rio felt terribly helpless. She didn't understand what he was asking. "Do?"

"Yes." His mouth twisted. "I've got a suggestion, if you want to hear it."

She nodded. "Please."

Wash studied Beckett, his expression hard. "What is it?"

"I say we leave her bones where they are. Don't move a thing. Restore the entrance to the cave and hide any sign we've been here. And don't tell anybody but the lawyer. When, or if, it becomes necessary, that'll be the time to produce her bones...her body. If your discovery gets noised around, you're apt to be in danger. Wash, too. All three of us, I expect."

Wash nodded agreement. "Or whoever buried her comes back to move the bones and destroy the proof. I think you're right. The sooner that attorney can get this through the courts, Rio, the safer you'll be."

Rio knew they were right although the knowledge started a sort of war within her. Part of her wanted to scream the culpability of her father, of the sheriff, probably even of her half brother, aloud to the world. To let everyone know immediately. But she wouldn't. At least not yet. She'd have to let this ride until the proper time for it to be revealed.

Bending down, she looked again into the cave, at those poor yellowed bones lying in the dirt. "Agreed," she said, and began rolling a stone so heavy she ended up needing Wash's help to place it at the entrance.

They heard nothing further of anything—or anyone —moving in the woods. But the idea had taught them a lesson. *Proceed with caution.*

AS IT TURNED OUT, the discovery of Juanita Salo's bones wasn't the only surprise of the day. Although, as Rio came to think of the adventure, she knew Wash was more surprised than she when Beckett made his revelation. He didn't even try to hide his anger. Anger at Beckett and anger at her. Mostly at her, Rio thought with more than a touch of bitterness, because it struck her as misplaced.

They'd finished restoring Juanita's grave and were at the creek washing sweat from their faces and dirt from their hands with water icy from the winter snow melt when Wash looked up and said to Beckett, "Where did you get to earlier, Ferris? Before Rio called to us. You crossed the creek to look around, but when you showed up, you were over by the trail." He shook his hands to dry them.

The burble of the creek almost hid Beckett's curse—though not quite.

But yes. Rio had been wondering some about that as well.

Beckett sent her a sort of questioning, shifty-eyed look.

"Time to come clean, I think," she said, which had Wash rearing erect and his expression turning first curious, then suspicious, and finally stiff.

"Come clean?" he repeated a little louder than necessary, and it was easy to tell his fur had been rubbed the wrong way.

Beckett didn't seem exactly pleased either, but Rio ignored both men's reaction.

"Yes." She met Beckett's dark stare with her own. "Tell Wash how you happened to arrive here at Painter's Bay. I must say, I'm curious myself. It's been ten days and I'm tired of being in the dark. Especially considering the circumstances."

"What circumstances?" Wash demanded. "What are you talking about?"

By the look on his face, Rio thought he must be counting down the week since he'd supposedly introduced Beckett to her and comparing it to the ten days she mentioned.

Appearing as if on the edge of protest, Beckett's shoulders dropped. He forced a tiny grin. "If you say so, boss lady." But then he turned and walked back toward the trail where he'd been when Rio cried out regarding the discovery of Juanita's grave. "Wait here," he said over his shoulder. "I'll be right back."

Wash made to protest, but Rio stilled him. She had a premonition. "We'll be here."

"He might not come back," Wash said quietly, but she shook her head.

"He will. Just wait."

And even if he'd rather not, his young brother was at the hotel. Beckett would never abandon Win.

They didn't have to stand there long. Inside five minutes Beckett reappeared. He carried a pack on his back with a couple bedrolls looming over his head, a second, smaller pack under one arm, and a rifle in his other hand.

Rio wasn't surprised and she smiled a little.

Wash's mouth twisted. His expression went stiff. "What's all this?"

"These belong to Win and me, lost when somebody tried to kill us when we came up on Hightower being shot. Only we didn't know it was Hightower at the time. I thought he might be an opium smuggler."

Wash interrupted. "An opium smuggler? Here? I understood they circled around south of us before heading east into Idaho and Montana."

Rio had the sudden thought that he'd been easily fooled then. Or more likely, suffering a case of ignorance being bliss. After all, Li Bai had been right in front of him.

Beckett ignored him. "We had to run and leave our things behind when the shooting started. I guess the shooter didn't think to look where we'd come from. Otherwise he'd have taken this stuff away or destroyed them. He'd shot Win, you see, when my brother ran forward to help Hightower. Not," he added, shaking his head, "that Win could've helped. Hightower was a dead man as soon as that bullet hit him."

"Your brother was shot?" Wash stared at Beckett, then, wonderingly, at Rio. "Not sick?"

"No. He's been here the whole time."

Wash's head swiveled to look around the little clearing. "Where were you when all this happened."

Beckett nodded toward the trail. "We were coming down from the main road heading toward Painter's Bay, following what looked like a frequently used path. We'd just set our packs down and unsaddled our horses when we heard a shot. Since it drew our attention, we noticed the flicker of the fire, here at the campsite. I figured to warn whoever was shooting not to point his gun our way, and we started over, but when we got closer, we could see the man was face down in the fire and not moving."

In the fire? He said *in*? Rio's eyes widened.

He paused and shook his head. "Win started running toward him thinking to help. He got hit before I could stop him. That's when I saw the figure of the man who did the shooting. I shouted at him but he kept firing. It was too dark to get a good look at him, and after he emptied his rifle at me, he took off. The wind was blowing and it was raining hard, if you remember. All I got was a general impression."

"Yeah?" Wash's suspicion hadn't abated.

"Yeah. A heavy-set fellow, unless that was due to his coat and rain gear. That's about it. Not enough to point a finger at anybody. But since this looked to be a flat-out murder, I figured to leave everything untouched and get help for my brother. He was bleeding badly. Bad enough I had to carry him the last part of the way. The hotel was the first place we came to where I figured there might be help." He looked at Rio with a faint smile. "And there was. You, Miss Salo. I figure Win would've been dead in another fifteen minutes."

Rio nodded, but said, "You were on foot. What happened to your horses?"

"They were livery horses we picked up just this side of the mountains. Gentle old plugs, but not used to gunfire. They pulled loose and ran off when the noise started. I've been hoping they made it back home to their stable, otherwise I'm gonna owe a certain liveryman money for two horses."

But he didn't seem too concerned about the cost, which struck Rio as a bit strange for an out-of-work timber cruiser.

Wash, too, since he stepped back from Beckett, pulling Rio with him. "You didn't report what happened to the authorities? To Donaldson?"

Beckett shrugged and led his horse over to where he'd dropped the packs and began loading things on the back of his saddle. "No," he said simply. "Especially after I saw the way he treated Miss Salo. I didn't know who to trust. And then, Win shouldn't have been with me at all. But what was I going to do? I couldn't leave him where he was with nobody to look out for him while I was on the job."

"On the job?" Wash eyes narrowed, his gaze as sharp and pointed as the tip of a sword. "How'd you know we'd need a timber cruiser? Or is there some other job we ought to know about?"

Beckett tied a knot in the saddle thongs wrapped around his bedroll and looked doubtfully at the other one. His horse had about as much tied on back as would fit. He sighed, seeming to come to a decision.

"Here's the thing, Ames," he said. "It's true I'm a fair hand at evaluating your timber for the market, but that isn't my main job nowadays."

Rio held her breath.

"No?" Wash said.

"No. I work for the United States federal government. I'm a customs agent. My job is to stop the opium smugglers from bringing in unstamped opium from the Victoria, British Columbia factories. The Seattle folks have been making a big push to shut the whole opium business down."

Wash's mouth dropped open. "A customs agent. So you're after Li Bai."

Shrugging, Beckett said, "I expect I am, though I figure he's just a middleman. I'll need to have a talk with him sooner or later. See if he'll tell us who is running the enterprise around here. That's who I'm after."

"Not him?" Wash sounded surprised.

Beckett shook his head. "The importers don't usually put a Chinaman in charge. They just have them sell the opium. Then the law comes down on the little guy and the big fish skates."

The metaphor—or whatever it was—boggled Rio's mind.

Rio could see Wash putting the facts together. About how convenient it had been to find a timber cruiser. About Beckett's secrecy about his brother. About a lot of things.

"Li Bai got beat up last night." Wash scratched the back of his neck. "Beat up bad. Whoever did it made a point to destroy much of the cook shack, like maybe they were looking for something. I think they burned some of Li Bai's stock. Or maybe it was a warning to me, indicating I should close my eyes to what's coming through the Salo woods. I don't know how eager Li Bai will be to talk to you. He didn't want to tell me who did the beating or why. Took some persuasion."

Rio gasped a little, thinking of everything else that had gone on last night, but this was news.

"Could be he's been holding back." Beckett said. "Taking a little off the top without telling his boss."

"Possible. I wouldn't know." Wash shrugged. "More likely, a simple warning to keep his mouth shut. That'd be my guess."

Rio had picked up Beckett's other bedroll and tied it behind her saddle. The least she could do, she figured, for a hotel guest who just happened to be a customs agent. No wonder he didn't hesitate to call the sheriff out. But if Donaldson ever suspected him to be other than a timber cruiser, Beckett had best watch out, government agent or not.

Wash, after helping Rio mount her paint, climbed aboard his sorrel. "I may have made a mistake last night," he said to Beckett.

"Yeah?"

Wash nodded. "Yeah. See, when I walked into the cook shack yesterday after I left the hotel, Li Bai almost shot me. I took the pistol away from him. Confiscated it, I guess you might say. And I still wouldn't trust him with it. The thing is—"

"The thing is what?" Rio asked, Wash having stopped in mid-sentence.

"I may have left him with no way to protect himself against whoever mauled him."

They made haste, after that, urging their horses through the woods without stopping to admire the scenery, and didn't even think about eating their lunch until they'd arrived back at the hotel.

Win and Boo came out on the back porch to greet them, Boo circling around the horses' heels and generally being a distraction.

"Everything all right?" Beckett asked Win even before he dismounted and began unloading their gear.

"Sure." Win frowned at his brother. "Why? You expecting more trouble?"

Beckett glanced at Wash who had collected the horses' reins to lead them to the corral on his way back to his cabin at the Salo compound. "Might be a possibility. I want you to be on the lookout. After last night..." He didn't finish.

Twenty

"I know how to keep my mouth shut," Win said to his brother. His lower lip stuck out. "You've hammered it into me hard enough. And I'm getting durned tired of hearing—"

"Tough. I don't care what you're tired of. After what happened out there in the woods, after hearing that gunshot, and after I told you to stay back while I looked around, you dashed ahead anyhow." Beckett began a rebuttal before Win finished his complaint.

"Well, don't I know it?" Win yelled. "You've told me often enough. And ain't I the one that got shot?"

That's when Rio held up a hand. The hand with a scraped and now bandaged palm, the sight of which seemed to stop the brother's argument in its tracks. Actually, she was glad Wash wasn't there to hear them going at it since he still didn't know everything. She couldn't help thinking it might be best if he never did. "Enough. Please don't fight. I've had enough awfulness for one day. I don't think I can bear anymore."

"Sorry," Win said. Then, "What awfulness?"

They hadn't told Win about finding the body of Rio's mother. An agreement that a secret between three was more likely to hold than a secret between four.

"None of your business." Beckett made short work of any reply she might have conjured and put a stop to Win's dogged questions. But evidently, since both Wash and Rio now knew about Beckett's mission here, the boy had the idea he should have more freedom to get around and to talk to people.

Beckett disagreed. Adamantly. "There's some things could get you, Miss Salo, and all of us, killed if it got to the wrong person's ears. Didn't the attack last evening prove anything to you?"

Win, being a smart enough boy, nodded, in spite of the look of petulance on his face.

All Rio wanted to do for now was to snuggle up with her dog and forget about everything. Even for just fifteen minutes. She intended to put those bones out of her mind and replace them with the picture she'd formed of her mother as she last remembered her. Warm, loving, protective. And always smelling of the good food she'd been cooking.

Maybe Beckett understood her desire because he tugged on Win's arm and insisted they collect the fishing gear he'd spied on the porch and see if they could catch a mess of crappies. "Maybe our chef will cook them up for us." He glanced at the chef.

"Maybe your chef will," she replied. "If you catch anything."

The quiet after they left seemed a blessing.

But even when Rio shut Boo and herself into the quiet of her bedroom, her insides felt coiled like the springs in a fancy new buggy seat. Ready to pop forth and hit her in the behind when she least expected it.

So instead of curling up on the bed, she got down on her hands and knees and wrenched up a certain floorboard. Beneath the board was a cavity about two feet long, six inches wide, and perhaps four inches deep. Rio didn't know who had created the space or whether it was deliberate or the result of a simple mistake in calculation when the hotel was built. She'd found it years ago when using a dust mop to clean the floor. A string had caught on a loose nail as when she tugged, the top board popped up. It had served as a hiding spot for her few treasures ever since. And now she'd put it to use hiding the money from Elias's armoire.

She drew the envelopes, bags, and documents she'd taken from her father's cache and set everything on her bed. Sitting cross-legged there with Boo resting his head on her thigh, she drew a breath and opened the first envelope she knew contained money. The same one she'd counted before, but she counted it again. The sum was accurate. She wrote the total on the outside of the envelope.

One thousand dollars even—mostly in one-dollar bills, which puzzled her—in each of the stacks bound with twine. "Where do you suppose this came from?" she asked Boo.

He shook his head and tried to scratch his shoulder, no doubt itching as it healed.

The bags of coins were deceptively small, but heavy for their size. Opening the drawstrings, she found one bag contained fifteen twenty-dollar gold pieces and the other twenty-three. Most were as bright and clean as the day they were minted. $760 she wrote on a slip of paper and put it in one of the bags.

"We're rich," she told Boo. "And I'm almost afraid to count the rest."

He answered by climbing all the way into her lap.

THE DINNER she offered her two hotel guests that night had them gaping in wonder, though Rio considered the meal below her grandfather's standards—or even hers by the time they had to shut the hotel because of her father's illness. She'd have to do better when she opened the restaurant for all-comers if she wanted to earn top dollar. First of all, she'd have to spend some of Elias's cache on supplies. Make a standing order at the grocery for Mr. Lewis to order in from Spokane for arrival on the Thursday train, just like they'd always done before. Except for the folks staying in the hotel, Friday, Saturday, and Sunday had always been the busiest nights of the week. It wouldn't do to run out of food.

As a trial run for Beckett and Win, she made squash soup with chicken stock and coconut milk, and put thin flakes of the coconut, sweetened a bit, in her fruit ambrosia, which she layered with orange slices into small crystal bowls with whipped cream and dusted with cinnamon as a special touch. She served the crappies the Ferris men had caught on their fishing venture sautéed to perfection and added a dab of tartar sauce with a sprig of early dill on the side. She roasted a chicken, made potatoes au gratin in small ramekins and made a spiced apple cake with a glazed walnut topping to finish the feast.

Seating her guests in the dining room, Rio donned a fresh apron and, metaphorically speaking, changed her chef's hat for a server's.

Finally, setting a small crockery plate with the cake in front of Beckett and another for Win, she filled their cups with coffee and stood back.

Win's reaction pleased her most.

"I've never had a meal that good before," he said, patting his belly. "Nothing that fancy. I don't even know what you call some of it. Like that soup. Or like that orange stuff."

"Thank you, sir." Rio had to laugh. "I call the orange stuff ambrosia."

"Ambrosia indeed. My compliments to the chef," Beckett said.

She saw the twinkle in his eyes. "I'll pass that on, sir," she answered gravely.

Rio started back to the kitchen, but as she passed from the dining room, the bell at the hotel door clanged a discordant note. As if that weren't enough, the door shook on its hinges as someone began banging on it. Whoever was out there had gone beyond simple impatience.

And Rio believed she knew just who. In her experience there was only one person around with the crass audacity.

Behind her, she heard Beckett get up from the table, his chair screeching backward. "Don't answer that," he said.

In the kitchen, Boo scrambled to his feet and began howling.

She really wished she could ignore the noise. But she couldn't. Not if she wanted to have a front door come morning. Defiance made her disregard Beckett's advice.

Shaking her head, she crossed the lobby to the door. Removing her apron, she dug the key from the ledge where it was hidden. Twisting the key, but leaving it in the lock, she opened the door a scant six inches.

"Yes?" she said to the man standing there, his fist raised as if to hammer her through the slate-tiled floor like a nail. One look and she knew she should have listened to Beckett. "Here again so soon? What do you want? You know the hotel is not open to the public as yet. It says so right on this sign. You'll have to wait until the grand reopening."

She'd put the sign up this morning, saying she'd open for business on Friday. So saying, she started to close the door.

Sheriff Donaldson, with his toady of a deputy following on his heels, shoved her out of the way as if she'd been no more than a grain of sand. Both men wore clothing splotched with water, a sure sign they'd come by boat, and that the person at the oars hadn't had the least idea on how to row without getting wet.

Rio fell back against one of the coat trees in the hall, a hook jabbing painfully into her shoulder blade. Startled into saying "Ow," she gripped the coat tree to hold it—and herself—upright. Then, louder, "What is the meaning of this? How dare you barge in without a by-your-leave? Please desist."

Hearing herself, she had the thought she sounded like one of the more stupid heroines in a gothic novel. *How dare you? Please desist?* Donaldson would do anything he felt like, as long as his victim was weaker than him, and she knew it. What she needed was a gun —and the boldness to use it.

A thought occurred to her. He wasn't beyond committing murder. He could murder her and blame it on someone like Beckett or Win. But if he tried, he might find Beckett a stronger opponent than he thought.

What did Donaldson want? Or rather, what did he have to gain? There must be something. Or why was he here at all?

Donaldson's grin jarred her, making her think of a wolverine's snarl. "You, woman, shut up and do as you're told," he said. "I'll be searching the room that used to be your father's for contraband, though I expect you've moved your frills in by now. Better than that little closet I seen where you slept. Raise a fuss and you'll spend some time in the jail. Only one cell in the jail, I'll have you know. Could be a drunk'll end up in the bunk right next to you."

The deputy giggled.

Fury buzzed Rio's nerves like a lightning bolt. "What are you talking about? Contraband? Such as what? You have no right to rummage through my property. What are you looking for, anyway?"

"You'll see."

She shivered as what he'd said struck her. Apparently, when he'd been here before, he'd taken notice of where her things were kept. The mere thought made her feel unclean.

Rio suspected he didn't have a real object in mind to look for. Contraband indeed! But then she knew. He was looking for the money from Elias's secret cache.

And maybe those letters too. Letters she hadn't yet gotten around to reading.

He started off across the lobby to the stairway. Spotting Beckett—silent, observant, maybe a little dangerous looking—standing in the archway to the dining room with his arms crossed, he stopped, startled. And so fast the deputy ran right into him. He pushed the man away.

"You." The sheriff eyed Beckett through slitted lids. "What the hell are you doing here?"

The look he turned on Rio accused her. "You said this joint ain't open for business."

Rio arched a brow. "Mr. Winter is a special case. The logging company needed a place for our timber cruiser to stay. I provided it. Not that it's any of your business."

The sheriff digested this information. "What about them barracks down by the sawmill?"

"What about them?" she answered.

"Why ain't he there?"

Rio didn't answer. She didn't want to mention Win.

Deputy Klinggaard, his nose pointing toward the kitchen, sniffed at the air like a hound dog. "Say, something sure smells good. I could use some of that stuff that smells like cinnamon."

Rio pretended not to hear him. If he expected her to offer him a piece of cake, all he'd get was disappointment.

Donaldson sent the deputy a look meant to quell him—and it did. "We're here on business. It's come to my attention your pa took opium. I mean opium beyond what the doc prescribed. Untaxed opium is illegal in this county and I'm gonna put a stop to the trade. I'm looking for the evidence. Whoever brought him that there dope is going to serve jail time and have all her property confiscated." The man seemed positively gleeful as he imparted this information.

He'd said *her*. Which meant he intended that person to be her. Rio knew it. Looking at Beckett, she could see he knew it too.

"In case you hadn't heard, Mr. Donaldson, my father is dead and buried. If you have otherworldly abilities, perhaps standing at his graveside would put you farther ahead when you ask for information."

He slapped her. Hard.

Rio reeled backward until strong hands grasped her arms and held her steady. "Easy," Beckett whispered to her before setting her aside. "That's enough," he said to Donaldson. "Touch this lady again and you're a dead man."

"I'm the sheriff. No smart-mouthed woman is gonna talk to me like that." Donaldson's voice rose into a whine, yet something about the *way* he said it indicated he had believed Beckett's quiet declaration.

Pain surged through Rio at the blow. Her tongue felt as if she might have chewed a chunk out of it. Blood flooded her mouth and set her stomach to churning. She thought maybe her face had been knocked askew. It must have, the way she felt. Blinking aside the tears seeping from her eyes, she saw that Beckett had unaccountably acquired a revolver from somewhere. He hadn't had it at dinner, but now the gun hung in a holster snugged against his hip. From the casual way his right hand hovered beside it, he knew very well how to use it.

The sheriff must have thought so too. Maybe he knew so. Last night's trouble rose in her mind.

"I said that's enough, Donaldson. Now or later." Beckett flicked a single glance at the deputy who stood staring at him as if dumbfounded, his mouth agape. "Get out. You and your little toady here. This isn't the first time you've used your badge as an excuse to intimidate this lady. I don't know what the idea is behind your persecution, but no badge gives you the right to strike her. You've been warned. Come here again and you'll be the one who is in trouble. Serious trouble."

"You can't—" Donaldson began, but Beckett shut the argument down fast.

"Try me." Beckett crooked a smile that wasn't really a smile. "You'll find I can."

Did a customs agent's authority override a local sheriff's? Rio wondered. She hoped so. Oh, how she hoped so.

Donaldson, his face nearly purple with rage, backed slowly away. At the doorway, he finally turned and, followed by his deputy, hastened toward the moored boat. He kept looking over his shoulder as if worried about a bullet in the back.

Even from inside, Rio could hear the sheriff shouting at his deputy. Something along the lines of "a stupid ass who can't even row a damn boat in a straight line." In that he may have been right and she saw the little boat skitter and dip before Klingaard got it controlled. She hoped they both landed in the drink. And that neither one could swim.

Finally, she turned to Beckett. "Donaldson didn't expect to find you here." She found it not only hurt to talk, but her speech was garbled.

Fortunately, Beckett had no trouble understanding. "No, but he knows I'm the one who did the shooting last night. He wouldn't have backed off otherwise. Seems the sheriff isn't as brave when he's fighting face-to-face against an equal opponent."

Gently, he tilted her chin and, examining her face, gritted his teeth. "You're going to have a bruise, but not, I think, a black eye. How are your teeth? Any of them wriggling? Your mouth is bleeding."

As she very well knew considering her mouthful of blood. "Bit my tongue," she managed, then spat into a handkerchief she pulled from her pocket. "Gah."

Beckett lent an arm on the way to the kitchen. "Win," he called. "Come out here. See if you can find some ice."

Win hadn't gone far, certainly not to their room where Rio supposed Beckett had told him to stay. In fact, she realized, it must have been Win who delivered Beckett's gun to him when the trouble started.

Rio gingerly seated herself on a kitchen chair in an attempt to regain her equilibrium. Donaldson's blow had made her a little dizzy.

In seconds, Win had used the ice pick to chip a piece off from the chunk cooling the icebox and brought the flakes to Rio on a plate. "Set 'em on your tongue."

She nodded. She would've smiled except for the blood filling her mouth. The sight would probably have scared a ghost.

Poor Win. Apparently, it had as he went off outside to look for a piece of driftwood to whittle. Or maybe to watch the boat making slow progress across the lake. Donaldson's voice still carried across the water.

Evidently, he hadn't liked the way his visit had gone.

Twenty-One

By Tuesday, Rio managed to speak without having to twist her tongue to avoid scraping the bitten spot on her teeth. Early in the morning, armed with a couple long lists, one which included the purchase of touch-up paint for the hotel facade that totaled an amount of money that made her wince, she and Boo hopped into a boat and crossed the bay to the landing in town.

Her first stop was at Dr. Clement's office where she found Molly on duty. Molly greeted her and took the money Rio handed over with something of a grateful air.

"I don't know," Molly said with a plaintive droop to her lips, "but though it seems James is as busy as ever, there's just not as much money coming in. Thank you, Rio, for being so prompt with payment. We thought you might have trouble paying, you know, because of how... well..." She blushed and added brightly, "I'm so glad you're opening the hotel again. We've missed treating ourselves to your dinners. At least, James told me that is your plan."

Rio was embarrassed for them both at having to consider finances. Having seen the doctor's name on a note in one of Elias's bags that had contained the gold eagles, she had an idea why the doctor was short. Not that she would've spoken of it for the world. The doctor's gambling losses were between him and his wife, though it crossed her mind to wonder who the doctor was losing to since Elias had become housebound. Still, a certain awkwardness made her keep the visit short.

The hardware store was second on her schedule, where she bought paint, along with oils and caulking and ropes to repair the hotel boats. Next was a large order at the grocers for foodstuff, the cost which made the storekeeper smile, and then on to the newspaper. She provided a front-page announcement saying the hotel would reopen on Friday and requested flyers to be put about with the news. Lastly, she stopped in at the bank and opened an account in her own name and directed the money from the Salo account be deposited there.

All of this took up her morning, but she felt well satisfied as she rowed back across the bay. Boo, tired but happy from the attention drawn by his bandage, rested between her feet all the way back while trying half-heartedly to nip the bandage away. "We'll take it off when we get home," she told him.

At the hotel, she found Win wandering the grounds and looking bored and at loose ends. Meanwhile, she had more than she could comfortably handle, which gave her an idea. She studied him, peering up at his greater height and considering.

"What?" Noticing her attention, he arched an eyebrow in an exact copy of his brother.

"How are you?" she asked, her expression making her as enigmatic as an owl.

"Fine. Pretty much healed up. See?" He swung his arms and stretched them over his head, demonstrating. "Why?"

"Well enough to take on a job? I'll pay you."

Win's face lit up. "A job? For pay? Sure." Then he frowned. "But not chopping wood. I don't think I'm ready for that."

"Not wood-chopping. How about wielding a paintbrush?"

He lit up again. "Yeah. I painted my uncle's bunkhouse last year. All by myself. Did a good job if I do say so, though Aunt Mildred didn't agree."

"She didn't? Why not?"

"Said it was the wrong color. She said a bunkhouse should be the same color as the barn,"

"What color did you paint it?"

"Blue. Kind of a bright blue. Stood out pretty good but I don't know why she blamed me. Unc is the one who got the paint and told me to have at it. So I did."

"Wasn't she mad at him?" Rio bit back a laugh.

Win sighed. "No. Just me. Because she said Unc can't tell blue from red and that I should've known better. She said I should've asked her, but shoot, going back and forth between them meant nothing ever got done around there."

Rio stifled a laugh. "Well, you'll find this paint is a dark green. The same color the boats are now."

"I'm gonna paint the boats?"

"Yes. I'll help you get them out of the water so they can dry first. Then you'll have to sand down the rough spots and re-caulk any that are leaking. Keep the one I used this morning until last in case I need it before the others are ready."

"Got it."

They settled into their separate chores. Win set to scraping the boats and poking cotton caulking into the most leak-prone areas, while Rio began sanding the woodwork on the hotel's facade. She wanted everything shipshape by Friday. And the way the two of them worked into the afternoon put them well on the way.

Rio had set aside her sanding supplies in favor of paint and brushes when it became time to put a beef roast in the oven. She'd fed Boo a couple generous scraps of meat and set onions around the meat with red wine poured over the top when she heard Win yell at her from outside.

Closing the oven door, she went outside. A breeze had blown up in the last while, blowing her hair around her face and sent dust whirling around the yard.

"What's wrong?" she called down to Win, still on the shore with the overturned boats. One had already had a fresh coat of paint applied and as the dust blew in a cloud, she hoped Win's hard work wasn't ruined.

But Win's attention wasn't on the boats or his paint job. He went out to the end of the dock and stood with his head cocked, looking in the direction of the sawmill and bunkhouse.

"Gunshots," he said, and he looked worried. "Over there, beyond the point of land."

"Gunshots?" she repeated. "The sawmill is over

there, but it's shut down by this hour of the afternoon. Are you sure?"

"I know gunshots when I hear them. Seems as if with the wind blowing from that direction, it brought the sound along with it." He paced around in a circle, then stopped. "I think I'd better go see what's happening."

Rio heard a shot now too. Just one. How many had there been before Win called her? And why should there be shooting over at the camp? It didn't make sense. But she shook her head. "If there's shooting going on, I don't think you should..."

He overrode her protest. "Yes I should. You said the sawmill isn't operating, right?"

"Right. They're only running one shift and it's past quitting time."

"Then there shouldn't be anyone over there at all, right?"

"If there is, they should all be resting." The boy was smart. And from the looks of things, accustomed to and ready to face trouble. Although the last time he'd heard shooting he'd been the one getting shot. One would think he'd learned enough from the experience not to go blundering in the vicinity.

"Well," he said, "Beckett and Mr. Ames, they won't be back for an hour or so yet. Somebody needs to see what's going on."

Rio hated to say so, but Win was right about that much. Somebody did. She did. Her responsibility. Just like she had to keep Win safe.

Boo, sensing the tension, ran around in circles barking, and Rio's lips flattened into a straight line. "Win, please do as I say. Take Boo inside and keep him in your room with you. I'll go over and take a look around the sawmill and bunkhouse. I'm sure it's nothing. Hunters, perhaps. Or...or...someone target practicing."

A thought wandered through her mind. *Target practicing on the Salo property? To what purpose?*

Win opened his mouth, gave her a funny look, then closed it again. "All right. Boo, c'mon fella. Come with me." The boy didn't argue for a change, evidently seeing the good sense in her demand.

Thankful she was wearing a pair of Eino's britches cast off years before he departed Painter's Bay, Rio dashed upstairs and found Elias's .44 Smith & Wesson. Checking the loads, she carried it with her as she ran out the door. It would take twenty minutes to walk to the camp. She knew the way and the time well from visiting Li Bai. But if she ran, she could cut the time in half.

I'll be back soon," she called down the hall to Win. Boo barked a reply from the Ferris's room, and satisfied, she hit the path through the trees and hurried. The wind pushed against her. Maybe even pushing the sense of dread she felt more firmly into her mind.

The trees hummed overhead. Bushes rustled. Grass flattened. She neither saw nor heard a single animal. The path was beaten hard underfoot and she ran fast until a limb, blown from an old pine, almost sent her sprawling. Five minutes and she was blowing hard. Ten minutes and she'd slowed to a trot. Fifteen minutes and she'd arrived at the edge of the clearing. Just ahead of her, despite dust and sawdust blowing through the air, Rio spotted the sawmill burner, a quiet, rust-colored monstrosity banked down for the night, rising into the sky above the mill at the edge of the lake. Closer to her direction was the buttoned-up bunkhouse. Doors and windows closed. It looked deserted.

Where, she wondered, were the Chinese sawmill workers? Why hadn't the gunshots drawn them out? Or where they all hiding?

Wash's cabin and one other were barely visible through the trees. They all looked undisturbed.

But the cook shack. The door stood open there. Could've been wind blown, she told herself. But somehow, she didn't think so. A rift of smoke came from the chimney. But it, like the bunkhouse, seemed empty. No one stirred.

Over toward the road, she thought—imagined—she heard something. Maybe the whinny of a horse. Maybe the pounding of her own heart.

Her eyes came back to the cook shack. *Something wrong there.* Nothing seen. Just felt.

"Hello," Rio called out. "Is anyone there? Li Bai? Is that you?"

She didn't hear the horse anymore.

"Hello?" she called again. "I heard shots. Is everything all right?"

This time there was an answer. Another shot. But it didn't come from the cook shack.

Then a second shot. Both from the woods. At her.

Again. A repeat from Sunday night. She stood frozen, disbelieving.

And while she stood agape, a bundle hit her at the knees and she went down to the ground into some tall grass. A heavy weight landed on top of her.

"Ain't you got sense enough to duck?" Win whispered at her. A harsh whisper, and she knew he'd hurt himself, leaping at her like that to save her life.

"J-just trying to judge where the shots came from," she lied, and as Win rolled away, she drew the .44 and took aim into the trees.

There. A shadow rider moved. The horse, a bay, one she clearly saw, with a distinctive white blaze down its face. Urged by its rider, it took a couple steps toward her. Taking care, she squeezed off a shot. The man shouted, a hoarse cry. The horse jumped sideways, spun, and fled. Rio shot again and, as Win yelled out a kind of victory cry, she saw the man slump, bending low over the horse's neck. He didn't fall, but didn't shoot again either. Then he was gone, beyond her sight.

Seconds ticked past, Rio had no idea for how long, while both she and Win just breathed.

"You got him," Win said, breaking the silence after a time. He rolled over and sat up.

She felt cold as ice, lying there in the grass. "Whoever that man is, he's the luckiest deplorable in these woods. I may have winged him, but your brother thought he did the other night too. This one, he always manages to dodge."

"Who is he?" Win asked.

Who is he? She knew. Oh yes, she knew, but would anyone believe her? Would anyone help her? "I don't know," she lied. "An unwelcome visitor who seems bound to do damage."

"Yeah." Win's voice shook. "But he missed both times, so I guess that puts you ahead."

She stared at him. He had a point. "Ahead? Maybe. But for how long? Win, we have to get this guy before he kills—" She broke off and rose to her feet. Looking toward the silent cook shack, her eyes narrowed. "Before he kills somebody."

"What should we do?"

"First off, the cook shack door is standing open. I think we'd best take a look in there."

"Beck told me the place was ransacked the other day. Why would anybody bother it again?"

"The cook is an opium dealer." She thought this was explanation enough.

Win blanched. "Does my brother know?"

"I expect he either guessed for himself or Mr. Ames told him." Rio strode rapidly across the open ground to the cook shack, trying to ignore the itchy feeling between her shoulder blades. It felt as if her muscles were hardening against a bullet.

Win kept pace, muttering to himself, but Rio held up a hand to stop him when he would've barged into the shack. Wide eyes questioning, he obeyed.

"Stand to the side," she said softly. "In case..."

He nodded, understanding.

"Li Bai, it's me, Rio Salo. Do you hear me?" She thought she heard movement, but it may have been an errant breeze stirring something inside.

Not a breeze, she decided a second later as a bullet thudded into a porch strut mere inches beyond her face. If she, or Win, had been in the doorway, they would have been hit.

"Li Bai, I'm here to help you." Even to herself, she sounded frightened. There was a strange kind of thud and then only real silence.

"Li Bai?"

They waited, she and Win, for as much as a minute before Win knelt down, poked his head around the doorframe, and peered inside. Rio took note of the way he sucked in a large lungful of air.

"What is it?" she asked.

Still kneeling, he looked up at her. "He's sitting in a chair but I...I think he's dead."

She stood still for a long moment, gathering her weakened courage and willing herself to take some kind of action. "Stay here," she said. "I'm going in," And she did before she could change her mind.

Passing from sunlight into the dark unlit room made her almost blind until her eyesight adjusted. Then she wished for the blindness back. There wasn't the destruction Wash had told her about from the last ransacking, but definite evidence of someone taking a thorough look around remained.

Rio took her time examining the room, if only to avoid attending to the other object. *Did one call a man's body an object?* Her eyes slid away.

"Miss Salo?" Win's voice came to her as if from some long distance. "Rio? Can I come in?"

She had to try twice for her answer to become audible. "Yes. Come ahead." Maybe having him here with her would make her braver. Together, they peered down at Li Bai.

What next? This is too much, too many dead bodies in less than a week. My father. My mother's bones. This man in front of me. Rio felt herself swaying and straightened her spine.

As Win had said, and she saw now for herself, Li Bai sat in a chair pulled up to the table. His arm was outstretched, pointing toward the door, and his hand lay on top a small revolver. A pocket pistol she believed the model was called. This one had a very short barrel. The thud they'd heard must have been when it dropped out of his hand after he fired it.

As for Li Bai, he was slumped forward. Blood drenched the front of the tunic he habitually wore, as he'd refrained from wearing white men's clothes except when he went to town. His mouth hung open, his queue lay coiled on the table like a black snake, the end in a pool of his blood. His eyelids were only partway shut.

Behind her, Win gagged as Rio touched Li Bai's throat, seeking a pulse. She knew the effort to be fruitless but did it anyway. It's what people did.

"What should we do?" Win asked.

Rio wished he hadn't asked her that because she didn't know. They couldn't report this to the sheriff, that much was certain. Who would believe her when she said she knew who'd murdered Li Bai. Besides, going by what she saw here, all he'd have to do is claim self-defense. Anybody could kill with immunity if they were defending themselves. Not that for even one instant pitting Li Bai and his tiny pistol against his killer could be construed as fair.

But if she couldn't think of anyone local to tell, now she knew Beckett was a customs agent, might that mean he had authority when it came to smugglers—dead or alive?

"We wait," she said. "We will close and lock this door and leave everything just as it is for Beckett and Wash to see. I expect Beckett might know what to do."

Win stared at her. He blinked and nodded. "Yeah. Beckett always knows the right thing. And—" He stopped. "I don't like it in here. Let's go."

Rio didn't care for it either. She shuddered. "Yes. Let's."

Twenty-Two

Beckett and Wash showed up just at dark, when birds were taking shelter in the trees and the good smells of Rio's dinner wafted through the open kitchen door into the night. The windstorm had passed. As it turned out, in taking the easier road in from the timber, the men had returned to the camp together.

Wash knocked on the doorjamb warning of his presence, then came on in as Beckett headed toward his room without pausing.

"I saw the note you tacked on the cook shack door telling me to come on over." He took off his hat revealing hair sticking up in points. His face was dirty and he'd been working hard through the day. "The note on the *locked* cook shack door," he went on. "Why is that? Do you know? Did Li Bai go off somewhere? If so, he didn't tell Chiang. Or me." He thought a moment. "Must've told the other men though. They were all gone, probably to town for supper."

She wasn't so sure of that. Her best bet was that

they'd all retreated to the opium den to sleep away their fear and their hunger. Some might never come back.

Not her problem and she was glad of it.

Rio looked up at him, the spoon in her hand dripping a butter and wine sauce unnoticed onto the floor. Boo, ever helpful, rushed over to clean up the droplets. Rio, eyeing Wash a little apprehensively, failed to notice the dog as she searched for words. "Li Bai, he didn't go anywhere. He's right there inside."

If Wash paid attention to her pale face, he didn't remark on it. "He's inside?" he repeated. "I knocked. Nobody answered. Rio—"

"He's dead. Murdered. Win and I...we...we—" She rushed the words, then stopped.

"You what?" He came close to shouting.

Beckett, with Win at his side, strode into the kitchen just in time to answer. "They barely escaped being murdered, as well, that's what, and it wasn't because the killer was feeling generous." He made a sort of bow to Rio, who stared blankly at him. "Win tells me you shot him. Wounded him and drove him off, actually."

Wash made a sound a bit like a tea kettle blowing a build-up of steam from its spout. "*You* shot him?" His blue eyes blinked. "With what? You mean you were carrying a gun?"

She'd brought the .44 with her into the kitchen after loading fresh shells into the cylinder. If the killer came back, she didn't intend to be caught napping. Wordlessly, she waved the spoon toward the revolver laying on a nearby counter—much to Boo's renewed gratification as he cleaned the floor again.

Wash eyed it. "Elias's old six-gun."

"She's a good shot too," Win said. "Sure made that feller change his mind about sticking around."

Win, Rio could see, during this last hour or so had regained his equilibrium after the shock of getting shot at and finding a dead man. She wished she could say the same.

"That was luck," she said. "Pure luck and a wonder."

The way Win shook his head made it clear he had his mind made up. "Didn't look like luck to me."

Though puzzled that neither man had asked yet if she knew Li Bai's killer, she hesitated to bring the question up herself. Men, she'd always found, were unpredictable. Even these two, both of whom she trusted, might question her reliability when it came right down to it. But still, it struck her as odd they hadn't asked.

Had Win already said something to Beckett? But she hadn't put a name to the man she'd seen to Win either. Not out loud.

Inviting Wash to stay for dinner, which she served in the hotel dining room, she managed to overhear some, though not all, of their discussion as she flitted in and out from the kitchen. The part she heard mostly centered on Wash's immediate concerns regarding getting another cook.

On the other hand, going by Win's guilty demeanor, she knew they'd spoken of the shooting when she was out of the room. Which was fine with her, Rio decided, as she handed around plates with more of last night's apple cake dressed with whipped cream and a caramel sauce. Let Win tell them the story.

"Promote Chiang," Rio advised Wash as she wiped crumbs into her hand. "Isn't he the logical person? He's been Li Bai's apprentice for a couple years and knows what's expected."

"I suppose." Wash sounded tired. "But if he doesn't have someone to serve as his apprentice, I expect I'll still have to find someone."

Rio had to smile. Wash liked to eat just fine and didn't miss many meals. Food always mattered to hard-working men. They liked their coffee too, and she dashed off to get the pot.

When she got back, Win had already polished off his cake and was waiting for his brother to finish. He may have been unaware of broaching the very subject everyone seemed to have been avoiding. "Beck?"

"Uh-huh?" Beckett grunted.

"We, Rio and me, that is, were thinking about who needs to know what happened today. Don't we have to report about that Chinaman getting killed to somebody?"

Rio stopped short, waiting for Beckett's reply. The heavy pot wavered in her hand, coffee sloshing until she found a place on the table to set it.

"That's the general process," Beckett said.

Win nodded, as if he'd already known that. "Yeah, well, since we've reported to you, you being a customs agent and all, are you going to take charge? Is that part of your juri...juris..."

"Jurisdiction?"

Win said, "Yes," at which Beckett fiddled with his fork as if he couldn't decide what to do with it. Could be that's how he felt inside because his reply, when it came, struck Rio as evasive.

"At this point, I'd say this should be a problem for the sheriff," he said.

He may have been answering Win, but he was looking at Rio.

She reached for Wash's empty plate but he clasped her hand and gave it a little shake. "You're not saying much, Rio, and I'm wondering why."

Pulling her hand free, she grabbed the plate and moved out of his reach. "Sorry," she said, turning to go. "It's been a rough day. That's all."

Wash snorted. "Rough day? Listen, we all know you must've seen the man who killed Li Bai. After all, you were shooting at him. I don't figure you were aiming blind."

But she had been, Rio thought. Sort of.

Beckett pulled the spare chair out from the table and told her to sit. "If you know who it was, you'd better say so."

She glanced at Win. He nodded at her. "You gotta tell them," he said, "because I don't know. Not for sure."

Rio supposed that was true. He'd always remained in his room when the sheriff came around. In fact, she had made sure Donaldson never saw the boy. Still she dithered. They were talking about a dangerous man. Hadn't they guessed that? What if her information got one of them killed?

Beckett smiled at her. "I figure it wasn't a friend of yours, considering you were shooting at him. So most likely, you're afraid there might be unpleasant consequences. How about you start by telling me something easy. Win says you both saw him riding away. What did the horse look like? What color? Did it have any distinguishing marks? Hope it wasn't white. White horses can be hard to identify."

Sighing, Rio understood what he was doing.

Working her up to the moment of truth. "No. The horse is a bay. Just a bay."

"Uh-huh. What else?"

She didn't say anything, which forced Win to take a hand. "It's got a white blaze. Goes all the way from under the forelock down to his nose. And it has a real short tail, like somebody chopped half of it off. Looked kind of funny. That right?" He looked to Rio for confirmation.

She nodded once, short and quick. Wash sat up straighter.

Beckett quirked an eyebrow at Wash. "I see that rang a bell."

"It did."

"The sheriff?" Beckett's query didn't surprise anyone.

Rio and Wash nodded, but it was Win who came to the point. "The sheriff? Can you arrest him, Beck? Or do you need to report to your boss, him being a sheriff and all?"

Beckett sat back, drummed his fingers on the table for a bit, then looked up. "I could do it by claiming he's in on the smuggling of drugs—and I think he is—but I'd rather not. Not just yet." He glanced at Rio. "If we can keep him from killing anyone else meanwhile, I'd like to have the governor weigh in on this and maybe have him consult *his* favorite judge. One he can depend on not being under either Donaldson's, or the smugglers thumb. I'll tell you now, they have some people highly placed in government circles working with them." He sighed. "Some folks—the more they have, the more they want. Meanwhile, I'll take the train into Spokane tomorrow and get some telegrams sent from there." He glanced at Wash. "Sorry to take the day off, but this has to be done right away."

"We've got a telegram office. They can do it and save some time. We're never going to get the crew to cutting timber if this doesn't stop." Wash frowned as Beckett shook his head.

"Not safe. I'd rather nobody knows we're on to Donaldson. What I want you to do, Wash, is to go ahead and report finding Li Bai dead. Do it this evening, please, if you can." He chuckled, taking Rio by surprise. "If you can find Donaldson anywhere. Could be he'll be making himself scarce tonight if Rio wounded him. But there's always that deputy. He'll do."

Turning to Rio, he said, "Do you have any idea whereabouts on his body your shot hit him? Do you think it might've been enough to take him down, even if not right then?"

Rio shook her head, but Win, sharp-eyed as a high-flying bird did. "Yes. Maybe. I saw blood on the back of his shirt." Excitement carried his voice higher by a degree. He poked his brother at a point just below his left shoulder blade. "Right about there. Bet if you can find his shirt you can prove it, right?"

Beckett grinned at his young brother. "Good thinking, Win, though I'd be surprised if he hasn't already burned the shirt. You've got the makings of a good cop. And Rio, you're friendly with the local doc, aren't you? Maybe you can check with him to see if he's treated the sheriff for a gunshot wound."

"I'll do that. Tomorrow. Right after I talk to the people who used to work in the hotel. I'll need employees by Friday."

The men may have forgotten the intended hotel

opening date, but not Rio. She refused to let Li Bai's murder destroy her plans.

THAT NIGHT, Rio finally read the letters she'd found in the secret compartment of Elias's armoire. The first, the one from Eino's relatives back east, was a letter demanding Elias return a particular piece of jewelry, a pendant made up of a large emerald surrounded by diamonds. The writer explained that the necklace had been in the family for a hundred years and they wanted it back. The letter stated that Edith, and Elias, both had known it was a piece to be handed down to daughters and that Edith's next oldest sister wanted it for her daughter now. If Elias kept it, it was under false pretenses.

Rio smothered a snort. One loud enough to make Boo sit up and look at her.

Surely that family had known Elias—or Eino—were not the type to give up anything of value. And it had been nearly twenty years since Edith's death. Why let the matter ride until now? It didn't make sense. The tone of the letter made Rio think Eino's visit with them had been less than satisfactory.

She set the letter aside. If Eino didn't show up by the end of the summer, she would ship all the jewelry she'd found in the armoire back to the family. She took no responsibility for it.

After that, she stared a long minute at the second envelope. For some reason, she got a sense of dread just by looking at it. The return address named a man she'd never heard of, but it was from a well-known Spokane firm of attorneys.

"I wonder," she whispered to Boo, "if my father was being sued by the family and he didn't want anyone to know. Otherwise, why would he have a letter from this person?"

Then, "Yes. I know. There's only one way to find out." Rio smiled at Boo and, after opening the envelope, withdrew the single sheet of paper.

What she found had her sitting up in bed, mouth open in astonishment and fury beyond anything she'd ever known. Her whole body heated up, as if she were being consumed by fire. This was worse, perhaps, than when Elias had confessed to murdering her mother, and then when she'd found the bones. She hadn't, after all, been totally surprised by any of that. Hadn't she wondered—surmised—for some years that her mother was dead and Elias knew it.

And she was glad Elias was dead. Glad!

The letter began by saying,

In reply to your letter of October 25th, I am sorry to say your request to sue for annulment, although I agree the solution you proposed would be cleaner, is untenable. As you and Juanita Seranno were together for eight years and have a daughter together, by law, an annulment of marriage is not possible at this late date. As to your other point, in which you state you believe the daughter was not fathered by you, that would be hard, if not impossible, to prove. Since she has lived under your roof to the age of twenty-one, your claim is sure to be denied. I would suggest you try for a divorce on the grounds of desertion by your spouse. Many divorces are granted for that very reason. However, that will prove a great deal easier if Mrs. Salo can be found and persuaded to attend court and agree to the terms. At that point, all property can come to you with a clear title and the girl can eventually be disinherited. If you wish to pursue this course, I will be happy to represent your interests.

The letter was signed,

Respectfully,
Elmer M. Lindquist, Esquire

Seething, Rio threw the letter down, then picked it up again before Boo could pounce after it.

"The old devil. How dare he?" She read parts of the letter again. "Ha! Hoist by his own petard! So this is why he had to back off. A dead woman can't appear in court. Not eligible for annulment and lacking one of the main reasons to claim divorce." Rio laughed, short and bitter. "I hope I'm not his child. I hope my mother had a moment of happiness with someone else."

Unfortunately, she knew it wasn't true.

What a fool she'd been, working all these years when he intended to boot her out without a thing the moment it suited him. He'd held off because when he got sick, there was no one else to care for him. It was funny really, that his precious Eino had apparently abandoned him.

But she wasn't laughing.

Grabbing Boo to her, Rio shed a few tears into the dog's curly white fur. "If I were a witch I'd put a hex on him. I'd grub him up out of that grave and dig the hole another six feet deeper. I'd plant him closer to hell, right where he belongs."

Her mutterings were lost in her misery. Boo licked away her tears.

After a restless, dream-plagued night and armed with this new knowledge of her father's perfidy, Rio went about her business with new purpose. Mrs. Golz, whose husband provided Rio with dairy products, both the little she'd used lately and the larger supply when the restaurant was up and running, was the first person on her list to contact. With the dairy, it meant the family began their day early, so she'd barely cleared away the remains of her hotel guests' breakfast than she, with Boo, set out to walk the mile to the Golz farm, located in a series of meadows west of the hotel.

The walk would do her good, Rio was thinking. Her and Boo both. Maybe she'd be able to walk off some of the ire still coursing through her veins.

Anna Golz greeted her with a short, rather stiff, handshake and, after Rio explained her errand, called two of her daughters, strong and stalwart like all of the

Golz's nine children, to come attend the women's conference.

"Blanche, Maria, I've come to ask if you will work again at the hotel?" Rio smiled at the girls, quite unaware of how haggard she looked after the angst-filled night. "I'm opening the restaurant on Friday evening, and hope to have reservations. The hotel will open as soon as I have guests. Anna, I hoped you could come back and work for me at least a few hours every day."

This had been their routine before.

The girls, Blanche and Maria nodded eagerly as they were both saving money for their hope chests. Rio, smiling to herself, didn't know if either one had a beau in mind, but if she did, the fellow had no chance of evading either of the strong-minded girls short of leaving the country.

Anna herself, maybe not as eagerly as her girls, added, "Now Eliza is also old enough and can serve at tables. Other girls have shown her how. Blanche is good cook. Maybe you will train her to be more? More like you."

Rio liked the way Anna bargained for her daughters. And a back-up cook would be good. She hardly had to think about it. "Agreed. A deal for all of you. Same wages as before." Blanche and Maria had been fully trained and were efficient. She'd have a new employee earning a top wage, but she had no doubt the new girl, Eliza, would prove equal to whatever task was set her. "Start tomorrow, please. The hotel has been neglected." She admitted this with a shamed air.

Anna sniffed. "My girls will soon put everything right. We will be there tomorrow. Early."

Rio's steps back to the hotel were lighter. Right up until Win turned to face her as she walked into the kitchen. She found him standing at the sink holding a towel-wrapped ice chip to his cheekbone, his face pale and his dark eyes blazing. He looked, she thought, exactly like Beckett when he'd been telling about the attack when Win got shot.

Her mouth rounded into an O. "Win! What happened? Are you all right?" Rio hastened forward, taking him by the arm and urging him to a chair. She pulled aside the towel and found a bloody gash on swollen flesh. She recognized the look of it, having had a similar one only a few days ago. "Donaldson was here?"

Win nodded. "Accused me of lying when I told him you weren't home. Sorry, Rio, I tried to stop him but he tromped all through the hotel. I followed him into your dad's old room. He was real curious about that big cupboard in there. He was poking and prying at it and I told him to get out. That's when he told me to shut up and hit me."

Rio hissed out air. He'd known—or guessed—about Elias's cache in the armoire. "Did he find anything?"

"No. But, Rio, I could tell by looking that he knows it was you and me yesterday. That you're the one who shot him. He looked mad when he saw me. Real mad."

"Apparently, he acted like it too, I guess. I'm sorry, Win. So sorry." She was frightened too. For him and for herself.

He shrugged. "Not your fault." He brightened. "Anyway, I reckon things might be evening up. Seeing him close up, I think—I'm sure—he's the one shot me, and now you've shot him. See, I saw he's right-handed, but he slugged me with his left. Made a face, too, like it hurt. I hope it did. Just wait until my brother sees what he did to me today. I figure the sheriff is gonna be real sorry."

Rio half-smiled. "Sooner than later, I trust." Her smile faded. "I just know none of us are safe until he is..." She hesitated. "Until he is either put in prison or dead." She knew which she'd prefer.

Twenty-Three

"I'm okay," Win insisted. "It hardly even hurts." Sporting his cut and bruised, though now bandaged cheek as if it were a badge of honor, he soon declared himself ready to get back to work. "Got any more chores for me to do when I'm done with the boats? Those'll only take me a couple more hours. And do you have more books I can borrow? I finished *The Call of the Wild* last night."

Rio, who'd been dreading the outdoor tidying up, was delighted with his ambition. Especially since Win seemed to have a work ethic that rivaled the Golz womenfolk. She enumerated her needs. "Rake the pine needles and cones from the path to the dock and burn them there on the beach. Examine the hitch rails and make sure they're secure. Every once in a while, we'll have someone ride or drive up on a half-wild horse that causes a big commotion. And if you'd put some old manure on the soil in the porch planter boxes, I'll get some flowers planted. Don't feel you have to do it all today. There's tomorrow too, before the restaurant opens."

Win's mouth gaped. "Were you going to do all this by yourself? Before me, I mean?"

"Well, yes. Wouldn't be the first time. And, yes, I do have more books. I'll get them to you this evening." Sending the boy off to complete the boats, she set about tidying herself for an excursion into town. A visit with Dr. Clement was only the second of her planned errands, although after Donaldson showed up at the hotel so early she wondered what, if anything, she'd discover. Win had said there'd been blood on Donaldson's back yesterday, but it looked to her that, according to the blow he'd dealt Win, he was hale and hearty this morning.

Too bad. She wouldn't have minded crippling him, if not permanently, at least for a while.

Leaving Boo to supervise Win, she took one of the boats Win had refurbished yesterday, and with its fresh paint now dry, she rowed over to town. Win had done a good job of the caulking, she noted, the leaks stemmed for now. Passenger's feet would stay dry, always good when the passenger was a lady dressed in her best for an evening out. And with the path raked, she wouldn't be dragging a skirt hem through the cones and needles either.

Which reminded her. She hadn't mentioned a boatman to Anna this morning, but she'd wager Anna hadn't forgotten the need. One of her sons would take on the job. One or another always did.

The wind had calmed this morning. The sun sparkled on the deep green water and Rio made good time as she pulled at the oars. At the landing in town, she moored the boat and swiftly made her way to Dr. Clement's office.

"Hello there," Molly greeted her as Rio poked her head inside and peered around. For once the place was empty.

"Is the doctor out on calls?" she asked, disappointed.

"No." Molly smiled. "Come on in. I think he's lying on the examining table having a nap." Her smile slipped. "Are you ill? You do look tired. I read one of your handbills about the hotel reopening on Friday. James and I are hoping he isn't called out at dinnertime so we can come eat in the restaurant. We've missed the opportunity these past months. The Bay Café here on Main Street is no substitute for your cuisine. I suppose you've worked yourself to a nub."

Molly, Rio reflected, hadn't guessed the half of it. "Yes, I'm tired, but it's a good tired. I just have a question for the doctor. Not about my health. About something that..." She paused, not quite knowing what to say now the time had come. Then it occurred to her that perhaps Molly wasn't under the same constraints as the doctor might be. Perhaps asking Molly would work just as well, particularly since the doctor's wife liked a good gossip. "Maybe you can help me."

Molly sat forward as Rio leaned over the desk. "If I can. What is it? You look very serious."

Rio pursed her lips. "I am serious. It's about a patient of Dr. Clement's. A potential patient," she amended. "I don't know for sure if he would've come to the doctor or not. But with your husband the only doctor around—" She left the rest unsaid.

The idea evidently tempted Molly enough to make her ask, "A potential patient?" A thought seemed to strike her then. She cleared her throat. "When do you think he...you did say *he*...might have been in?"

Hopeful, Rio took a breath. "Yesterday. Late afternoon. Maybe even in the evening if—" She faltered, then went on. "It's regarding a man who may have been shot. A slight wound only, I think."

"Shot?" Molly's eyes rolled toward the back room where the doctor was napping. Her gaze came back to Rio and she nodded once. "I'd left the office by then, but when James came into the kitchen later, he told me he'd been delayed by a patient. I asked the patient's name, but he wouldn't tell me, and he didn't say anything about a gunshot wound. But I could see he was bothered by something and he had blood on his shirt sleeve."

Disappointment rolled over Rio. She'd have to try to pry the information out of the doctor after all. "Darn," she said.

Molly's eyes rolled upward as if doing some heavy thinking, then clicked her tongue in an indication she had more to say. "The thing is, I know James hasn't had a chance to file his patient records from yesterday as yet. He got called out to a ranch several miles from town before he even finished supper and was worn out when he got back sometime in the middle of the night." She grinned. "Which is why he's napping on the examination table right now."

She studied Rio for another long moment. "Is this truly important, Rio? Is it why you look so worried? Because you do, you know." A smile briefly flashed. "Be careful. You don't want your face to freeze like that.

And if you don't start eating more of your own cooking, you're going to melt away." She straightened her own healthy figure, and added, almost as if the words were forced from her, "I might be able to get that information for you if you really need to know."

Rio almost trembled with eagerness. "I really do, Molly. It's important."

Molly took a deep breath before heaving herself from her comfortable chair behind the desk. Standing, she shook out her skirt. "Wait here. I'll be back in a few minutes." She started off, then stopped. "Sit down. If anyone comes in, just tell them I'll be right back."

Nodding, Rio eyed a chair. She didn't sit though. Instead, she spent the time pacing slowly around the waiting room. Fortunately, she didn't have to wait long. A mere five minutes crept past according to the loudly ticking schoolhouse clock behind Molly's desk before the woman slipped back into the waiting room and came over to where Rio stood gazing blankly at an eye chart on the wall. To Rio's alarm, she wore a grim expression on her face and her mouth was pinched tight.

"Well," Molly huffed. "Well."

Rio looked up and tried a smile. "I don't like the sound of that." A failed attempt. Molly must not have found anything. Or if she did, decided she couldn't say. And from her expression, the doctor most probably would remain mum besides.

Molly was staring at her. "How did you know?"

"Know?"

"About the man with the gunshot wound."

What could she say? Admit that she'd been the one

to do the wounding? She took the plunge. "Because he was trying to shoot me."

Molly's jaw dropped. Her eyes went wide. Hands on ample hips, her coolness vanished. "He was shooting at you?"

Rio nodded. "And I shot back."

"Then that means—wait. Did *you* shoot him?"

Rio nodded again.

"You give me a name, Rio. Even if it's only a guess. If you're right, I'll let you know. If you're not, we can forget this meeting ever happened."

"Thor Donaldson." The name, though Rio whispered, resounded loudly in the silent room. A name that came of its own volition. What would Molly say? Or do?

Seconds went by, then Molly clapped her hands. "Jackpot," she said, but it didn't exactly sound as if Rio had won a prize. "And now you'd better go before James wakes up. I don't want him to know you were here." Finally, she smiled, faint, but there. "I'd give good money to hear how that all came about."

Rio clasped Molly's hand. "Maybe someday I can tell you. You and the doctor come for dinner at the restaurant on Friday—or whenever you can. On me. A small thank you."

This time Molly's smile lit her whole face, but when Rio glanced in the front window as she started down the boardwalk toward the post office, she saw the smile had already changed to a grimace. Molly was afraid.

IN A SPARSELY POPULATED area like Painter's Bay, rural mail delivery occurred only three times a week. Not expecting a delivery on what was an off day, Rio still hoped by now to have gotten some response to her restaurant opening flyers.

"Check your box," Mr. Burton, the postmaster, called to her from the beyond the counter where he was busily sorting through more mail.

Peeking through the little lock box's glass window, Rio's spirits soared. The receptacle overflowed and when she retrieved the contents, it made a reassuring mass on the bottom of the shopping basket she'd brought. She hadn't time to look through them now, as Mr. Burton hurried over carrying another small handful of letters with the hotel name on them.

"Plan on my missus and me for supper on Friday, Miss Salo." He beamed at her from behind his service counter. "We've been hoping you'd open back up now Elias has passed on. What's on the menu, if I might ask? Not fish, I hope. Me and Ella Sue are hoping for that there Boeuf Wellington you fix." He smacked his lips. His pronunciation of the unfamiliar French word brought a smile to her lips.

She'd already planned for the Beef Wellington, knowing it for a community-wide favorite. There were a lot of English expatriates hereabouts. "Count on it," she said. "You'll catch the boat at the landing as usual starting at six?"

"We will." The man was practically giddy. "Delighted. Ella Sue's been waiting for the opportunity to gussy up. She's got a new dress. A right pretty one."

Rio continued on to the grocery to order the ingredients she'd need for the opening. The restaurant at

Painter's Bay had always served meals a little differently than most restaurants. Only two entrée dishes were on the menu, and patrons could have their choice. The same price was charged for either. Dessert was always included, no matter how elaborate. No one ever went away hungry or dissatisfied.

The grocer, keeping a tablet beside the cash register he'd done years in the past, had a list of people signing up for reservations. Rio found herself hoping some of these requests were for meals on days other than Friday. But of course, she was used to the vagaries of the business—or would be again when she got back to the routine.

The butcher was next—most important. He was ready for her, having read her flyer.

"Got some fine tenderloins," he said, "the best I've seen for a while. What about a turkey? Don't often have them birds at this time of year, but I got in two young toms."

Rio, who'd planned on roasted chicken, happily agreed on the turkeys, and went away with the promise her order would be delivered Thursday afternoon.

Satisfied her work in town was done, she went back to her boat for the row across the lake. It was breezier again, putting white caps on the rising waves, making her work at the crossing. While the restaurant opening had been on her mind earlier, now it went straight to Sheriff Donaldson, then to Eino, and on to Mr. Brackman. Had he followed through by filing the will, as he'd said he would? Was all the paperwork in order, ready for the revelation of Juanita's bone and burial site?

She shuddered, the oars missing their rhythm and hovering in the oarlocks. The boat spun, startling her as water sloshed over the low gunwale. Gulls who'd followed the boat, squawked alarm and flew away.

After a moment, she recovered her oars and began her even stroke again, worrying now about Wash and Beckett out in the woods. It was almost an anti-climax to arrive safely at the dock and tread a finely raked and swept path up to the hotel's front door. Win's work.

It only occurred to her later that night, when she was in bed and should've been sleeping, that not one soul she'd talked with today had mentioned Li Bai's murder to her. And yet, they must have known he worked for Salo Timber Products, the same as Bill Hightower. Did none of them question such a coincidence? If murder could ever be a coincidence. Weren't they even curious?

Another thought occurred. Did the folks hereabout even know about Li Bai? Or did they simply consider him, as a Chinaman, not important enough to wonder about. Or had Donaldson kept the death a secret?

ON WEDNESDAY, Wash met with Beckett around noon just as the crew was settling down to the hearty mid-day meal. The woods were quiet just then. No sound of men calling to each other or to the horses as they worked. No crash of falling timber. No scrape of saws. The men had been noticeably silent since Li Bai had been killed. Wash couldn't tell if it was because they were missing the cook or reveling in his absence. Or just worried one of them might be the next to die.

With his superior command of English, Li Bai had

been their mouthpiece. What would happen to them now?

Meanwhile, Chiang, inscrutable as a statue when around his white boss, had easily taken over both the cooking and the clean up. His recipes were not as flavorful as Li Bai's had been, but the crew seemed to take it in stride and had voiced no complaints that Wash knew of.

Chiang also, he'd found, worked well alone. A good thing, since the only person to apply for the helper job had been female. He'd had to tell her no. He wasn't bringing a female into a camp of horny loggers, although he'd gotten an idea from a feral look in her eyes that she may have been gunning for just that.

It had struck him that Li Bai's proclaimed need of a helper had been due to his extra activities as a procurer of drugs and possibly, most probably, of women. Wash figured he'd been a real fool to let Li Bai hornswoggle him for so long.

Sitting by himself away from the men, Wash finished his meal in short order and got up to dump his plate in the wash bin. Beckett, who'd borrowed a horse from the hotel stable this morning, rode into camp just then, raised his hand in a salute, and dismounted. Wash was glad to see him. Remembering what had happened to Hightower, the cruiser's lateness had begun to make him nervous.

Beckett poked around in his saddlebag, coming up with the notes and tools he'd borrowed to complete the cruising job. Walking stiff-legged, he gathered everything up and brought it over to turn in his work to Wash.

"This is it," he said, indicating the tools. "I think

you'll find everything in order. According to the totals, it appears you'll make a tidy profit on this piece. This is a fine stand of timber."

"Glad to hear it. You gonna be heading out now Li Bai is dead?" Wash asked, thinking that with the Chinaman gone, the smuggling would end. "You and your brother?"

"Not until I have whoever is head of the smuggling around here under arrest. It wasn't the Chinaman, you know."

Startled, Wash's mouth dropped open. "Not the Chinaman? Then who?"

"That's what I'm still trying to discover. Is there anyone so opposed to the smuggling as to kill for his ideal?" A wry look crossed Beckett's face. "Unless..."

Wash didn't much care for that. "Unless what?"

"Far from opposed, what if somebody saw a Chinaman making money hand over fist and killed him so he could take over the smuggling."

Wash's gaze went back to the crew who seemed to be eyeing them in return. "If that's so, it doesn't appear to have made *them* happy." Could this be the reason for their dour silences?

His gaze following Wash's, Beckett smirked a little. "No. It doesn't. Could be our smuggler has made a big mistake. Maybe caused enough resentment to put himself in trouble."

He shoved the paperwork and bag of tools over to Wash. "I hope you'll keep up a pretense of needing me around until I can put an end to this. I'd hate to see a war start."

"You suppose whoever is running the opium den will demand more money than Li Bai did? Sometimes I hear what I take is grumbling from the men." Wash nodded toward the silent group who watched them with dark questioning eyes. "But I don't know what they're saying and Chiang, who at least speaks some English, isn't translating for me. Each man is probably wondering if something will happen to him if he speaks out."

"Strikes me as a problem of not getting their drug at all." Beckett's response was dry. "Can't blame them, I guess, if that's what it takes to keep them on the job. I wish to hell I could park Win somewhere safer. So far, he's been shot from ambush and beat up by a crooked sheriff, all on Salo land. It's tough, being in this business and being responsible for a kid brother."

Wash nearly laughed. In his observation, Win did pretty well at being responsible for himself, which he'd expanded to include looking after Rio. Consider the other day when he'd tackled her, saving her from a bullet a second before it would've plowed right through her head.

"Win's a good kid," he said. "But I don't know how people hereabouts will take it if he fingers Donaldson for Li Bai's murder. Donaldson will have his own story, you know. One that puts him in the clear. And people will pretend to believe him. They're afraid to do otherwise."

Beckett huffed, half snort, half laugh. "I run up against that a lot in my job. Agents, most of us, do our best. Even so, too many men fall in with the smugglers. Easy money. They figure, what's the harm? Folks are just trying to make themselves feel good. They say it's like sex or eating a good meal." He paused. "But it isn't. It's a dirty business."

Sighing, he started over to his horse. "I've got to go into Spokane this afternoon and talk to some people. Will you tell Win and Rio I plan to be back tomorrow afternoon? At the latest. Sooner, if I can."

"I'll tell them." Watching him ride off, Wash had the thought that Beckett—and maybe Rio, too—had bitten off more than they could chew. Smugglers, murderers, missing persons. What next?

Twenty-Four

Rio found four envelopes in her mailbox when come noontime on Thursday, she and Boo strolled over to the road that circled the lake a little south of the hotel. Three of the envelopes contained requests for reservations, though none, a little to her relief, for Friday's opening. She already knew her tables would be filled throughout that evening. One of the envelopes contained a reservation for a room for an unspecified duration.

"Hmm," Rio said to Boo with a satisfied air. "Business may be looking up."

Boo put a paw on her skirt and grinned.

The fourth missive was from George Brackman. She pounced on it eagerly, ripping open the envelope before she even got back to the hotel. Standing in the shade of a massive old ponderosa pine where a chipmunk chittered at Boo, she flipped open the folds of the letter.

My dear Miss Salo, she read, I have brought your mother's will, plus a copy of your grandfather's, before the court, so all is in order and proceedings to prove your ownership of the hotel have begun. Fortunately, the judge is an acquaintance of mine, and after seeing how much time has passed with you in limbo over this, he has promised to expedite the process. Anything to do with Elias Salo's estate remains to be seen, but as long as you can be legally declared the sole owner of the hotel retroactively, I doubt you need to worry about that as it is beyond your scope. As I told you before, the hotel belonged to first your grandfather, which your mother then inherited at his passing. Her will is specific that the hotel belong only to you. According to the record, your father conceded any claim to ownership and had no rights over it. The judge is taking steps to declare your mother deceased. I do not foresee any problems with this.

Regarding your father's estate, no filings have taken place as yet. I would suggest you and Mr. Ames carry on as you have been doing since your father became ill and until his death. If anything changes, I will be in touch. Meanwhile, look for me to pay you a visit within the next few days with papers for your signature.

Respectfully yours,
George Brackman, Attorney at Law

Thoughtfully, Rio refolded the paper and put it back in the mangled envelope. She needed to speak to the attorney in person and ask his advice about the sheriff. where they were located. The three of them, Beckett, Wash, and herself, hadn't wanted to tip Donaldson off regarding the discovery. Not to anyone, though Rio did trust the attorney. He had, after all, on his own volition contacted her about her mother's will.

Eino, in the case he ever did return to Painter's Bay, would try to contest the will. She felt certain of that. His greed would drive him, just as it had always driven their father. Revealing the body would prove her claim though it seemed wise to keep the location secret. For now, at least, until just the right moment.

"Not forever, Mama," she whispered. It was as if she told the tree tops in a message to be wafted to wherever her mother's spirit had gone. "We'll beat him yet. I promise."

A warm breeze lifted a ruffle on her apron. A light tug. Boo barked.

Message received? Rio liked to think so.

Back at the hotel, Rio marked down the names in the

reservation book, noticing for the first time that the person requiring a room had sent scant information. A certain Q. Callahan would be arriving on Monday and was asking for a stay of an unspecified length of time. No Mr., Miss, or Mrs. to identify the Q of a first name but she thought the handwriting looked masculine. No address to either send a confirmation or satisfy her curiosity as to where the person was coming from. And nothing about why. The whole thing was a little unusual.

She shrugged and wrote it down, then turned to face Blanche Golz as her new helper cook called out. Her new *sous chef*, Rio amended. Her own mother had called her that when Rio, as a small child, had been learning how to help cook in the restaurant and not just make family meals.

Blanche, who'd been busy in the kitchen, had hurried out when she heard the paper rustling.

"There you are." Relief suffused the young woman's face. Her cheeks were red with tension and perspiration dampened her hairline. It wasn't easy, cooking over a hot wood stove in a strange kitchen for the first time. "Good. I have questions. The recipe for stuffed turkey says use basil. I do not know basil. I know parsley. I know sage." Her old-world accent was revealed as she practically wailed the last.

Rio put down the pen. Her own question would be answered when the person, whether man or woman, arrived next week. Meanwhile, she'd have to school Blanche on identifying the herbs on the spice shelf not only by sight, but by smell. It wouldn't do to use sage and she was sure Blanche would be inclined to use that instead of the sharper, brighter basil.

Not in her special recipe.

"I'll show you," she said, but was interrupted as a loud knocking began on the back porch. The butcher's son had rowed himself over to the hotel with the turkeys and the beef tenderloins, which he put in the icehouse for her right away. She gave him a dime for his extra help and sent him on his way before turning to Blanche again.

But she'd barely begun with the tins of various herbs when the grocer's representative, an older man, half-crippled in a logging accident, showed up with an assortment of foodstuffs in his delivery wagon. He, a rather cranky fellow, was not so helpful in carrying things in as the butcher's boy, but the Golz girls, as Anna had promised, were as good as any man.

In another half hour, Blanche finally took whiffs from a canister of dried basil from Rio's garden, and declared, "Ah. So this is what makes your stuffing so different and so good. No mistaking this one."

What a relief to find a sous chef so willing to learn. Some of Rio's fears lightened.

And then, at last, it was Friday.

RIO STOOD in the doorway between the kitchen and the dining room, watching with satisfaction as Maria, arms laden with heavy plates—some featuring the Beef Wellington, some roasted turkey—served another family dressed in their best who sat at a round table in the center of the room. The table, surrounded by six chairs, was occupied by a complete family; mother, father, two sons, one small daughter and an aged male parent. The daughter, her cheeks pink with excitement, wore a frilly dress that matched her cheeks.

Win, bless his heart, had dressed in one of Eino's outgrown suits and taken over seating people, and during a lull when all the tables were full, came to stand beside her.

"Hah," he said. "And you were worried nobody would show up. Is it always like this?"

Rio patted her flushed face with a snowy handkerchief and smoothed the perky half-apron she wore. She'd trade for the cover of the big chef's apron when she returned to the kitchen. "No, or I don't know how I would've survived. We were always busy, but this is...is almost overwhelming." Although with the Golz ladies, they were coping nicely.

Win, over his first nervousness in this new job, laughed. "Folks are sitting out on the porch waiting their turns. Most of them are being fairly patient. Good thing none of them are my Uncle Henry or you'd have heard about keeping him waiting." His face puckered. "Some of those men are going on their second drinks from the bar. Hope they don't get too drunk while they're waiting." He touched his bruised cheek, the gash still covered by a small bandage. "Wouldn't want any fights either."

"Trust Mr. Turner not to pour with too heavy a hand." Rio agreed with Win's assessment. The bar had been a last-minute addition to the evening, only put in action when Mr. Turner showed up unexpectedly asking for his old bartending job back. It wasn't much of a bar and never rowdy, having been fitted into a small alcove off the dining room. More a courtesy to those who simply enjoyed a drink before dinner than for serious drinking.

Turning, Rio planted a kiss on Win's cheek. "You're a champ to help out, Win. Thanks so much. And poor Wash. He worked in the woods all day and now he's rowing the second boat back and forth across the lake. Aaron Golz coming from one direction while Wash is going the other."

Win touched his cheek and blushed a fiery crimson.

The first seating of patrons had gone from the second to the third when Dr. Clement and Molly finally arrived. The doctor was carrying his brown medical bag, an indication he'd come directly from a call. Molly was wearing a lovely blue dress that flattered her figure and enhanced the color of her eyes. The doctor viewed his wife with pride as they settled to their dinner. For the first time since opening there was one table standing empty, and some of the din had diminished. A situation that changed when a commotion sounded at the open door and two men entered, one lagging behind the leader. He swaggered self-importantly into the middle of the dining room, stopped between tables and slapped his hand down on the nearest one with enough force to make the dishes rattle.

The folks sitting there stiffened as if frozen in ice blocks.

Rio, having switched aprons again for another round of hosting duties and ritual greeting of customers, also froze. Donaldson hadn't seen her yet, as she paused in the doorway leading into the dining room. She sucked air into her lungs with an audible gasp, and her heart began pounding. Trouble brewed, obvious at first look. She stepped back, hiding at the passageway edge.

Thor Donaldson—and his idiot deputy, Klingaard, who aped him—glowered around the room, eyes searching as though seeking a victim on which to pounce. They didn't appear to have come for dinner since both were dirty and rank enough their smell, forced inside by a breeze off the lake, preceded them.

A woman at the table near them waved her hand in front of her nose.

The deputy raised his head and, as if scenting the air, pointed his nose toward the kitchen. Like a hound dog, Rio thought. A particularly ugly, and hungry, hound dog.

The sheriff paid no attention to his deputy. He tilted back his hat with one finger and surveyed the diners. His brows drew together into arrow points and he looked distinctly displeased about something.

His narrow-eyed glare came around. He was looking for someone in particular, she knew.

Me. They're looking for me. Rio felt it in her bones.

Every muscle in her body tensed and hardened, as if to repel the attack she knew was coming.

As more people noticed him and his peculiar actions, diners put down their knives and forks and went silent. Finally, it appeared Donaldson had the attention he craved.

He should've been here sooner, Rio thought. He'd have had a larger audience.

But this seemed to suit him well enough. Possibly because he didn't know the difference.

Donaldson didn't speak. Not at first. Perhaps he believed that if he could force her into coming forward on her own that he would've won the opening gambit of whatever game he was playing. Or that somehow, she was meeting his terms and answering to his demands.

Not much of a game, in Rio's opinion.

Whatever he wanted to call it, Rio was determined not to participate. Or not the way he wanted, anyway. But she had to do something.

Stepping forward in silence, she smiled around the room and, as if she didn't see him, walked toward the nearest table. The postmaster and his wife, she realized. Mrs. Burton indeed wore a pretty dress, just as her husband had told Rio she would. On the inside, Rio's stomach roiled and she shook all the way down to her shoe soles. She hadn't thought she needed to carry a gun in her skirt pocket. Not tonight.

She may have been mistaken.

The couple watched her approach their table, gazes shifting from her to the sheriff and back again. Mrs. Burton's fingers clenched around the stem of her water glass. Quickly, she took a sip, then smothered a cough in her napkin.

Mr. Burton reached across the table and clasped his wife's hand. He, brave soul, was the one who broke the stillness of the large room.

"You've made us a fine dinner, Miss Salo. We've missed your expert cooking. Glad to have you back. Real glad."

Rio managed a smile through lips that felt stiff. "Thank you, Mr. Burton; it's good to be back. I've missed serving the hotel's loyal customers during this difficult time." Her voice hardly shook at all although it sounded a bit choked. "Mrs. Burton, what a lovely dress you're wearing."

What is he going to do? What? Why is he just

standing there? He's like a grinning demon about to take a bite of my soul.

Wild thoughts raced through Rio's mind. Raced around and around.

An old-time rancher from five miles down the road hurriedly shoveled the last of a piece of raspberry-filled chocolate cake into his mouth and got up from his seat by the window. He had to step around Donaldson to get to the cash register to pay, and he did so without looking into the sheriff's face.

The sheriff deliberately bumped him. "That's right," he said. "Clear out if you want to miss the fun." He winked elaborately. "Never know but what there might be some excitement in a minute or two."

She should speak, Rio thought. Reassure these people who'd come to have dinner at the hotel. But how could she reassure anyone when she was scared half to death herself? What did Donaldson mean to do? Arrest her? Shoot her?

Perhaps the same thoughts had occurred to Win because he began moving quietly toward the kitchen. Hiding? Going for help? She hoped so since he could very well be on the sheriff's list for revenge. She doubted Win's youth mattered one whit to Donaldson.

It was the deputy who noticed Win's movement, and he nudged Donaldson for attention.

"Hold it right there, sonny," the sheriff ordered, his voice as harsh as the sandpaper used on the boats. "I'll get to you next." He drew his gun and pointed it at Win. At least he didn't pull the trigger.

Yet.

Win stopped. His dark eyes went wide as he stared across at Rio.

She'd have to take a hand, she realized. She couldn't let this madman loose on the boy, let alone the whole crowd of people in her restaurant. Couldn't let her friends or her employees pay the price of this man's crazed actions.

So she called out, doing her best to keep the tone light. "What on earth do you think you're doing, Sheriff? Can't you see you're scaring the ladies with your drawn gun?"

And the men too, who were mostly unarmed, though she didn't say so.

The words came, and people nodded. Surely, he must see that public opinion was against him.

What brought Donaldson here at this time, when it stood to reason she'd be surrounded by a lot of people? Was he simply trying to ruin her business? It just didn't make sense. The man had always treated her with contempt, and at the end, he'd seemed to hate Elias even though at one time they'd been, not friends, but some kind of allies. She'd never known for certain what bound them together, although she could take a guess. But this? Had he gone insane? Was he drunk? Under the influence of some of his own opium product? What did he hope to gain? She'd come to realize every single thing he did was meant to bring him some sort of reward. What could it be?

"Perhaps," she said, the suggestion she was about to make terrifying her as she spoke it aloud, "if you need to speak to me, we could go outside where we can be private." God knows she didn't want to go anywhere private with him.

He grinned as if aware of those feelings. "Why? You got things to hide, missy?"

Her eyes narrowed. "I don't, Mr. Donaldson, but you do. We both know that."

Rio took a step away from the Burton's table. She was panting, she realized, unable to catch a real breath. Which is no doubt what made her squeak just a little as she said, "If you're here to shoot me, Mr. Donaldson, I suggest you allow these good people to leave before you begin spraying bullets around."

Quite suddenly, her voice returned and steadied. Got louder, too. Loud enough to fill the room. If she was going to say this, she wanted everyone to learn the truth about their sheriff. And perhaps, somehow, if all these people heard what she had to say, it would keep her safe. He couldn't, not really, kill a whole roomful of people. Not with one pistol with six bullets.

"After all, you're not much of a shot when it comes to a moving target, are you? You managed to murder Mr. Hightower by shooting him in the back as he sat at his campfire. You murdered Li Bai when you caught him by surprise in the cook shack. But you missed me, when I heard the shots and ran to see what was happening. I, on the other hand, while not a good shot, managed to put my mark on you."

It was, she decided, as if all the air had been sucked from the room. Anyone in the midst of movement stood still.

Donaldson shook his head as if he couldn't believe his ears. Which was nothing. Rio couldn't quite believe she'd said it either.

"Lies," Donaldson roared, his face turning purple as he raged. He waved his gun to encompass the room. "All lies. Don't you believe a word of it. She did it. All of it. Hightower, the Chink, even her own pa."

The deputy stood behind Donaldson, his mouth sagging open and shaking his head like a bewildered bull. He drew his gun but then stood holding it as if unsure if where to point it.

Somebody, a woman, said, "Did he say Miss Salo shot Mr. Hightower?"

"He did. And her father too," someone else said. He didn't sound as if he believed it.

"And a Chinese person?"

"I don't believe it." The sentiment echoed in the space as it was repeated.

"She said she shot *him*. The sheriff." A woman who sounded approving spoke loudly.

"Nobody shot me." The sheriff's denial came too quickly. "I wasn't even at that cook shack."

"Then how would you know where Li Bai was killed?" Rio said. "Since I'm told no one was able to find you to make a report. And you never came to investigate."

"Yeah." The town blacksmith, his frown puzzled, spoke up. "A day or so later I heard *you* telling Klingaard not to bother going to investigate. Said you was tired and nobody cared about a damned Chink anyhow."

A swell of murmurs rose.

Donaldson stared around at the blacksmith. "Shut up." He eased the hammer of his pistol back, holding it cocked and pointed first at Rio, then at the blacksmith.

Every drop of moisture in her mouth dried. Her tongue stuck to the roof of her mouth. And worse, Dr. Clement, who'd remained sitting as others rose, effectively hiding him from Donaldson's view, rose from his chair. Very slowly, as if he'd rather not. And so did Molly.

The doctor stared at Donaldson. "Some of these accusations I don't know about, although accusing Miss Salo of going out and shooting Mr. Hightower is quite ridiculous. What I do know is that Elias Salo died of lung cancer. The *only* thing that killed him was incurable disease. As for saying nobody shot you, Donaldson, that isn't true either. You came to me with a bullet wound on the same evening Li Bai was killed. Not a serious wound, but I cleaned it up and put in a few stitches since it was bleeding quite profusely." He looked up and stared out over the silent watchers. "Miss Salo just said she is the one who shot him. I can't attest one way or another to that, but somebody sure as...most certainly...did."

Rio loved him for what he said. And feared for him.

Donaldson was shaking his head. "Don't believe him. It's not true."

The doctor glared. "So, now you're calling *me* a liar? I think folks know me better than that." Then he said, which Rio thought might not have been a good idea, "Besides, it's easy enough to prove. Stitches are hard to hide. How about you take your shirt off and show us, Donaldson. Let everyone see. They'll be interested in the back of the left shoulder blade."

Fury suffused the sheriff's face. He fired off his pistol, the sound overwhelming in the crowded room. Women screamed. Men yelled. Several people began running for the doors. Those closest to the kitchen headed for the hotel's back door. Those closer to the front crowded through two at a time and without bothering with the steps, jumped from the porch.

The bullet, Rio saw, had landed about two inches in front of Molly Clement's toes. It made a hole in the hem of her dress before plowing into the floor. Molly swayed and the doctor jumped to hold her upright and then pushed her toward the exit.

Rio turned to watch, relieved when they both made it outside.

But by then, Donaldson had turned the gun on Rio again. "Now you," he shouted, almost as if he'd shot Molly dead. "I'm taking you to jail. You'll hang. I'll make sure of it."

What she saw in his face terrified her. If he took her from this room, she'd be dead. She knew it. Knew that was his intention.

Why? The question rocketed through her. So she asked. "Why?"

"You," he said, his voice going quiet as the room emptied and except for Klingaard, they were alone. He grinned, a hateful sideways slant of his thick lips. "You're the last one in my way."

"Your way? Your way to what?" Rio couldn't move. Why bother? There was nowhere to hide as the sheriff jerked up his pistol and fired.

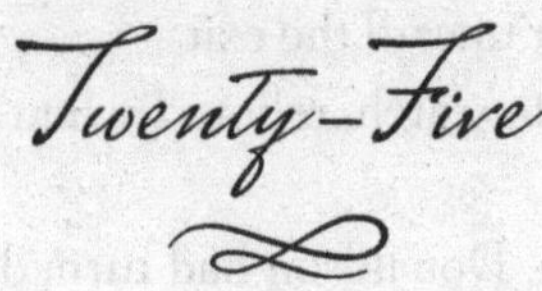

A second gunshot came from just inside the front door, not that Rio was aware of it. Mainly because she had fallen to the floor by then, her legs having gone right out from under her. For several seconds she wasn't even aware of having fallen. Only she was suddenly lying on her back looking at the ceiling with no notion of how she'd gotten there.

Then she was aware of everything.

Of blood sopping through the blue fabric of her skirt and turning it deep purple.

Of the legs and feet of the few who came to stand around her.

Of more screams.

Of a man moaning.

And of pain. Her own pain, a feeling of fire consuming her legs and wondering why she didn't lose consciousness. Or at least faint. It would be a blessing.

Faces swam above her.

Wash—how had he gotten here so fast? Last time she'd looked, he'd still been rowing back across the lake.

Win—why didn't the boy stay back? The idiot sheriff was bound to go for him next. But try as she might, Rio couldn't force out the words of warning.

And oddly, she saw the rancher who'd been the first to depart. Why had he come back? Foolhardy man.

Slowly, some things became clearer. Like Dr. Clement bending down to kneel beside her—if only he could do something for the pain before the scream gathering in her throat burst out.

And the two women, Molly Clement and Anna Golz. Stalwart Anna saying, "Lift her up, a couple of you men. Careful now. Let's get her to a room. Got that bleeding stopped yet, Dr. Clement?"

The doctor saying, "No. Hold up. Let me get the tourniquet on."

The pain swelled as the leather strip he used as a tourniquet tightened. She heard herself whimpering.

Anna again, sounding angry now. "Move back, people. You're sucking every bit of air out of the room and Miss Salo needs all she can get."

And somewhere, Beckett's voice, growling and angry, telling somebody, "Go ahead. Try it. I'll be glad to put a bullet in you too."

Rio wanted to laugh except she figured it would hurt too much. Though fuzzy in thought, it came to her that, though rather late, he'd gotten back from another meeting in Spokane just in time to exact his authority as a federal customs agent.

The will to laugh faded as a couple men, obeying Anna's instructions, started to lift her. She cried out. Everything went black for a minute or so before opening her eyes long enough to see Wash's face above her own as he carried her toward the room Beckett and

Win occupied. The closest, as she well knew. Someone was holding her legs so they wouldn't jostle.

Wash, gentle as a mother, deposited her on one of the narrow beds.

"Everybody clear out," Doc Clement was saying, "except you, Molly, and you, Mrs. Golz. I'll need your help. Yes, you too, Mr. Ames. You've gone as pale as Miss Salo and I don't need another patient."

Rio heard chattering from the Golz girls before Anna spoke sharply to them. Then the doctor again, saying, "One of you girls bring a basin of hot water and some towels. Molly, can you fill a syringe with morphine, please? A small dose. Rio is a small woman and I don't want to give her any more than she needs."

Rio tried to shake her head. She didn't want morphine, not after her experience with Elias and his constant shouting for more. She didn't want to be like him. Rolling her head brought the bump from where she'd crashed to the floor in contact with the mattress and she only moaned. She felt the prick of the rather dull and very painful needle in her arm—

And that was that until sometime in the night when she awakened. In her own bed, groggy from the drug and thirsting for a drink of water. Plenty of it and preferably cold.

The room was quiet. Cool. Dark.

Boo lay beside her, his head resting on her chest. Sensing her awakening, he raised his head and licked her chin, which made her smile. "Hello, little friend. Thank you for staying with me." Or that's what she tried to say.

Though she'd spoken quietly—more of a croak, she realized, than a recognizable voice—the man seated a few feet away got up and leaned over the bed. A moonbeam caught him in its light.

"Wash? What—" she said, startled into moving her legs. A mistake, she discovered, but at least she had legs to move. Once, before she'd passed out last night, she'd wondered about amputation, the idea tearing at her.

"I'm here. Don't worry. Clement says you'll be all right, that it's not as bad as it looked at first and probably still feels. Can I get you anything? Do you need...a woman...in here with you?"

Why did he sound embarrassed, she wondered, and then, oh. Maybe she didn't need a woman's help yet, but she probably would soon. Anyway, what woman would come? Molly? Anna? One of the girls?

"Thirsty." Her dry tongue stuck to the roof of her mouth. "Please?"

Water waited on the little table beside her bed. Wash helped her sit—a pain-filled process—his body warm and strong holding her up as Boo moved aside and she drank.

"Better?" He eased her down again.

Rio nodded. "I...I'm not sure what happened," she said. "Did he get away?"

"Donaldson? No. Far from it." He tucked blankets back around her. "But sleep now. We'll talk tomorrow."

With that, she had to be satisfied. So she slept.

WHEN RIO NEXT AWAKENED, it was to sunlight filtering through thin muslin curtains covering the window instead of moonlight. Before she thought, she threw back the blanket cocooning her and started to stand. Which was, she discovered, a bad idea. Very bad. To prove it, she fell back on the bed, dizzy, sick, and frantic to get to the bathroom.

With the sharp pain came remembrance—and Wash's promise to enlighten her this morning. He was gone from the chair beside the bed, and evidently Boo had gone with him. Just as well, she thought, because she desperately needed a woman's help to get to the bathroom, and that woman's help to wash. She could smell the stench of blood since she was still partially clothed in the undergarments she'd been wearing last night.

Opening her mouth to call out, she spotted the cowbell from her father's room, placed now on her table. She eyed it with revulsion but picked it up and gave it a shake anyway.

From below, she heard Boo bark a response. Soon footsteps resounded on the stairs. More than one person was on their way up. Maybe more than two. She shivered, though the room was warm, and drew the blanket over her. Fear? Apprehension?

To her astonishment, Mr. Brackman was the first person through the door. He took one look at her and turned color, first red because she was, after all, in a state of undress though fairly well covered by the blanket, then white. Most probably because she looked like death warmed over, Rio supposed. Well, she admitted. Why not? Lord knows she felt just like that.

"My heavens." He swallowed. "My dear Miss Salo, you...you look..." He shook his head.

"Terrible?" Rio supplied. "Hideous? Like I might be a ghost?"

He appeared slightly relieved. "At least you can joke."

She hadn't been joking.

Beckett was next, and Rio could tell he was displeased about something. "Is Win all right?" she asked, swallowing her anxiety for the boy.

But he nodded. "Physically yes. I'm thinking he might have nightmares for a while."

If so, Rio knew that he wouldn't be the only one.

And the final person into the room was Anna, as brisk and competent as ever as she hastened over to the bed. "You fellers scat," she told the men. "Can't you see Rio needs her comfort seen to. Just look at that disgusting er...dress. It's stiff with dried blood."

Mr. Brackman and Beckett moved aside as Anna reached into a corner and drew forth a strange object that appeared to be a cross between a step stool on wheels and a child's push toy. "The doctor sent this contraption over for you first thing this morning." She eyed it doubtfully. "You're to hold on to these here things that look like handles and kind of walk it wherever you need to go. It'll help keep the weight off your legs and prevent you from falling. He sewed the wounds up tight, but he doesn't want you bending or moving much for the next several days so go slow." She surveyed Rio every bit as doubtfully as she had the contraption. "Ask me, I'd say you won't feel like moving much anyhow. Best to stay in bed and rest."

Rio stared at her. "Several days? My hotel," she said, faint with the despair that flooded in. "My restaurant. The guests."

"Don't you worry," Anna said. "Me and the girls will handle the work. It won't be up to your usual standards, I suspect, but folks will understand. They've got plenty to talk about, I assure you. After what happened last night, they'd just better not complain. That's all I can say. Now, let's get you up and to the facility."

"Yes. Let's."

Just thinking of it made the facility more urgent. But how could she not worry? Even getting a good hold on the contraption was hard enough, but oh, how good it felt to tend all her needs and with Anna's help, wash away dried blood and sweat. The effort exhausted her. When she got back to her room, she found someone had changed the linens, cleaned and straightened everything that needed cleaned and straightened, and opened a window to the fresh air. Anna's girls at work, she knew.

Wash, unshaven and wearing last night's clothing, joined the other two men as they filed back into the room once Anna gave the word. Each of them bore a coffee cup in his hand, and all but Brackman who took the chair, stood and waited for her to settle in bed. She surmised Wash'd been rousted from his own bed after spending the night watching over her.

Anna, promising something to eat, left her with the men. For long moments, they said nothing and avoided meeting her eyes.

"I could use some of that coffee," Rio said at last. She didn't know about food. Her stomach felt much too queasy to try eating and she didn't really know about the coffee. But maybe that had been an excuse for Anna to leave the four of them alone. There was a whole lot that had happened last night after she went down, and she needed to know what.

"Sheriff Donaldson?" Her dark gaze went first to

Beckett. "I thought he was going to kill Win—after he killed me."

Beckett huffed a laugh, short and bitter. "Planned on it, I expect. He's not a man for facing an armed opponent. Not unless their back is turned."

Which, Rio decided, might mean most anything. "I think we all know that. Win?"

Ignoring this as if she hadn't spoken, Beckett pointed to Wash. "You go first. I wasn't there for the first part."

Wash nodded, flushing a little. Always a quiet man, he wasn't used to being the focus of attention in any way beyond his duties as foreman of the woods crew. "I was already close to shore after returning some folks to town when I saw Leonard Pickens run out of the hotel and start waving at me to hurry up. Figured something was wrong, so I added extra muscle to the oars. I'd just tied the boat up when I heard the first shot. Next thing I knew, a whole slew of folks came pushed on out of the hotel hollering and screaming and scared half to death. I ran on ahead up the path and got to the dining room just as Donaldson shot you." His voice went lower. "I saw you fall. Figured you were dead. God only knows who Donaldson had in mind to go next, but yes, probably Win. He was waving around that big old hogleg he carries in a careless sort of manner—so I shot him."

Rio stared. "You did? You had a gun?" She'd never known him to openly carry a weapon, aside from when he was in the woods.

"Yes, ma'am." Wash stated the obvious. "Ever since Hightower was killed."

She hadn't even known. "Is he, Donaldson, dead? I

thought I—" Rio knew herself to be coming over shaky again.

"Not yet, though the doctor says he's in a bad way." Beckett had the answer. "He's in Clement's surgery with a guard over him for now. If Donaldson survives until train time, we'll take him into Spokane to the hospital there. Meanwhile, he's awake. I figure on getting him to answer some questions for me while I have him here. The deputy, Klingaard, or whatever his name is, is in a cell at the jail. I'll be talking to him too, when I leave here. He's pretty scared over what Donaldson did here last night. Figures we might blame him—and I figure he carries some fault."

"Is he scared enough to tell the truth?" Brackman asked.

Beckett's dark eyes flashed; his anger easy to see. "I think so. If he's not now, he will be."

"Just be careful," the lawyer warned him. "Don't give the court any cause to dismiss the charges."

A lift of Beckett's lips turned into a wry smile. "I know the drill," he said. "Learned my lesson on keeping a man unmarked a long time ago." He turned to Wash. "What else?"

"Nothing much else to tell." Wash shrugged. "Donaldson was down on the floor, thrashing around. He'd dropped his gun and I saw the old rancher pick it up and hold it behind his back where nobody could get at it. Klingaard just stood there with his mouth hanging open and stuttering like a turkey gobbler. He didn't know what to do." He looked back at Rio. "Beckett came running in from the back around then, so I left the sheriff and the deputy to him and came to see what..." He faltered. "See if you—"

Rio forced a smile. "I remember you staying with me, helping. Thank you." She remembered being glad to see him. Remembered his deep, familiar voice as a comfort as the pain in her wounded legs became more and more intense. Remembered him picking her up to take her to a room and ignoring the blood that poured over his arm. The shirt he had on still bore the evidence.

They all turned to Beckett, who leaned against the side of the dresser. He shrugged. "Pure chance brought me back to the hotel in time to see any of this. I think Wash filled you in on everything noteworthy. As far as I'm concerned, I had no choice but to use my authority as a customs agent and make the arrest. I'd intended to wait a little longer, to tell the truth. Make sure of my evidence. But with what he did in plain view of about thirty witnesses last night, there is no need for delay. That's it." Beckett folded his arms and shut his mouth.

"No, that isn't it. Can anyone explain why the sheriff was so determined to...to kill me? And why he'd do it in front of everyone? It doesn't make any sense. I need to know." Moving restlessly and wincing at the pain in her stitches, Rio tried to shake her head and flinched from that as well. By this time, she knew the leg wounds consisted of a deep furrow across the back of each thigh. It occurred to her she'd been standing sideways to Donaldson. If she'd been head-on, the bullet might have shattered the bones. Even cost her a leg.

For a moment, the room seemed to close in, crowded by the three men in it with her. And Brackman's presence still needed to be explained. But first, Beckett.

"No more secrecy," she demanded.

"Nutshell only," he said. "And not to be noised around. You hear?" Beckett's glare took in not only Rio but Wash and Brackman besides.

Solemnly, they all nodded. Rio went so far as to cross her heart.

Beckett took a breath. "Opium has been pouring into this country from across the border. Up in British Columbia, where it is legal, Victoria has dozens of warehouses and processors all too happy to ignore our laws here. The drug has a tariff of around six dollars a tael, so you can see smuggling is a lucrative business. But our government is taking action on it. Not only the loss of tax money, but addicts are a growing problem, especially in cities like Seattle, all the way to San Francisco, and even inland, like Spokane. Their main route runs right through Salo land."

"Our land?" Rio was aghast. She hadn't expected smuggling of this magnitude.

Brackman's eyes had widened. "How long have you been onto this?"

Beckett shrugged. "Quite a while. A couple months ago we got word of a large shipment coming into Seattle by sea, being divided, and fanning out in all directions." He hesitated. "My assignment included policing the smugglers' route through Spokane and up into Idaho and Montana. But then our uncle, with whom Win has lived since our father's death, passed away and with his widow moving in with her sister, Win had nowhere to go. So I brought him along—a spur of the moment kind of thing—when it became necessary to track the smuggler's shipment. We followed the smuggler right up until he handed off to his local contact."

He sighed. "Remember the night Hightower was murdered and Win got shot and wounded, it was storming. We'd lost the track in the rain and decided to make camp, not knowing we had company until we saw Hightowers's campfire. We didn't approach. I thought at first he was the smuggler. But then we heard the shot and we ran over and spotted the man lying in the fire dead. Win took off to see if he could help before I could stop him, which is when he got shot. I dragged him away, but by that time, the shooter had taken cover in the woods.

"My concern was my brother, which is how we ended up here in the middle of the night. I..." He shot a look at Wash, then Brackman. "I compelled Miss Salo to keep our presence quiet, and when the timber cruising job came up, I took it. It gave me an opportunity to talk among the Chinese workers, since they are the smuggler's primary target, though there are plenty other folks around here caught in the opium trap. That's all I'm going to say, except that Win—and I, to a lesser degree—had only gotten a quick look at the shooter. Trouble is, it was dark and raining. Neither of us could swear to the person's identity."

"And that person was Thor Donaldson?" Brackman's lips tightened. "The sheriff."

Beckett's lips tightened. "Yes. I've been going out at night, watching, visiting with people, acting like a customer. Some of his opium dealers have been willing to talk to me. He was, so I'm given to understand, a man given to cheating the men working for him. Li Bai, for one, which is why Donaldson killed him. I think the sheriff was beginning to suspect I, or someone from customs was on to him. Then Rio and Win spotted him when he killed Li Bai, so he figured he had to kill them too. Why he thought he could commit murder in plain sight of everyone in a crowded restaurant the other night is anybody's guess."

Wash made a growling sound. "Too much of his own drug?"

"Maybe," Beckett said. "Anyway, we've got him, if he lives long enough to stand trial. I sort of hope he doesn't. A man like that will serve his time and come out of prison worse than when he went in."

Rio's breath went out on a gust that shook her. "Then it's over?"

Beckett nodded. "Wind up the details and it will be. For this area, at least."

Brackman cleared his throat with a noisy rumble. "My news is almost an afterthought compared to that, Mr. Ferris. I congratulate you. If I were a criminal lawyer I'd ask to take the case for prosecution."

They laughed, then he added, "But I'm not."

Rio had the idea she heard relief in those words.

"So," he continued, "here is the deal with both Elias Salo's estate and the late second Mrs. Elias Salo's private property. Fourteen years ago, Juanita Salo inherited her father's property when he, Benedict Serrano, died. Benedict had made Elias a rather large loan in order to bankroll the Salo Timber Products logging operation. In return, Benedict acquired title to this hotel. At the same time, Elias signed papers giving up all husbandly claims to the property and stating the hotel would belong solely to Juanita upon Benedict's death. Juanita, on my recommendation, made a will assigning the property to Rio. And so things stood, years passed, and when Miss Salo's twenty-second birthday went by without me hearing from her, I thought I must take action. I had heard something about Mrs. Salo's disappearance with all the accompanying rumors at the time it happened. So at this point, I began an investigation."

The men sat, ears pricked no less than Rio's own. Mr. Brackman had never given her all these details. A shadow at the door to her room showed Rio that Anna Golz was also standing there, still as a post, listening.

The attorney smiled warmly at Rio. "The inheritance, declaring Juanita deceased, deeds and whatnot are all in the hands of the court now. It may take a short while to clear, but be assured it will. I admit the progress would be both smoother and faster if we knew for certain your mother is dead, but we deal with what we have. No judge worth his salt will deny your claim, my dear."

Rio's gaze shot to Wash, then to Beckett. They nodded.

"We found her grave," she said. "If that's what you want to call it. Her grave and her bones."

Brackman's jerked erect, his eyebrows shooting upward. "Her grave? Her bones? Why...what...where?"

"We can show you." Rio glanced down at her legs. "Well, Wash and Beckett can. I guess I won't be riding anywhere for a while. We left the burial place entirely intact, just as we found it. The proof is there that the bones belong to her."

"You're sure?"

"Yes." Rio thought a moment. "But I wish I knew why Thor Donaldson seemed to be a part of my mother's death. Why part of this whole vendetta against me. Why would he have been? He and my father certainly weren't friends. More like they hated each other."

Hesitantly, Wash raised a hand. "Both of them were bullies. Both wanted to be the big man. Both were greedy beyond measure."

"But why Donaldson? What did he know?"

"I looked into his background," Beckett said. "Fourteen years ago he'd just been hired as a deputy sheriff and he headed up the search for your mother. Or what should've been a search. I'm not sure, but I think your father paid him to turn a blind eye to the details."

"Ah." Suddenly, it all made sense. An answer to everything. Even, in a cross-eyed sort of way, an answer as to why her father hated her. Guilt and greed.

Twenty-Six

Ten days later, though Rio's wounds healed quickly, a fever she successfully fought off had left her weak. Even so, stubborn beyond measure, Rio took up the reins of authority around the hotel again. Admittedly not to her normal strenuous schedule, but she was learning to leave certain things to the competent people who worked for her.

On this bright morning, aided still by Dr. Clement's contraption, she walked out onto the hotel porch. Mostly just to rest her eyes from the bookwork involved in keeping a list of supplies for the restaurant up-to-date, but she needed the air too. And so did Boo, who brought her a stick to throw for him. A quarter-hour of vigorous run and fetch play had them both worn out. Already today Rio had made up an order for the menus she and Blanche together had planned and checked the laundry for clean towels. Plus a couple of the other hundred and one things necessary to running a hotel.

For one thing, Anna Golz had said she was giving up on doing the hotel wash and that she could recommend one of the local Chinese laundries. Rio didn't blame her. She wouldn't want to wash all those sheets and towels either, no matter how much she got paid.

At least overnight guests hadn't overwhelmed the place in the short time the hotel had been open. In fact, the one longer-term reservation she'd gotten just before the opening had sent a message saying he, or she, had been delayed. Frankly, it had suited her. Right now she preferred the few overnighters.

Though still very early, two of the hotel's boats were already out on the lake, each rented by a couple fisherman trying their luck in the deep still water. Every once in a while, she'd hear someone shout with glee. It made her smile. The one thing that turned her smile upside down was that Beckett and Win were gone. A week after she'd been shot, Beckett had gotten a telegram, packed up his brother and their belongings, and with no more than an hour of notice, taken the train into Idaho. To the mines up near Kellogg, she thought, but wasn't entirely sure.

She missed him with a sad sort of longing she couldn't bring herself to identify. And Win. She missed him too, of course.

"Rio? Where are you? I need help."

The familiar plea came from behind her, and although the words might have sounded worried or plaintive, the voice was quite calm. Blanche, calling to her from the kitchen, was trying out Rio's recipe for omelets this morning, to be cooked upon demand.

"In our house," Blanche had protested, "we serve simple scrambled eggs. Everybody eats them up. Are they not good enough?"

And laughing, Rio had replied, "Not fancy enough.

This, Blanche, is a hotel and we're doing our best to raise the cuisine above the local café's fare. One can charge more for omelets. Same basics, different form. Got it?"

And Blanche, though showing a bit of disapproval, nodded. She was coming to prefer cooking elaborate dinners. Either way, she was a fine cook and eager to learn—and she understood about money.

Rio, somewhat reluctantly, had let Blanche in on her recipe for extra-fluffy eggs in the omelets, which included just a tiny bit of her biscuit mix beaten in to help the eggs hold their airy shape. They shared kitchen space when Blanche prepared the noon lunch offering while Rio baked a couple rhubarb pies and made dinner rolls in fancy shapes. Blanche's sisters Eliza and Maria served in the dining room, then went home to their own concerns until it was time to come back for the evening meal.

The day wore on.

Wash came for the dinner service that evening, saying he was tired of the food in the camp cook shack. "Soy sauce," he said disgustedly to Rio when she inquired as to how the new camp cook was working out and ask whether the pie was any good, rhubarb being one of his favorites. "It's a wonder if my innards aren't preserved until eternity what with all that salt."

She laughed up at him. She wouldn't tell him, but she'd been known to use soy sauce herself. It was one of the things that made some of her soups so tasty and gave the broth a rich color besides.

Since she was able to sit on a stool at the counter in the lobby where the cash register was set up, she took his money as he paid for his meal. He always insisted on paying. He'd eaten with her a few times when Elias was sick and they ate in the kitchen, but this was her business and he wasn't a mooch.

He fished money out of his pocket and handed it over. "Are you ready for the probate hearing tomorrow?" he asked.

"Yes." So she said, but Rio couldn't help but be nervous about it. "Are you?"

Wash needed to testify before the judge as well as to the finding of Juanita Serrano Salo's bones. Beckett had left something called a deposition.

Shrugging, he smiled a little, his blue eyes bright. "Easy for me. All I have to do is tell the truth. About everything. I'll pick you up in the morning in plenty of time to catch the train to the city. Okay?"

"Okay." She smiled back, glad to have his company. He was the most steady, dependable man she'd ever known. She'd liked that kiss they'd shared just fine, she thought, thinking back to the day of her father's funeral. Liked it a lot, though she hadn't actually heard harp strings and angels sing. But it had been Wash. It had been nice.

And hadn't happened since.

Had she done something wrong? She couldn't help wondering.

RIO, tired to the bone, made use of her contraption as she made her way across the lobby, intent on locking the hotel's front door for the night. If anyone needed her, they could always use the bell. It was clearly marked.

But she fervently hoped nobody would. She needed her sleep.

The lobby lights were dimmed, and the hotel silent. There were only a couple of rooms occupied on this Tuesday evening. Both were rented to traveling salesmen who were no doubt asleep by now as they'd made a point of visiting the nook dedicated to drinking men. One man sold Monarch cook stoves. He'd tried desperately to sell her one, showing her a lovely, tiny replica of the real thing. She'd been tempted. The other man sold whiskey. She bought a case of what had been her father's favorite—after she had her bartender take a taste to make sure plain rotgut wasn't being foisted on her. It wasn't. While a little expensive, many of her customers liked to brag about their supposedly superior brand of beverage. It always made her grin to herself. She'd tasted some and could barely tell the difference.

Boo kept pace with her, darting about the contraption's clumping feet, growling and biting at the sound-muffling rounds Wash had put there to keep the thing from thumping too loudly on the highly polished wide plank floors.

He stopped suddenly and looked at the door. Rio nearly ran over him as she fished in her pocket for the key.

"What is it, silly Boo?" She held up the key. "I nearly ran you over. Is there a raccoon on the porch?" She thought she heard a little something as Boo's ears flicked again.

Even so, the firm knock on the door startled her as she'd just leaned forward to insert the key. She stepped back, her heart pounding.

It reminded her too much of the night Beckett and

Win arrived. Or the times Thor Donaldson had come, blustering and intimidating with his coarseness and his threats.

She placed a hand over her racing heart, even as Boo began barking.

The knock came again.

Rio wished she was carrying her gun. She hadn't, not since the sheriff had died of his wound.

"I'm not afraid," Rio whispered, maybe to herself, maybe to Boo, maybe to the universe. "I'm not afraid."

"Hello?" someone—a man—said from the outside. "Is anyone there?"

Boo, she considered, had pretty much given them away. Taking a steadying breath, she opened the door.

A man stood there. He carried a valise in one hand, the other was tucked inside his jacket. Rio couldn't see him very well as it was dark, but she thought him about Wash's age, dark hair and light-colored eyes. Well-dressed.

Her voice trembled just the least little bit. "Can I help you?"

He studied her a moment, those light eyes taking in her, Boo, the contraption. "Yes," he said. "I'm Quinn Callahan. I've got a reservation."

Rio's breath gusted out, not noticeably, she hoped. "Indeed you do. Come in, Mr. Callahan, and I'll get you registered. You caught me just in time as I'm locking up for the night. I'm Rio Salo, the proprietor of this hotel."

He smiled and a charming dimple showed, but she was already turning and didn't see it.

"What luck," he said, and followed her in, reaching

down to let Boo smell his hand as she locked the door behind them.

Author's Note

As you are surely able to tell, I've left room to continue Rio's story. You want to know what happens with Eino, (pronounced A-no, or so I'm told) don't you? Well, I do. Stay tuned.

We always hear about prohibition, as if the outlawing of booze—and a rather inadequate job the authorities made of it as smuggling was a thriving business—was the only thing the Ladies Temperance League had to worry about. But before the prohibition movement here in Washington, a decade or so earlier the opium trade proliferated and the women took action. Opium was on a par with our present-day fentanyl problems, if not quite as lethal. Learning about the sordid business interested me greatly and provided a fine background for my characters to contend with. If you'd like to look up the history, here's a site to help with that: http://www.historylink.org/File/22666. Then there's the legality of marriage annulments. And divorce. And deserting a spouse. And inheritance laws.

Oh, and I had almost every person in my writer's

group ask what a timber cruiser is. Well, for those who don't know, here's the job description in a nutshell: *Timber cruising is the process of tree selection and measurement that determines the volume and value of usable wood in standing trees.* This is done before the logging crew comes in and starts cutting timber.

Wow. Such a lot for my heroine to contend with, she doesn't really have time for romance—although she'd like to.

I am not a historian and have no interest in becoming one. I do like to put real experiences and concerns of the times in all of my books, and there's quite a bunch in this one. But it's a book meant solely to entertain, and I hope it serves the purpose.

Thanks for reading.

A Look At: The Woman Who Built a Bridge

A WESTERN ADVENTURE ROMANCE

A 2019 Spur Award Winner

Shay Billings is pleasantly surprised when he finds a new bridge over the river, cutting miles off his trip into town. When he's ambushed and left for dead, the bridge builder—a mysterious young woman with extraordinary skills—jumps to his rescue.

January Schutt just wants to be left alone to hide her scars. Living like a hermit in a rundown barn, her life is turned upside down when she takes in the wounded Shay. And when she allies with him and a few ranchers to defend their homes against Marvin Hammel, a power-hungry tycoon intent on seizing their land and water, she finds herself in the midst of a battle over water rights. But has she chosen the right side?

Facing danger, newfound love, and difficult choices, January must discover her own strength and the true meaning of justice as she navigates the treacherous waters of loyalty and survival.

AVAILABLE NOW